RADIO WAVES

A Post-Punk Novel

Shawna-Lee I. Perrin

Print ISBN: 978-1-64719-251-8
Epub ISBN: 978-1-64719-252-5
Mobi ISBN: 978-1-64719-253-2

Published by BookLocker.com, Inc., St. Petersburg, Florida.

This is a work of fiction. Any semblance between original characters and real persons, living or dead, is coincidental. The likenesses of historical/famous figures have been used fictitiously; the author does not speak for or represent these people. All opinions expressed in this book are the author's, or fictional.

Library of Congress Cataloging in Publication Data
Perrin, Shawna-Lee I.
Radio Waves by Shawna-Lee I. Perrin
Library of Congress Control Number: 2020924471

Printed on acid-free paper.

Booklocker.com, Inc.
2021

Dedication

To my dad for instilling a lifelong love of books and rainy days.

To Dave for always drawing out the real me.

To Joy Division's Ian Curtis, Peter Hook, Stephen Morris, and Bernard Sumner for the relentless inspiration.

Chapter 1

August 31, 1979 (Labor Day weekend)

The sea wall along Marblewell Beach had crumbled in a couple of places since the last time I'd been there in the spring. The tide was low, with a warm, late summer breeze, and we walked on the beach side of the wall. Adrian stopped walking, took my left hand in his, and held it up to examine.

"The ring looks perfect on you, Viv," he said. "The diamond brings out the sparkle in your eyes."

The sinking sun coated everything in a syrupy haze. I rolled my sparkly eyes and put my hand down at my side.

"Have you always been this corny?"

He tilted his head and grinned, the skin in the creases around his golden-brown eyes crinkling. "I know – you're too punk rock for all this mushy stuff. But give me a break, will you? Thinking about us getting married brings it out in me."

I tucked a piece of hair behind his ear. "Sorry, Ade. That's very sweet."

He put an arm around me, and we walked to the Lobster Pot Bar & Grill. The hostess checked Adrian's name off the reservation list. She led us through the indoor dining room, with its many tables draped in red and white gingham tablecloths. The ceiling seemed lower.

"Did you guys redo the dining room over the summer?" I asked.

"No. It's been pretty much the same since the owners opened it twenty years ago," the hostess said.

"It seems smaller. Or shorter, or something," I said.

The hostess shook her head. "We've tried to get them to do some updating, but they're not interested. Mr. Kendall thinks everything moves too fast these days, says people like having one thing they can count on staying the same."

She seated us outside at a picnic table by the long railing overlooking the bay. I rubbed the cheerful gingham tablecloth between my fingers; its airy cotton gave this place a feeling of permanence, unlike the disposable vinyl tablecloths that every other restaurant used. Still, I was glad I wasn't the one trying to get butter and shellfish stains out of these.

"It's nice being here before all the other students," Adrian said, taking my hand across the table. "Hopefully not everyone else had the same idea to come early, and we can beat the move-in madness by a few hours tomorrow."

Adrian lived in Connecticut. Earlier in the day, he had met me at my house in Stonewald, in the northwest corner of New Hampshire, and I followed him two and a half hours across and down the state to Marblewell. We each took our own cars because we had too much stuff between us to fit it all in just one; my milkcrates stuffed with records and books dominated my trunk and back seat, and Ade's ironed shirts on hangers were laid flat and carefully stacked in his. We were staying overnight in a nearby hotel.

"Or," he continued, "maybe there's still time to get out of campus housing? Find a little apartment together downtown?"

"My parents are helping put me through college," I said. "The least I can do is respect their wishes of not 'living in sin like a hussy.' You have your room, I have mine, and everyone is comfortable thinking we're not having sex because we don't live together."

"Yeah, but we're getting married, and it's almost the 80s - everyone's living together first now."

The truth was, I could have moved in with him, with no argument from my parents. Getting engaged to Adrian was my single greatest achievement in their eyes, and they'd allow just about anything to make sure I didn't screw it up. But I'd seen girls I knew move in with their boyfriends, fiancés, or husbands, and they were automatically in charge of cooking, cleaning, and ironing in addition to whatever paying job they had. No matter how great the guy, living together changed the girls; they didn't laugh as much and sighed a lot more. I didn't think Adrian would expect me to be like Donna Reed, vacuuming in heels and pearls, but I wasn't ready to find out just yet. Anyway, trying to get through my last year of college and keep up at the radio station as both a DJ and Music Director would be all I could manage.

"They're afraid that if you're getting the milk for free, you won't buy the cow, and the cow will end up a bereft spinster sleeping in its childhood barn."

"Please don't compare yourself to a cow, Viv."

"I'm taking a 400-level metaphor class this semester. I'll have something better by December."

He laughed and shook his head. "I'm just so happy to see you."

"Me too, Ade," I said, but couldn't shake the nerves that had been making my neck ache since we'd gotten into town. He'd been staring at me more than usual, like he was trying to figure something out.

The waitress came and took drink orders. I initially ordered a beer but changed it when Adrian ordered red wine. Beer was what my friends and I drank. Wine was what people who were going to get married and own a fondue pot someday drank.

The wine came, and we ordered food. Adrian raised his glass and said, "To our last year in college, to our engagement, and to growing up and starting our life together."

He didn't even smirk when he said it. "*So* earnest," I said, and clinked his glass. I took more than a sip, slightly less than a gulp. It tasted like warm, metallic blood. I wrinkled my nose and said, "Mmmmm."

"It's an acquired taste, just like you," he said with a wink. "You'll get there."

I'm an acquired taste? I cleared my throat. "Yeah? They teach you that in Connecticut?"

He fidgeted with his napkin. "Maybe."

The breeze wandered across the deck, lifting the edges of the tablecloths and filling my nose with the scent of salty air and water. Adrian was looking out at the bay and the boats as they chugged by. His hair had gotten slightly shaggy over the summer, and he looked rested and dreamy-eyed. He wore a Beach Boys t-shirt and his old Levi's. Had he always been into the Beach Boys? I didn't remember that he had.

Our waitress brought salads and cups of chowder. Adrian ripped open the tiny bag of oyster crackers and dumped them into the soup, poured the dressing over his salad, and listed off all the things he had to get done the next day: get a haircut, go to the bookstore to get his textbooks so he could get a jump on the reading, organize his desk, get to the grocery store to stock up on healthy snacks… He asked me what my plan was.

"I guess bring my stuff up to my room, unpack some, then go to the radio station, see who's around," I said.

"Oh," he said.

I searched his face. "Did I say something wrong?"

"No. It's nothing. I just…" He looked up. "Our first full day back here, and you're already planning on spending it at the radio station?"

All my friends were at the radio station, and I hadn't seen any of them over the summer. I missed them terribly.

"I wasn't planning on being up there all day," I said. "You have a lot of things you want to do, so I figured I'd have some time while you were busy."

He poked at his salad in the small, clear bowl shaped like a lettuce leaf.

"Ade?"

"I was wondering if maybe you were going to skip that this year. Senior year is a ton of work."

I shook my head. "Of course I'm not 'skipping' that this year. Why would I?"

"Viv, please don't get mad."

"I'm not mad." No, I was furious he'd even think such a thing.

"You're scowling at me," he said. "I'm not trying to be a jerk, I just – it takes up a lot of your time, and you were struggling to keep up with your classes last year. And also... Ah, forget it."

"No. What?"

He set his fork down. Looked at the table, then back up at me. "A bunch of your exes are still around up there."

"A 'bunch'? How many people do you think I've been with, exactly?" I was trying to be funny and lighten the mood – however, he wasn't laughing. Ade hated to think about my romantic life before him. "It's all ancient history anyway."

"Not *that* ancient."

"Like a year and a half."

"I just think it's weird. I hate the thought of you hanging out with guys who have seen you naked."

"I can't do anything about what happened before we got together, Ade," I said. "But there's nothing to worry about. They're all like family now. I mean, they're *nicer* than most of my family, but – anyway, all that's over. Besides, some of *your* exes are still around the paper, right?"

"Yeah, but –"

"And I wouldn't ask you to not do that this year because I know it means a lot to you, like the station does to me. Plus,

I'm not worried because I trust you." I smiled at my impenetrable logic.

He held my gaze, and gradually, his expression lightened. "Yeah. OK," he said.

I wasn't asking permission. "Good," I said, and took a bite of a mealy tomato.

When I looked back up at him, he was grinning. I looked around to see if I was missing something funny.

"Hey honey? I have some really exciting news."

"*Honey*?" He'd never called me that before. "What's that?"

"I'm trying something new."

"Well, don't. I'm not some 50s sitcom housewife."

"Why are you so grouchy tonight?"

I unclenched my jaw. "I'm not."

He arched an eyebrow, then shook his head. "OK, no more 'honey.' Anyway… I was going to wait to tell you, but I'm just so excited, I can't. I got an early acceptance to Connecticut Teaching University. They have a program that's pretty much a fast track to school administration."

"You mean like a Principal? You want to be a *Principal*?"

"Yeah, some day."

I knew he was planning on teaching, which was one of the most admirable things a person could do. But Principal… Principals thought they had some right to make the rules, and the idea of being married to one… I'd definitely have to dress way different, like in sweater sets and pumps and shit like that. I committed to talking him out of it before he started grad school.

"In the meantime, though," he continued, "I'll get a TA job to pay bills while I go to school, and I'm sure there will be some secretary jobs in the department for you – with your English degree, you'll be a shoe-in."

My hands trembled. I put them in my lap and fidgeted with the cloth napkin. "Secretary?"

A few years ago, before I got my summer job at home in a nearby bookstore, I asked my dad if he could get me a job as a secretary at the construction company he worked for. "Oh, Jesus," he said. "You don't want that job. It's long hours, hard work, and they get treated like shit by those stuck-up assholes who work in the office all week. I don't know how they put up with it."

"Just for a little while, until we have kids and everything," Adrian said. "We should probably wait until I get my Master's, and till we get married of course, so your parents don't murder me."

I blinked at him.

Connecticut. Secretary. *Kids?* I couldn't picture going to punk shows in dimly lit clubs with kids clutching at me, demanding snacks and sticky drinks.

"Are you ok?" He reached for my hand, but it was still shaking, so I didn't give it to him.

"Um," I said. "This is – this is a lot."

He shook his head. "What do you mean it's 'a lot'?"

I stood. "I have to go to the bathroom. It's an emergency." I could just barely hear him saying my name over the sound of my own rapid-fire breathing. I picked up my pace toward the ladies' room.

Once in the stall, I sat down, dropped my head into my hands, and tried to calm my breathing. But it came in ragged gasps, and I realized I was sobbing.

Connecticut. Secretary. Kids. Like, next fucking year? I knew he had plans, and I figured I'd go along with them eventually, but I didn't think it would happen so soon. When would I ever get to travel and see all the things I wanted to?

I stood, opened the door and went to the mirror. My eyes and cheeks were red and swollen. My side-braid had come loose, and my hair hung wild around my face. I looked worse than I thought.

I've never gotten lost wandering around London. I've never seen David Bowie live. I've never sent postcards to my brother from somewhere that has different stamps than us. Never... Oh my God, how do I get out of this?

A woman wearing the Lobster Pot waitress uniform opened the door and caught her breath at the sight of me staring myself down in the mirror. She paused for a moment, then composed herself.

"Are you Viv?" she asked.

I nodded.

"Your fiancé asked me to check on you. He was worried you were sick."

I cleared my throat. Took a deep breath. Forced a smile. "I'm fine. Just didn't feel good for a second there. Nauseous."

"You must have had the chowder," she whispered. "I'll tell him you'll be along."

I nodded again. The waitress left, and I re-braided my hair, splashed cold water on my face, and constructed a veneer of sanity that would hopefully last until I could get some time to think. I returned to the table and sat down. Ade asked if I was all right. I couldn't remember the last time I'd been less all right.

"Viv, we have to talk about this."

"I just feel really queasy," I said. "I'm cold, then hot. I think I have to go back to the room and lie down."

Our waitress brought our dinners out. Ade started to say that we would have to take them to go, but I stopped him, reminding him that he hadn't had lunch, and should stay and eat. He admitted to being hungry, so reluctantly agreed.

"I'll be fine," I said. "It's a short walk, and I'm not dizzy. I just feel like I'm gonna throw up, and the smell of food is making it worse."

He leaned over his plate, and said in a low voice, "Do you think you're pregnant?" He was smiling. He seemed excited.

"No. Nope. Uh uh. The pill is very effective, and I never miss a dose. It's just nerves. Stress. All that stuff."

"Oh," he said, and sat back in his chair. His shoulders slumped and the corners of his mouth dipped to a frown. He looked down at his hands, which were fidgeting with his napkin.

I just need some time to think. "Take your time. I'll see you back at the room."

He looked up at me, his brows knit together. "You seem like you're freaking out, and I don't understand why."

"Not freaking out," I lied. "Just don't feel good."

He chewed on his lower lip while he studied my face, keeping eye contact for far longer than I was comfortable with. For a moment, it seemed, he could read my thoughts. I gave him my very sincerest smile, then turned and left, stepping slowly so as to not actually flee.

On my walk back along the beach, once past the sheltering bay, I didn't realize that the tide was coming in. Fast. I looked down and saw that my sandals and the hem of my skirt were soaked. It was getting dark. I stopped walking, and turned to face the advancing waves, capped with luminous white, stretching to the grey-pink horizon. The town lights twinkled on. Gulls screamed overhead. The saltwater was frothy and cold. Seaweed caught on my ankles.

The longer I stood in the water, the less the cold took my breath away. I admired each wave getting a little higher each time as it crashed down and headed toward me. The cold of the sea worked its numbing magic from my toes up to the water now swirling around my knees. The retreating water tugged at my legs a little more insistently each cycle. It was sweet and intimate.

I was lucky to have Ade. So lucky. No one else had ever wanted to spend the rest of his life with me, and Ade was better than I deserved.

***

We'd met our freshman year; the student paper was around a corner and down the hall from the radio station. We didn't give much thought to each other, though – just enough to say "hi."

"The newspaper kids," as we referred to them, tended to be more preppy and overachieving than most of us music nerds at the station, but there were a few people who did both, and so we all pretty much knew each other. Plus, we shared the chattering dot matrix printer that was somehow directly linked to the Associated Press's news service and spat out news stories and weather on thousands of feet of paper, so we had a somewhat reluctant alliance.

Near the end of my sophomore year, the guy I'd been seeing for almost four months told me via a letter slipped under my door that he was going to study in Italy in the fall, and that he thought it would be "easier on both of us" if we went back to being friends. Yet every time I ran into him up at the station, he wrapped up whatever he was doing and left quickly. I never got a chance to talk to him about anything. I didn't want it to be a big deal, but it was.

One Thursday during the week before finals, I was filling in for a friend's shift at the station because he was running late. I went to grab the news, and Adrian was already in the room, sifting through the piles of paper that had collected in pale grey ribbons on the floor.

"Hey Adrian," I said. "Got the *Reader's Digest* version there somewhere?"

He handed me the short summary of the day's events to that point. I thanked him and turned to leave.

"Hey, Viv?" he said, and I turned back to him. "I noticed that you seem kind of sad this week. Want to have some dinner with me? Let me try to cheer you up?"

I couldn't imagine he meant it like a date, and I wasn't ready to go on any dates again, anyway. My whirring thoughts must have been apparent on my face, because he said, "I'm sorry if that was too forward. I'd just really like to get to know you better."

"Why?" I blurted. *Jesus*. I was terrible at this.

He smiled. "I just – I think you're cute. You seem really cool. And it's just dinner."

My already-tenuous confidence had taken such a beating that spring, and his words were so very welcome. Unlike my friends and crushes, who wore a lot of garish-toned Grandpa sweaters over band t-shirts, Adrian never wore anything ironically; he always dressed like he might meet someone important he'd need to impress.

"OK," I said. "Sure. When are you thinking?"

He looked at his watch. "It's almost five now. When are you done up here?"

I thought I should probably try to clean up a little bit before going out with someone like him, put on something nicer than my beaten-up old jeans and thinning black sweater. "Keaton should be here in another half hour, but I should probably go back to my room and change. Or brush my hair at least."

He smiled again. "I think you look great. Don't change a thing."

I felt myself blushing, so I knew I had to make a hasty retreat. "My song's ending soon, and I don't have anything else queued up, so..."

"Oh, yeah, of course. I'll come back around 5:30?"

"Sounds good," I said. "See you then."

When Keaton came racing into the studio, apologizing for being late, I told him it was fine, but I was glad he got there when he said he would because I was going to dinner with a newspaper kid.

"Well well," he said. "I didn't think you even knew anyone outside this hallway."

"Don't be goofy. It's just dinner."

He was barely holding back his laughter. He did a very fancy bow and said, "Yes, m' lady."

I rolled my eyes and when I went back out into the hallway, Adrian was there waiting. We went to a small Italian restaurant downtown that I'd never been to. He even insisted on paying. I smiled more that night than I had in weeks. We went out a couple more times before the end of the school year and wrote to each other a few times over the summer break.

When fall came around, we were almost inseparable in our spare time between my radio station duties, and his classes, academic clubs, and the newspaper. Adrian was straightforward, reliable, and often mentioned things we could do together in the future. He made me feel more like a grownup, or at least like I could be one someday. Before Adrian, the guys I usually fell for often "joked" that I was too similar to them, and because they hated themselves, we couldn't last long. I'd stopped laughing at that joke a while ago. Adrian was exotic to me because of his normality.

While my parents hadn't met any of my previous boyfriends, they had met a few of my radio station friends one weekend when they'd come to visit me at school; my family's resulting descriptions included words such as "dirtbag," "bum," and "freakshow." I'm sure Mom thought I was planning a future specifically designed to blot out all the good in her world. So, when I eventually showed up at home with Adrian one weekend and my mother's usual pursed lips and disapproving head shakes transformed into a toothy smile and girlish giggle, I felt like I had finally done something right.

The school year went by fast, and before I realized it, we'd been a couple for longer than I had with anyone. I felt accomplished. I hadn't cried in quite a while.

On my 21st birthday in May after school was done, Adrian came to visit me at home in Stonewald. He proposed, with a diamond ring and everything. I said yes because there was no reason not to. And I was pretty sure I loved him.

Still, I was scared; it was so adult, so final. I wondered what I'd be like in five years. Later that night in my old bedroom on the second floor, I lay awake. The wide-open windows allowed an occasional breeze, but the air was mostly stifling. It was in those blessed, breezy moments that I heard the familiar whistle of a train passing through the night. The tracks followed the river on the Vermont side; I'd been hearing that whistle since I was little. Ever since my dad had told me about freight hoppers jumping trains undetected, seeing the country on schedules dependent only on the trains rolling through, I thought about them whenever I heard that whistle, wondering where they were headed, where they used to call home, and what they were riding to or away from.

The moon had been full a couple nights back, but its glow still spilled brightly into my room. I held up my left hand, the diamond glittering like a busted disco ball.

I wondered if the freight hoppers would let me go with them and teach me how to disappear when I wanted. Maybe someone could teach me how to play guitar or harmonica. Maybe I'd end up out West with the golden light, working as a typist for money when I needed it, hopping trains again when I was sick of it. Or maybe I could get a job at one of those weird little radio stations that Hollywood Joe had told me about before he graduated last year.

It was the end of wondering what and where I might be when I grew up, because now I knew: it was mapped out on my left ring finger and Adrian's lists. There was little room for any hard times or struggle in this version of the future, which should have been a relief. But as much as I tried, I couldn't shake this feeling of creeping terror. I told myself I would get over it. That I just needed a little time to get used to it. It wasn't like I had any better plans, anyway.

***

Looking into the waves, I wondered what happened when people got swept out to sea; if hypothermia or drowning killed them first. Hypothermia and its enveloping forever sleep sounded like the better of the two. I'm not sure how long I stood there, wondering what that would feel like.

Over the din of the ebb and flow, I heard shouting. I was dragged backwards. Then I sat on dry sand, and a tall, weathered-looking man in rain pants kneeled in front of me, examining my face and holding me by my shoulders.

"Young lady, the sea will steal you away if you're not more careful. You walked pretty far out there. Are you all right?"

I looked down and saw that my whole skirt was soaked. I'd lost my sandals.

"Yes sir, I'm all right," I said. "Sorry to have caused any trouble."

"No trouble, I'm just glad you're ok. Do you need help getting home?"

"No sir, I'm close by. But thank you."

He nodded, stood, and walked back to his boat. He brought over a small, plaid wool blanket and wrapped it around my shoulders.

"It's getting cold," he said. "This isn't much, but ought to help you get home without freezing to death."

I thanked him for his kindness and conjured up what I hoped was a reassuring smile. Barefoot and fighting back tears, I trudged back to the hotel, hid my wet clothes in a trash bag and tucked it in a pocket of my luggage, showered to warm up, and got into bed, where I lay staring at the bumpy, cigarette smoke-stained ceiling for only a few minutes before Adrian unlocked the door and came in.

"Viv? Are you feeling better? Do you need anything?"

Yes. I do. So much.

"So much better," I said.

"Oh, thank God," he said. "Because I think I'm really sick."

He ran to the bathroom, and soon I heard retching. I pressed my palms into my eyelids until I saw white explosions. I got up and went to help him.

"Oh my god," he gasped. "I think it was the chowder. I knew it tasted weird."

Chapter 2

When we got to campus in the morning, Ade pulled his Volvo into a parking spot in the lot near my dorm, and I pulled my rust-red Pontiac in next to him. I got out of my car, but Ade was bent over his steering wheel, and I could see his back moving up and down with labored breath. I tapped on his window, and he jumped, then rolled it down. His skin was pale grey and had a sheen that looked like it smelled of stale bread. His lips were cracked.

"Jesus, Ade," I said. "Move over. I'll get us to the lot behind your dorm and make sure you get upstairs without passing out."

His shoulders lurched forward with a body-shuddering dry heave, and he slid over to the passenger side. "This is horrible. I've never been this dehydrated."

We got to his dorm's small lot, where there were only a couple of cars; their hazard lights were blinking, and they were parked in No Parking zones near a propped-open side door. I helped him bring some sheets and blankets, sweats and t-shirts, and his bathroom caddy up to his room, brought him some water, and slipped away once he was settled into bed.

I decided to head to the radio station before going back to unpack my stuff. I walked along the campus's main walkway, gazing at its carefully scattered garden beds glowing with cedar mulch and autumnal mums in shades of orange, yellow, and scarlet.

When I got to Kennedy Hall, I was relieved that my key still worked on the back door. I ascended the narrow black and white-speckled stairs with fading chrome tread guards, gripping the handrail that had always been curiously sticky, and looked through the small, square window in the industrial-strength steel door on the second floor, but I didn't see anyone, and all the doors in the long hallway were closed. I swung the door open and walked about halfway down, taking in the walls covered in stickers and posters of records that had come out in previous years. It was always a relief to see that our little museum of punk rock and chaos had gone untouched over the summer; the building's janitor kept threatening to tear it all down and throw it away because it was "unsightly and lazy-looking." As far as I was concerned, that hallway was the most perfect art installation in the world.

I let myself into the music directors' office and thumbed through the nearly-toppling stacks of records that had come in over the summer; each record had to be listened to, summarized on a small rectangular label slapped onto its cover, and screened for profanity before it could go into rotation for airplay.

One that had come in was *Unknown Pleasures* by a band from England named Joy Division. I'd read a little about them in my music magazines, and was captivated by the stark, chilly atmosphere of their black and white photos. Music journalists said their live shows were "emotionally jarring," and described their music as "often glum." Being glum myself lately, the record seemed like a good match.

I walked down to the listening studio, flicked on the overhead light, closed the oversized, heavy door, sat down in the creaky desk chair that was older than I was, and put the record on the turntable.

The first lyrics asked if someone else could ever make him feel the things that normal people do. My heart leapt at this unexpected bit of empathy. I plugged in the headphones so I could be closer to these sounds that were unlike anything I'd heard before. The urgency and quickness of the instruments were pure punk, but the sound was far more sophisticated and complex, with the bass right up front; the low-end instrument, typically obscured behind everything else, here instead carried the melody, making every song feel like a catchy funereal dirge.

And then there was this voice: seductive and dark and crooning, reaching out with fingers stretched behind a glass barrier, and everything around him, echoing, distant, gaunt. He sang about conquistadors, used metaphors I didn't quite grasp, and referenced characters in old stories I didn't know the names of. But when he sang of love, desolation, and his inability to get beyond that glass barrier, it reached me in a way that drilled down into my marrow.

I had every reason in the world to be happy. I wasn't alone anymore. I had the ring. I was supposed to feel triumphant.

Unknown Pleasures raged quietly forward. It was a record of questioning, of perpetual discomfort with the savage, normal world. It wound its way into my bloodstream with each rotation of the vinyl disc.

The closer I got to the post-college life of actual adulthood, the more terrified I was of it – of tamping everything down, of being a *good wife*, of giving my body, mind, and soul over to pregnancy and birth; never mind the intense work and lifelong commitment of being an actual mother. As much as I connected to the singer's voice, low as a grave, I knew there were further horrors that awaited me as a woman that even he couldn't understand.

Nonetheless, this record was as close as I'd found to how flat and suffocating the trappings of such a life had begun to feel. I hadn't expected to find an aural portrait of what had become my deepest fears and most fervent dreams, but there it was, and the darkness of it all scared me. But it also gave me hope that if they, and he, could make this flawless, haunting thing out of their depths, that maybe I could make something beautiful out of mine, somehow.

The week that followed was a long one. I showed up to classes. I showed up to one meal or another. I showed up to Adrian's bed a couple times when he asked me to, but kept my single, solitary room to myself. I got better at making excuses why without making him feel bad or worry. I signed up for a Friday night shift at the radio station, hoping that it would keep my weekends free from travel to places I didn't want to go, like Connecticut.

I just need a little more time to adjust.

Chapter 3

Late Friday morning, I walked downtown to an appointment to get my long hair trimmed. It was a mild late summer day, just barely on the warm side.

I got there early, so sat and waited, drinking cool water from a paper cup. I leafed through hairstyle books, noting the abundance of long, flowing hair, blue eye shadow, and shiny lip gloss. Nothing I was interested in.

I wanted a change, to snap out of this claustrophobic daze I'd been in all week. My hair had always been the same: dark auburn, one length, just below the shoulders. I wondered if changing that might help me see and be seen differently; to give me the push I needed to move on from the past and into my future. It worked in the movies.

I decided to get it cut like silent film star Louise Brooks; my friends Keaton and Lenny were obsessed with her, so I went with them any time one of her movies was showing at a movie house downtown. I loved the severity and authority of her look, with no soft edges; the short, blunt bob angled toward the face, with straight-across bangs. Steely gaze. Square, set jaw. Louise was punk rock for her time.

"That's not how the girls your age are wearing their hair now, hon," my stylist said. "You want to keep the length you have, but cut layers so you can feather it. It would look so soft and pretty on you."

I didn't want to look soft. I wanted to look striking.

"I'd like the bob, please."

The stylist sighed and said fine, but warned me that it would be a big change. I figured the new 'do could pass in both extremes: maturing, responsible fiancée, or fearless trend-bucker.

When she was done cutting and styling, my discarded hair carpeted the black and white linoleum below like dead pine needles on the forest floor. She spun me around to see. Where Louise's look was angles, alabaster, and the mystery of sophisticated femininity, mine was apple cheeks, freckles, and a gal who still liked a good knock-knock joke. Louise's eyes were dark and deep, and mine were silvery and almost reflective. I couldn't hide behind a curtain of hair anymore. When I turned my face to examine the chin-length cut, I swear there was a little cheekbone I hadn't ever seen before. As I struggled to decide how I felt about this very different vision of me in the mirror, a grin spread across my face.

"I love it," I said.

Walking back through Marblewell, I smiled at strangers, successfully hopped through a hopscotch court in pink chalk on the sidewalk, and helped a small, elderly man across the busy Main Street. When we reached the other side, he turned to me and said, "Thank you, Miss. You know, you look just like the girls I used to ride around with in my jalopy as a young man." I beamed at him, wished him a happy day, and continued back to campus. I was meeting Adrian for lunch at the commons before he left for his best friend Steff's bachelor party weekend.

I saw him standing outside, waiting, and I sidled up next to him. He glanced at me and went back to looking at the main walkway.

"Ade?"

"Yes?" he said, looking back at me.

I grinned. "Do you like it?"

His eyes widened. He stammered, "*Viv*? Holy shit – I didn't recognize you. Is that a wig?"

"No," I said. "I got a haircut. Like Louise Brooks. Isn't it neat?"

"Who's Louise Brooks?" He squinted as he studied my head. "That's really your hair?"

I looked down at the ground, feeling stupid and exposed. I rubbed the back of my bare neck. It was cold.

"Hey, hey, I'm sorry," he said. "It's just so... Ok, don't worry. I'm sure it will grow back before the wedding."

Not if I don't let it. "Are you telling me that, or yourself that?"

"I didn't mean – It's just so... *Severe*. I'm sorry, I'm just in shock."

I folded my arms across my chest.

"Can we go eat?" he asked. "I have to leave in a half hour to get there on time."

I nodded.

He chomped on his usual: a turkey sandwich with mayo and lettuce on wheat bread, a green salad, and a sliced apple. He sure did like his lunch. He looked at the sports section of the paper someone had left behind. I pushed Choco-Bites cereal and milk around in a bowl. He told me I should eat something healthier. I nodded.

He had to go, he said. He loved me, he said, he's sorry he made me mad. He just needed some time to get used to it. He'd see me Sunday, he said.

I stood outside the commons, shook off the tears I felt creeping in, and decided to go across campus to the radio station, review some records, and take my mind off things.

I climbed the uneven stairs to the third floor, dropped my backpack on the ancient pea-soup-green couch in the lounge, and slipped into the narrow, long bathroom, covered in layers of stickers and graffiti of varying quality and crudeness.

I looked in the mirror, its glass hazy with age and second-hand smoke. The straight bangs threw a focus on my eyes that I'd never had before. I liked it, damn it, even if Ade didn't.

I left the shelter of the little bathroom, grabbed the top three records in the Awaiting Review stack in the Music Directors' office I shared with my friend and co-Music Director, Keaton, and brought them to the tiny listening studio.

I put the first record on the rickety turntable, placed the needle down carefully, and a soft melody unfurled itself from the speakers. Acoustic guitar. A gentle, male voice sang two verses over the repeating melody. On the chorus, a sweet, yet strong female voice sang the octave higher.

Per usual, I listened to the first third of each song. Then I wrote my short review on the rectangular white sticker on the cover:

FOLK

Sensitive man plays acoustic guitar, sings about not liking war, liking love better, why doesn't everyone else, etc. Sensitive, high-pitched woman's harmonies concur. Trite, insufferable. You know, FOLK. No swearing. All songs safe for airplay, hippie kids' birthday parties, and vegetarian potlucks.

Folk music of this ilk set my teeth on edge because I couldn't trust anyone making music these days who wasn't angry and anxious; how dare they say that love could fix everything? What bullshit, when love itself needed fixing. I put the record back into its jacket and set it aside.

A loud knock at the window in the door made me jump. Lenny. He grinned. I did too, and motioned for him to come in.

***

Lenny was the first person I ever met at WCNH three years earlier, in the fall of 1976; I'd just barely arrived at the University of Coastal New Hampshire in Marblewell, and heard it had a student-run radio station. I'd always loved radio, since my very first memory. I didn't want to wait a second longer than necessary to see a real, live radio station, so I'd gone and found it myself: Kennedy Hall, near the edge of campus, up a flight of stairs, down a long, narrow hallway, and into a room that looked like a lounge of some kind.

Unbeknownst to me, Lenny had stood behind me as my wide eyes took in every sight they could: the small radio with one speaker sitting on a large, rectangular table with patches of varnish long gone, the ashtray stuffed with cigarette butts crouching nearby, the electric blue walls with multicolored slashes and splashes, like a furious amateur Jackson Pollack painting. The music coming from the radio ravaged its insides, clamoring to shatter the tiny, round speaker with growling volume: garbled, ink dark, terrifying heavy metal.

"Can I help you with something?"

I turned and froze, as if I'd been caught stealing. He wore black high-top Converse, black sweatpants, a green t-shirt, and a grey corduroy blazer with wood buttons. He was a few years older than me, probably early twenties. His light brown eyes were sharp, but his face was kind. He held a can of Tab in his right hand and took a sip.

"Are you looking for someone?" he'd asked.

I shook my head.

"Are you here to sign up for training?"

"Training?"

He sighed and set his Tab on the table. "Do. You. Want. To. Be. A. DJ?"

"Can girls *be* DJs?"

He squinted and said, "Are you a time traveler? Were you teleported here from the 1950s?"

I blinked at him. "No?"

"Well, all right. Let's get started."

***

Lenny and I hugged, and he asked, "How was your summer, darling?"

"It was kind of weird," I said, and held up my left hand. "I got engaged."

He cocked his head, and said, "Have I met this guy?"

"Only once, last year sometime," I said. Ade had only hung out with me at the station a handful of times since we started dating. He tended to stick to the newspaper hall because he didn't know my friends well and said he always felt like they were judging him. He was right. The ones who remembered him, anyway.

"Huh. I don't remember him." He crossed his arms and smirked. "You seem very resigned – sorry, I mean, *happy*. Congratulations."

I shrugged. I waited for him to say something else, but he just continued to wait, with that knowing look he had, for *me* to say something.

"What? Jesus. Tell me what to do."

"I can't do that," he said. "But you do have a certain trapped raccoon quality about you, with the darting eyes and restless limbs, which can't be a good sign."

I glanced down and saw my right leg bouncing like I was playing a kickdrum.

"Your hair, however, looks fucking fantastic," he said. "I love it. Maybe a little red lipstick, though. Ok, I'm heading out. See you soon." We hugged again, he kissed my cheek, and left.

I looked down at the stack. The cover on the next record had a picture of a man and woman with kind smiles, each holding an acoustic guitar, wearing white shirts and braided ribbon headbands, standing in a meadow. I decided to go back to my room.

On my way out, I saw that the studio door was closed, and the ON AIR sign wasn't lit. The little break room radio had been turned off. The schedule for the semester hadn't been decided yet, so I wasn't sure if we were off the air. I peeked in the window to scope out the scene. No one was in the DJ chair, but the overhead lights were on, and a record was spinning on a turntable. The lights on the broadcast board were glowing, and the needle of the outgoing volume control bobbed in the safe zone, so someone was on, but must have been in the record library getting more to play. It was then that I noticed Serenity crocheting in another chair. *Shit.* That meant Blaze must be doing a shift.

Blaze and Serenity had moved into town from upstate New York about a year and a half ago. They were community members, not students. No one knew what they did for work. Blaze had gotten his DJ license. Serenity always sat in the studio with him, smiling and crocheting something brown. At general meetings, they would stand up, hand in hand, and petition for the folk record reviews to be left to them, because the words that non-folk fans (like me) wrote "hurt our heart chakras deeply," and as a result, they'd been "plagued with insomnia and a general malaise" in recent weeks. The thing was, those records had to get reviewed in order to be put into rotation, and those two weren't around enough to make much of a dent in the growing stack. I kept doing the reviews. Others did, too.

And much like my opinions about folk music itself, my feelings about Blaze and Serenity were irrational and unfounded, but unshakeable; how could they be so calm all the time? So peaceful and smiley? A few of us suspected that they must have a wicked mean streak in them just under their peacenik surfaces; we were certain that our reviews would have a cumulative effect, and one day they'd snap and shriek and call everyone motherfuckers. I wasn't sure why I wanted to see this so very much. Maybe just to know beyond a doubt that their kind of calm was just an act.

Just as I was about to turn and run the record back to the office, Blaze emerged from the record library and caught my eye. He rushed to the door to let me in. Serenity stood, set her crochet pile down, walked over, and stood next to him.

He wore his standard warm weather uniform of faded jeans with holes in the knees and an old, nearly sheer Newport Folk Festival t-shirt. Serenity, with her small, thin frame, wore a purple, billowy dress.

"Viv," he said. "Welcome back!"

"Thanks, Blaze," I said. "Serenity. How was your summer?"

She looped her arm through his, clinging to him like a folk-art Bond girl.

"Fine, fine," he said. "Hey, there's something we need to talk to you about."

Serenity leaned over and whispered something in his ear.

"You sure?" he asked her. She looked at me, squinted, then looked back at him and nodded.

"Ah. OK, then," he said. "Never mind. It can wait."

I'd never heard Serenity speak, not one word. Others said they had, but I think they just heard the wind and mistook it for her voice. She stood there, blinking at me.

"What just happened?" I asked.

Blaze looked back at Serenity. She nodded. He looked back at me.

"Serenity says your aura is weird right now," he said. "And that I should wait."

"My *aura*?"

"Yeah, you know – your body's energy field. It gives off light. Serenity's very sensitive to those. She says yours is all cloudy right now. We'll wait till it clears up."

"Right," I said. "I'm just going to put this in the New bin, and I should get going."

I walked into the studio and put the record right in front and turned to go. Blaze went over to look at what I had just put there.

"Oh, wow!" he said as I turned to go. "New Peace Brigadiers!"

I walked down the hall, slow enough to give him time to read my review. Would this be the straw that made the façade crack?

"God *damn* it," I heard him mutter. "*God damn it*, Viv. Please just stop…"

Instead of laughing, like I always thought I would when this moment came, I had the urge to flee. It wasn't funny; it was kind of scary. I grabbed my backpack from the lounge, picked up my pace, and turned out of sight just as I heard them shuffle back into the hall.

When I got back to my room, there were two notes pinned to my door. One said, "Your mom called. Call her back." The other said, "Your mom called again. VERY URGENT."

I exhaled and unlocked my door. I'd gotten in the habit of not wearing my engagement ring unless I was going to be around Ade because wearing it made me very uncomfortable; I was afraid that attention-seeking diamond would catch on something, break off, get lost, and then I'd owe him money for the rest of my life. I deposited it on my dresser, dropped my book bag on the floor, and trudged down the hall to the payphone.

"Hi Mom. It's Viv. You called?"

"Oh, Vivian, yes. You were going to call me this week sometime, remember?"

"I've just been really busy with classes and the radio station and stuff."

"You're at the radio station again? Do you have time for that?"

I rolled my eyes. *It's the only thing that brings me joy, so yes.* "It's fine, Mom. One of the notes said there was something urgent. What's up?"

This was the invitation that she needed to go into excruciating detail about all the things I needed to start deciding on for the wedding. She asked if I had a pen and paper handy to make a list. I said I did. I did not. Some of the things to start moving on included a date, a venue, the colors (for bridesmaid dresses, flowers, the groom's accessories, whatever those were, for tablecloths and napkins and invitations and and and), if I was going to wear her wedding dress or look for a new one and if so, where, the shoes, the cake, the cake toppers…

"What are cake toppers?"

"Those little statues of a bride and groom that sit on top of the cake."

I shook my head. "Do we *need* those?"

She scoffed. "Your cake would look naked without them. There are so many choices now, not like when your father and I got married. I've seen some very clever ones in catalogs – you can really show off that *individuality* of yours with some of these. But you'll need to order them soon to make sure you get them in time. I assume you're getting married next summer?"

"We haven't gotten that far yet, Mom." I opted not to tell her about everything else Adrian had told me he had planned.

"Vivian, churches book weddings way in advance – some years in advance, so you need to – "

"Wait, churches? We never went to church. Why would I get married in one?"

"Well, where else are you going to get married? A farm? A movie theater? That damned *radio station*? Of course you'll get married in a church. It's just the way it's done."

I leaned against the wall and stared up at the ceiling. "Mom, I have to go now. Someone's waiting for me."

"Oh, I know, Vivian. You're always in high demand. But this wedding isn't going to plan itself. Pick a weekend to come home so we can go through these catalogs and magazines and start making decisions. And I want your sister to help, so the more advanced notice we can give her, the better. You know how busy she is with the kids."

A chill rocketed up my spine at the mention of my sister, Sherry. She was so bossy, we might as well just let her plan the damn thing, which would be fine by me. Everything I'd decide would be wrong, anyway.

"OK, Mom. I'll be in touch next week."

"I'll believe it when I hear it."

We hung up and I went back to my room feeling like a heavy, frilly, stupid, useless weight had been placed on my chest as I lay down and fantasized about smashing tiny brides and grooms with a sledgehammer until it was time for my radio shift.

Chapter 4

"Good evening, Marblewell. The time is 7:01 p.m., and you are listening to WCNH, 91.3fm, the sound of the University of Coastal New Hampshire. It's Friday night, my name's Viv, and from now until 10, or when you decide to leave your radio, whichever comes first, you'll be listening to This Song Could Save Your Life. But first, the news."

I read the first few stories that the printer had spat out a few minutes earlier: an Irish Republican Army bombing killed the Queen of England's cousin; another IRA attack a couple of days later killed at least 18 British soldiers. Everyone everywhere was worried about gas. But when I reached the next headline, I stammered.

"Also, President Carter was… Oh. I'm… Sorry. Hang on, listeners, let me make sure I'm reading this right. Uh, let's go to this PSA with some tips on how to hitch hike safely."

I quickly scanned the paragraph, acutely aware that the 30-second public service announcement would end soon. It still read like the beginning of a joke, but I had to press on. I heard a tap on the glass in the door and turned to see my friends Izzy and Dean waving. I waved back, the spot ended, and I flipped the mic back on.

"And we're back. All right, here's my best summary of what I see here: President Carter went fishing, when a rabbit began swimming toward his small rowboat. Alarmed, the President used an oar to splash water at the rabbit, who did, evidently change its course, and swam away in the other direction. The President was shaken, but unharmed, as was the rabbit. So. That's the news."

I glanced back at the door to see my friends' faces red from laughing, and felt my own composure quickly crumbling.

"So, kicking off This Song Could Save Your Life, like I do every week, is an extra special song that saved *my* life when I first heard it careening down the hallways here at WCNH, because it sucked me further into this strange world of radio, and a whole new slew of weirdos I now call my friends - here's the first punk single ever, 'New Rose' by The Damned."

I hit the start button, flipped the mic switch, checked the levels, waved Izzy and Dean in, and stood up. I hugged them both.

"I thought you were in the city this weekend," I said.

"Dean's gig got canceled," Izzy said. "The place got shut down last night."

Dean sang and played lead guitar for a Rockabilly revival band called The Royal We. He and Isabella met two years ago at one of their shows in Manhattan, and it was love at first power chord. They traveled between New York City and Marblewell most weekends to see each other.

"It's definitely cocaine-related," Dean said. "Rumors have been flying about that place for years. Figured I'd come see Iz while it's still warm enough to go to the beach. Way less crowded here than the city this weekend."

"Holy shit, I can't believe your hair – you look like a movie star!"

"Ade hates it."

"You look great," Dean said "Like a punk rock flapper. He'll come around."

I lined up the next few records. Izzy came and stood next to me. "You ok? You seem mopey."

I told her about Ade's plans for our future and my mother's plans for our wedding. I believe I used the words "trapped forever in a mediocre, boring suburban hellscape."

Izzy wrinkled her nose. "Connecticut? Maybe it's close enough to Dean and me that you could come hang out, get away from the pearl-clutchers?"

"I asked about that. Ade said we'll be on the other end of the state. Then he said, 'Besides, New York City is too dangerous for you to wander around by yourself.' It's like my mom designed and grew him in a lab to her specifications. And did you know that he wants to be a *Principal*?"

I became vaguely aware that Dean was talking to a couple of people in the hall.

"I've got to be honest: that does not surprise me," Izzy said. "So… What? You're just going along with it?"

My breath quickened again, and I got that hot swell in my chest. "I don't know, Iz. I don't know what else to do."

"I think you do," she said.

"Yeah, I know. I have to talk to him."

"Just don't let him bulldoze you. It's your life too, and you deserve to have a say in it, right?"

I nodded, but I didn't really know what I *did* want anymore, let alone how to explain it. It had all gotten so jumbled up. All I knew were all the things I *didn't* want, and there seemed to be more of them every damn day lately.

Dean called me over, and introduced me to Noel and John, who he'd been talking with for a few minutes. They were brothers from England; Noel was a freshman, might want to become a DJ, and John, his older brother, was tagging along to get a break from their family and "the over 40 crowd."

"Viv here is my favorite DJ," Dean said. "She's been doing this for the entirety of her college career and can answer any questions you have."

We all said hello and made nervous, fleeting eye contact. John was striking; he looked like he could be in one of my favorite bands straight out of the pages of the British music magazines I mooned over. Short, almost black hair, big dark blue eyes. And an aged Wire t-shirt that clung to or hung off him in the exact right places.

I pointed at the shirt. "Have you seen them?" I asked.

He met my gaze and grinned. My knees tingled.

"Last year," he said. "They're fantastic. You?"

"Yeah, in New York, when I went to visit these guys." I gestured toward Dean and Izzy. "They were *so* good. My ears rang for days."

"Mine too." He didn't look away this time. "Were you the one playing the Damned and the Buzzcocks a little while ago?"

I nodded.

"And probably the first person to report on the potential killer rabbit threatening our President," Dean added.

I laughed. "Oh man. All I could think about was how my Republican uncle will use that against me at Thanksgiving this year. He'll say, 'Did you know *your* President is a goddamn fraidy cat?' Like anyone would know what to do if a rabbit was *swimming* at them."

"Song's ending, Viv," Izzy said from the other room.

"I should do a readback while I queue up my next song – you guys mind being quiet for a minute?" They shook their heads.

I dashed back into the studio, grabbed the stack of records I'd pulled earlier, skidded into the chair just as "Paint It Black" wrapped up, turned down that turntable's channel, hit stop on the player, turned the mic on, and read back the long set of music I'd played as I grabbed another public service announcement to throw in the cart machine – this one about eating fruits and vegetables – and queued up a long song. I turned the mic back on.

"So, kids, make use of that fine salad bar in our dining commons. Don't be like me and eat Choco-Bites cereal for dinner several times a week. Next up, we have Public Image Limited to remind us how good dance music is done. Here's 'Public Image' on This Song Could Save Your Life."

Izzy laughed, and said to the boys in the hall, "And *that* is my friend, the consummate radio professional."

They applauded. I blushed.

Izzy looked down at her watch, and said to Dean, "We better get going."

I glanced at the clock. It was almost 8. "What are you guys doing?"

Dean rolled his eyes. "Seeing 'Jaws'."

"*Again*?"

"It's the best movie ever," said Izzy. "Love that shark eating those preppy rich dicks."

I stood and hugged them goodbye.

"The dark-haired one has his eye on you," Izzy whispered.

"I noticed that, too," whispered Dean. "Want us to stick around?"

"I'm fine," I said. "And I can't say that I mind."

"Saucy little minx," said Dean with a wink.

"See you at lunch tomorrow?" asked Izzy.

I nodded, and they left.

"How do you do it?" said Noel. "I would have panicked if a song ran out and I wasn't ready yet."

"The worst that happens is there's some dead air, you queue up the next song or PSA, jump on the mic, make a self-deprecating joke, hit play, and you're fine."

"But your friend is right," said John. "You're really good at this. I'd listen to your show every week if we got it back home."

"Thanks," I said. I found it hard to look away from him. "I should probably go pull the news."

I ran down to the news wire printer outside the bathroom, tore off the latest, and quickly skimmed it to pick out which stories to read. I went back out and glanced up to see them talking a little further down the hall. John looked at me and smiled. My knees tingled again. I smiled back, then ran to the studio and closed the door. Holy hell, he was so beautiful it hurt to look at him almost as much as it hurt to not look at him.

When I finished reading the news and weather, and pushed play on the turntable, I glanced up at the window in the door. He was there, looking unsure. I waved him in.

"Sorry to bother you," he said.

"You're not," I said a little quicker than intended.

"Noel's been here for not even a week and has a date tonight. He's always been popular with the birds. Anyway, I don't know what to do with myself. Would you mind if I hang around here? I promise not to get in your way."

Please do get in my way. "I don't mind," I said. "Have a seat, if you like." I assured myself that I was just having fun. Just like the old days, except I wouldn't follow through.

He sat to the right of the DJ area, in the rickety old Windsor chair that had been in the same exact spot since I'd stepped foot in there three years ago. So many other things had been moved or gone missing from the studio in that time, but this chair stayed put. Some people said it was haunted and they "didn't want to fuck with that." Everyone agreed it was fine to sit in. But leave it there. I was about to ask him if he believed in ghosts, but decided to err on the side of not sounding crazy.

He flipped through the records I'd pulled to play and grinned. He said, "You'd love it in England. Our radio stations are much closer to the stuff you're playing. I hadn't realized just how good we have it until I heard mainstream radio here."

"Oh, I know," I said. "It's awful. How long are you here for?"

"Going back tomorrow. Second-to-last round of university starts week after next."

"Why is your brother coming to New Hampshire, of all places?"

He shrugged. "Our parents are worried that if Noel goes away to university at home, he'll be blown up by the IRA or slashed to ribbons by a street gang. Unemployment's up, so crime is too. We have an Aunt and Uncle who live near here, our step mum thinks it's safer, and Noel's always been a little obsessed with America, so he's giving it a go."

"And *you're* not scared of getting blown up or slashed?"

He shook his head. "Can't live life as a shut-in, can you? Besides, I'm in an area where not much of anything ever happens anyway."

"Hang on," I said, and flipped through the stack of records for the next song, trying to find one that would cement me forever in the memory of this luminous boy. Then I saw it, placed it on the turntable, and positioned the needle.

"What've you got up next?" he asked.

"It's a surprise," I said. "Trust me."

"Completely," he said.

I picked up the *Unknown Pleasures* record jacket. I had written my review in an ecstatic fervor:

This is the sound of something from very far outer space echoing back in response to our own howls, trying to see if maybe we're not really alone in the universe. Every song on this record says, 'You're not.' NME *calls this 'post-punk,' whatever that means. No swears. Safe for airplay.*

I realized I was testing this guy at least as much as much as trying to impress him. I lowered the needle and turned to observe his response.

His eyebrows shot up. "I didn't think anyone in America had even heard of them. I'm going to see them next week and I'm so excited I can barely sleep."

I gasped and covered my mouth with my hands. "I have never been more jealous of anyone."

As the shift passed, I told myself that I was just being nice, and there was nothing to feel weird about. But in between raving to each other about this band or that, I occasionally glanced up to see if he was watching me; he usually was, and he'd smile and settle his gaze elsewhere with a quick laugh.

When the next DJ showed up just before ten, I said goodbye to my presumed listeners, put on one last long song, and gathered my records to put away.

"Come see the record library," I said to John. "It's the crown jewel of this place."

It was small; four rows of floor-to-ceiling hand-hammered two-by-four and plywood shelves, each one packed to capacity with records, with narrow paths in between. The room's only window's shade was drawn, and the air conditioner clattered away like a pan of Jiffy Pop with a tracheotomy. Light green liquid pooled on the floor below. It would probably evaporate eventually.

"It's cramped," I said. "But it's alphabetized. And we all work our asses off to make sure it's exhaustive. Go on, think of a record and see if it's here."

He looked at the shelves, wonder evident on his face.

I beamed, not trying to hide my pride in this tiny space that I had helped grow over the years via record shopping trips to Boston on the station's dime. John seemed positively in awe, which made me even prouder.

He went to a shelf, scanning it for something. He ran his fingers over a few records, looking for one in particular. He grinned and pulled out an almost-new-looking record jacket.

"This is Joy Division's first record. It's only got four songs, but it's so fucking good. Have you heard it?"

"No," I stammered. "I didn't know they had anything before *Unknown Pleasures*."

"You'll love it," he said. "Is there somewhere we can go listen?"

"There's a listening studio down the hall," I said. "Just let me put back the records I pulled."

As I moved along the rows, re-shelving everything, John lingered, looking through the shelves. There were a few arm brushes, blushes, and sorries.

"Well, that's that," I said when I was done.

He stood still and close, looking at me with those eyes suspending quiet rains and fathoms of seawater. He tentatively put his hands on my waist. I was eye-level with his sculptured clavicle and the small hollow at the bottom of his throat. My breath caught in my chest.

I can't do this. This isn't something a good person would do.

I took a step back. He jammed his hands into his pockets.

"I'm sorry," he said, and searched my face. "I misread what I thought were signs."

"No, you didn't," I said. "They were. But - "

Just then, I had a vision of every weekend after this one: trying to acquire the taste for wine, making lists, picking a date, picking a dress, picking bridesmaids and tablecloths and plates and flowers and those ugly stupid fucking cake toppers, reassuring everyone how goddamn happy I am.

Fuck it. I want to break everything.

"Never mind," I said.

I threw my arms around his neck and kissed him. A jolt of electricity shot through the length of me, and I closed my eyes, pressing my body against his. I inadvertently pushed him up against a stack of records, mumbled an apology, and he laughed and continued kissing me. My elbows tingled now.

We paused, catching our breath. I whispered, "Want to listen to that in my room?"

"Absolutely."

It was a short walk to my dorm, but I was nervous, so it felt longer than usual. I hoped that no one I knew would see us. But there was a small, quieter part of me hoping someone *would* see us, either irreparably ruining everything with Adrian, or scaring me into chickening out of doing what I very much wanted to do with John.

I asked if he lived on campus at school. He said he used to but was renting a place with a friend this year. I did not know what to do with my hands, so I grasped the record with both, carrying it like a shield.

"Do you have roommates?" he asked.

"No. I keep some pretty zany hours, so it's easier with no roommate."

"You like it here?" he asked. "In Marblewell?"

"It's all right. Better than home. I love being so close to the ocean. And to people who haven't known me since I was born."

We reached the main door of my dorm, and I got my keys out. The lobby was busy tonight, with girls and several boys lounging on overstuffed, worn couches, watching tv and eating snacks from bowls or bags. I saw a girl from my floor glance around, take a big gulp from a gold-colored cup, and giggle. The whole lobby smelled of cheap vodka, Hawaiian Punch, and popcorn.

"Do I need to sign in?" he asked.

I glanced over at the front desk, the guest register open on top. The girl working the desk was on the phone and hadn't seen us in all the Friday night commotion.

"No," I said.

I looped my arm through his and guided him to the wide staircase with gleaming mahogany handrails and thick green carpeting.

When we reached a landing with no one around, he turned and pulled me against him. We kissed, he ran a finger along my spine under my shirt, his hand hovered on my lower back, and every single one of my nerve endings lit up like fourth of July sparklers. The grand old stairs and the snaggle-toothed chandelier cast us in an otherworldly light, like a shattered autumn moon. I pulled him up another flight of stairs.

When we got to my room, I switched on the table lamps on the periphery; I didn't want my freckles or the crook in my nose from a slam dancing accident illuminated. I glanced over at my windowsill – the six-pack I'd gotten earlier in the week had four left.

"Want a beer?" I asked. "It's warm, but it's, you know, beer."

"Love one. Thanks."

I twisted off the tops and handed him one. We clinked the bottles.

"To new friendships," he said. "And Joy Division."

"Cheers," I said. "Speaking of which, I can't wait any longer to hear this."

I told him to sit where he liked, brought the record to my turntable, and lowered the needle. When I turned around, he was sitting on the floor with his back against my bed, watching me.

The singer, Ian Curtis, shouted a series of numbers ending in "Go!" The jagged guitar kicked in. The bass and drums rolled over me like a tsunami. It was violent, urgent, immediate. Like I'd been blindsided and knocked down by a spectral stage diver, elbows flying. It was everything I fell in love with about punk, and I hadn't thought of them as a punk band, but they fucking nailed it.

John was laughing. "You all right? Your eyes are huge."

"What the hell?" I said. "I didn't know they could do *this*."

He held his hand out, and I took it. He pulled me down, so I straddled him. I wrapped my arms around his neck, and he slid his hands under my shirt and down the back of my jeans, rubbing my tailbone with a thumb. We kissed, and even that warm, shitty beer tasted better for having touched his mouth.

He slid his hands up my sides, brushing my ribs before flinging my shirt to the other side of the room, and I was *so* glad that I'd decided on my black lace bra that morning instead of the tan elastic one. I moved my hands along his lean, strong sides and chest, where my hand lingered before pulling his shirt over his head. He kissed my neck, flicking it with his tongue, and I had never wanted anyone as desperately as I did at that moment. But that side of the record was only two songs, and it ended soon thereafter. I caught my breath and cupped his face with my hands.

"Just let me turn it over," I said.

He exhaled and leaned his head back on the bed. "Fucking short records."

I got up, went to the record player and turned it over. Side two shot out like a Tommy gun.

"Maybe we should hold off on more of *that* for now. Two songs isn't much time."

He sighed, smiled, and said, "As you wish."

We sat side by side with our arms looped together, heads leaned against each other, and it was like the songs entered our bloodstreams through a thousand pinpricks. The waiting thrilled me. He rubbed my arm, slow, and I trailed my hand over that clavicle. I was taking to this harlot thing with great ease.

"It's like electricity, isn't it?" he asked.

"What's that?"

"The record."

"Oh. Yeah," I managed, and kissed his shoulder.

"You're making it difficult to sit still and listen politely."

"Sorry," I whispered.

Side two ended almost as suddenly as it had started. We stared up at the ceiling. In the dim light, its water stains looked like feral roadside flowers in bloom.

"That," I said, "is one of the most perfect things I have ever heard."

He nodded and said, "What shall we listen to now?"

"Something longer?" I asked.

"Yes, please."

My stomach fluttered like it used to back when I had still been interested in sex. I went to my record crates. I couldn't focus; if I'd been thinking clearer, I would have picked a Ramones record for its flawless blending of ironically romantic 50s style crooning and melodic punk rock. Instead, aching to feel him against me again, I grabbed the first record my hand landed on: The Fall, *Live at the Witch Trials*. I hesitated; it was not a record known for its melodic or sexy nature, but rather its janky rhythms and brilliant, angry poetry sneer-shouted by Mark E. Smith.

John got up on the bed and watched me put on the record, then walk slowly over with a raised eyebrow that questioned what he thought.

He laughed. "Interesting choice. I've never... done this sort of thing to this record before."

"I can borrow a Bee Gees record from someone, if you prefer."

He scrunched up his nose and shook his head. He took my hand and pulled me on top of him. I leaned close and kissed his neck, breathing in his intoxicating warm orange and herby smell I was sure would cause me to spend nights tossing and turning while remembering it in my dreams. I stood, pulled the rest of my clothes off, and kicked them to the side, and John did the same. When he pressed his nakedness against mine, I bit my lip to try to keep from rushing any of it.

He lay back down on the bed and pulled me on to him, his fingers hovering on the bend of my hips. I glanced over at my dresser and spotted the small shadow of my engagement ring hunching there like a prissy chaperone. I scowled at it, spread my thighs wider, and leaned down to kiss him.

The record started getting weirder and louder, which gave us an oddly ferocious focus on each other in between fits of laughter.

#

I lay on my back in my tiny twin bed with my leg dangling over the edge, stars threatening to burst through my skin. John was on his side, wrapped around me. I was staggeringly stupid from the first orgasms I'd had in a long time. I started thinking about how to tell Ade, and if I should tell John, and what might happen, and what I was going to do until John kissed my cheek and popped the thought bubble.

The rain started. My bed was right under the window, and a mist blew in through the screen, sprinkling our faces and shoulders. I could just barely hear the train whistle from downtown.

"Just like home," he said, tracing my nose with a finger.

"What's that?" I asked.

"The rain," he said. "It's almost all the sky does in England."

"I love the rain," I said. "It's an excuse to stay inside, read, and drink warm things. Avoid scantily-clad sportball players chucking things indiscriminately."

"Sportball?"

"It's my friend's term. It's just… Balls. For sports we don't understand. Sportball."

He propped himself up on an elbow, looking down at me. "Where are you going after this?"

"I guess to the bathroom," I said.

"Sorry, I mean after university?"

Connecticut was another planet just then.

"I'm," I said, "not sure. You?"

"Probably London. Maybe Manchester. I'm stuck in the Midlands for now. Not exactly a hotbed for aspiring artists."

"You're an artist?" I asked.

He told me that he was studying art, that he drew in ink, made his own frames, and glued small, random toys he found at second-hand shops to the frames to offset the seriousness of his portraits. He said that finding a city to live in would be the only way he could make a real go of it. That he didn't want to give up on it.

"It's a ridiculous dream," he said. "But fuck it, you know? Other people have done it, and it's not like I want to be famous – just make a living of some sort. And if I fail, ok, *then* I can go back to working as a clerk shuffling papers from one cabinet to another in a poorly lit office building. But what's the point in never trying?"

"Your parents must be thrilled," I said.

He stifled a laugh. "Your sarcasm is duly noted."

"I'm sorry," I said. "You just keep getting cooler, and the only way to stop myself from saying so every ten minutes is to make a stupid joke."

"You think I'm *cool*?" he asked.

"Geez, John, I don't know. Kind of."

"The feeling's mutual," he said.

He kissed me and I got dizzy.

"What about you?" he asked. "What's your ridiculous dream?"

I thought about saying that I wanted to be a writer. The English degree, and all that, and it would make me sound more serious. But if I was honest, I knew that wasn't it, because I hated writing. So, for the first time in a long time, I said the honest answer out loud.

"I'd be a DJ," I said. "Not at parties, just on the radio. That's what I do better than anything."

When I looked over at him, he nodded. He didn't even smirk.

"My first memory was of listening to the radio," I said.

"Tell me," he said, and lay his head on my shoulder.

So I did.

***

I sat sprawled on the floor in our kitchen, coloring and eating cheese puffs from a small bowl with Donald Duck on it. I was four years old. My mother stood a few feet away at the ironing board, laboring on one of my dad's dress shirts, with a pile of clean, un-ironed ones in a basket towering on the counter to her left. Sunday mornings were always set aside for ironing the week's clothes. She wore a denim skirt and a white blouse with small, pink flowers and tiny green leaves. Her short, copper hair was in perfect, shiny curls and she was smoking.

She glanced over at my crayon work and said, "Vivian, try to stay in the lines. You're covering up all the pictures with your scribbles. I might as well give you a blank piece of paper instead of paying for coloring books." She poured a cup of coffee and went upstairs to get more hangers from the closet.

I looked down at my book: the thick black lines that formed a horsy, a doggy, and a house were faint under my streaky blocks of brown, red, and waxy yellow. This formerly perfectly nice picture was ugly now because of me. My upper lip quivered, and my cheeks got hot. I put my crayons back in the box and shoved them aside.

The little, single-speaker radio sat on the other counter near the sink. In the moments that followed, a song floated over to me through the air, drying my tears and pulling me up and over to the radio. I stretched out my arms toward it, the sound filling my ears and skull so completely that it spilled over and down into my shoulders, arms, hips, knees, and feet, moving them like I was its little Marionette. I laughed and laughed while I danced. Then a silky voice without music behind it came over the speaker, and I got very quiet.

"That was 'Suspicious Minds' by Elvis Presley. If you didn't dance to that one, you'd best check your pulse. You're listening to WNNH, the sound of Northwestern New Hampshire. I'm Jumpin' Jimmy, and up next, we have a little ditty by a sweet Southern belle who some are calling 'The female Elvis.' Here's Wanda Jackson."

"Wanda Jackson," my mom said from the doorway. "I can't stand her." She came over and switched off the radio. "What are you doing over here?"

I yelled so loud my throat hurt, “Bring it back! Bring the voices back!”

My mom’s face sharpened. “*You* do *not* yell at *me*.”

I flailed my arms because I didn’t know yet that that would only make her madder. “Bring them *back*!” I reached toward the radio but couldn’t get my arms that far back on the counter.

She grabbed my wrists. “Go to your room, Vivian. *Now*.”

I looked back and forth between her and the radio, willing Jumpin’ Jimmy to help me. But he didn’t, so I went to my room and cried until my head hurt and my eyes were swollen. But just before I fell asleep, I thought: *That was magic. I want more.*

***

I glanced at John, expecting to see that glazed-over look of boredom Ade got when I got lost in a memory like that, but he was propped up on an elbow and studying my face in the low light. He touched my cheek with his pinky and ring fingers. “I used to color outside the lines too,” he said. “Do you still listen to Elvis?”

“Sometimes. I play that song on my show every so often, but a lot of people up there think Elvis is cheesy, so I act like it’s a joke and I’m playing it ironically. I’m not, though. It still makes me feel like anything is possible and people don’t have to settle for a relationship they’re not happy with. That they can change it, or walk away. I mean, I didn’t think all that stuff when I was four. Just years of repeat listening and thinking and… Experiences.”

“I know the song but hadn’t thought about it like that. I’ll have to listen to it again.” He twirled a section of my hair around his index finger. “There’s this radio show in England that you'd love – the Peel Sessions, it's called – I listen to it any time I can catch it."

"What's it like?"

"John Peel, the host, has bands come into the studio, and he records them playing a few songs live. It's better than a concert recording because you get all the rawness of a live performance without having to sit through the cheering and some twat singing along out of key right in your ear. He's had so many great bands on – The Damned, The Jam, and of course, our boys, Joy Division. Then he talks about music news and new releases, things like that."

"Sounds like someone already has my dream job covered."

"Maybe he wants a hilarious, sarcastic American co-host? I'll tape some and send them to you, if you like. Consider them research."

"I'd like that," I said. "So, what's England really like? Punks everywhere, great bands playing in abandoned factories and all the stuff *NME* says?"

"Some parts, I suppose, but not so much where I am," he said. "More so in the bigger cities like London and Manchester. Punk's lost its edge a bit, become more a uniform: ripped jeans, expensive leather jackets, dyed, spiked hair. Not long ago, there was more creativity, less conformity."

"I'd rather be around that kind of conformity than the boring crap we have here."

"Have you ever thought about visiting England?" he asked.

"I almost went for a semester last year, but it didn't work out."

I had gone so far as to get my passport and pick out some classes at one of the schools in England that was part of UCNH's exchange program. But a budding relationship with

Ade, as well as a series of frantic, borderline threatening, phone calls from my sister telling me I would make my parents sick with worry if I went, likely sending them to early graves, had caused me to change plans. I tried not to think about it much.

John traced his finger along my forehead, cheeks, and mouth. "I bet you'd love London," he said.

"I have no doubt. I've always wanted to go there. Do you get there a lot?"

"Not as much as I'd like, but I have some friends there who have helped me get to know it better when I'm able to go. It's like any city, you just find your place in it."

I turned toward him. I wanted to remember what it was like to think maybe I *could* do it. Maybe I *could* go and find my place in it.

I remembered his brother. "Is Noel looking for you? I just realized that we up and left without waiting for him."

"Oh," he said. "Right. Would you hate me if I told you that he wasn't actually going to go back looking for me?"

"I don't think so. What do you mean?"

"I kind of," he said, and burrowed his face into my shoulder, "told him I was hoping to... Spend more time with you. That I'd see him later. Possibly tomorrow. I'm sorry."

I laughed. "Don't be sorry. I was hoping to spend more time with you, too." *Oh my god. What am I doing?*

He kissed me, and I let my mind again erase everything outside my room, outside my bed and his lips and his warm arms.

We stayed up late talking. When we couldn't fend off sleep anymore, we got as close as we possibly could, limbs draped over each other, still mumbling about songs and art and a future I wasn't sure would ever apply to me.

Chapter 5

In the morning, as the light grew beyond the drawn shades, I lay on my side against him, deliriously close. His chest rose and fell against my cheek. I'd been awake for a while, being horrified with myself yet not wanting him to leave, and wondering about the logistics of maybe even leaving with him.

I inhaled his sleepy, soft scent, picturing where he might have bought whatever made him smell like he did, making my mind swim; some small drugstore with a name I'd never heard of on a crooked cobblestone street, red door with a bell that rang when he stepped inside, his pretty, focused face scanning the shelves, then paying in pounds and pence. Nothing like the fluorescent-lit Woolworth's where I got my boring deodorant that smelled like baby powder.

I wrapped an arm around his waist, wanting to be even closer, hoping that lessening the space between our bodies would drop me into a different world than the dreary, demanding one hunkering outside, tapping a foot, checking its watch and to-do list. He stirred and yawned.

I should get up, I told myself, get dressed, and chalk the previous night up to sowing some slutty oats I hadn't realized were still laying around. Forget it ever happened.

Or, lob it like a Molotov cocktail straight into my engagement.

"When are you meeting your brother?" I asked. "I mean, if he's *really* your *brother*."

He grinned and glanced over at the alarm clock on the nightstand. "Noon. Not for hours."

He slid his hand down to my lower back and kissed me. I wanted him again already.

#

I pulled on a black, hooded sweatshirt with a zipper up the front. I wasn't ready for him to leave. I wasn't ready to get back to everything else. Wasn't sure if I'd ever be.

"Want to get some coffee? Or tea? That's what your people drink in the morning, right?" I asked.

"I've grown quite fond of coffee," he said.

"I know a place," I said. "Want a clean shirt? You can wear one of mine if you want, they're all just regular t-shirts."

"I'd appreciate that, but I may not be able to get it back to you," he said.

It was an ugly reminder. But an important one.

"Right," I said, "so we should make this a cultural exchange. You leave me your Wire shirt, because I don't have one yet, and I've always wanted one. And I'll give you one of mine."

"Yeah? What've you got?"

I rooted through my t-shirt drawer. "For American bands, let's see. Ramones, of course. Mission of Burma - "

"Never heard of Mission of Burma," he said. "What are they like?"

"They're from Boston. You know how when you're dancing to a fast song, and you're not sure if you're going to be able to keep it up because you're exhausted, but you do, because the song is stronger than your weakness?"

His eyebrows raised up as my sentence rambled on. "Actually, yeah."

"Every song of theirs I've heard is like that. They just sound like what would happen if you opened the pressure valve on all the things you stuff down every day."

He tilted his head and searched my face. “Can you play them for me?”

In an attempt to play it cool, finally, I pretended not to notice his reluctance to get out of bed. “I would, but they don’t have a record out. They just play live a lot. A friend of mine taped one of their shows, but I haven’t gotten him to copy it for me yet. I guess you’ll have to trust my judgment.”

“I do,” he said. “Completely.”

I pretended not to be mesmerized by his oceanic eyes. “You sure do smile a lot.”

“Sorry,” he said. “Not very British of me, is it?”

“No. What a let-down.”

I glanced at the clock. 9:30.

Something caught my peripheral vision. I looked over at my dresser. The gold band and sticky-up diamond glowered at me in the pale light. I glowered back, strode over, opened my top drawer, and swept it in.

“What was that?” he asked.

“Just a,” I said, “spider.”

“You swept a spider into your drawer?”

Shit. Had he seen it?

“Well, yes,” I said. “That’s... where I keep my spiders.”

He furrowed his brows but laughed.

I again fought the urge to take everything back off and jump into bed with him.

“Should probably go soon if we’re going to,” I said. “There’s a place off campus that I like. It’s just a little walk.”

Esmerelda’s Diner was a townie place, about 20 minutes from campus. I liked to go there because it was just far enough away that other college kids didn’t tend to. I’d only been there with Adrian a couple times when we were first dating. He didn’t like the food or the coffee, so we never went back together.

John sighed, pulled down the covers, and grabbed his clothes off the floor. He slipped into his jeans and stood there shirtless with his hands in his pockets. I'm not sure how long I stared before he spoke.

"Could I take you up on that clean shirt?" he asked.

"Right," I said, "of course. Here you go. Do you have something warm too? Like a flannel, or something? It's probably cooled down a lot out there with the rain."

"All my things are in Noel's room," he said. "I didn't plan ahead all that well, I'm afraid."

I handed him the warmest flannel I'd brought back with me from home. The arms were a bit short on him. He looked all that much more striking, like some perfect creature from another world accidentally sent to this small one.

"You say *I* smile a lot," he said.

"Americans always smile. Even when we're having a rotten time."

"Good, then. We're on the same page. Just being polite."

We kissed again and left.

Esmerelda's Diner had been in business since 1957, and by the looks of it, like a lot of places in Marblewell, had never had a remodel or renovation. Its clean, but time-dulled chrome edging and Formica surfaces always made me feel like I was stepping back into the way my parents always talked about the past, without acknowledging all the ugly things about it: before President Kennedy was killed; before the Manson family murders; before Watergate; before Elvis died. Before abortion was safe and legal; before black people couldn't go to the same schools or drink from the same water fountains, for Christ's sake, as white people. Nostalgia was complicated.

I glanced around to see if there was anyone I recognized. Aside from a few regulars I only knew by face, there wasn't.

John and I ordered coffees at the long breakfast counter and carried the thick mugs to a booth in the back. Most of the people there were in their thirties and up, people who lived in and around Marblewell. The large windows that lined the front and sides of the diner were open. A light drizzle had just started back up, making the air smell of coffee, bacon, and late summer rain. Roy Orbison's "Dream Baby" sauntered out of the jukebox and around the room.

I ran a finger around the rim of my mug and glanced down at the floor. His faded black high-tops touched the toes of my scuffed-up, big black leather shoes. When I looked up, he grinned.

"Are you hungry?" I asked. I hated eating in front of people, but my stomach had been growling all morning.

"Famished," he said. *Thank God.*

A waitress came to take our order. We decided to split a large plate of extra crispy bacon with two orders of toast made from their homemade bread.

When she walked away, John reached across the table and held my hand. "I wish we had more time."

"Me too," I said, as a hot bubble rose in my chest. "You're flying out of Boston?"

"Yeah. Around three, I think."

I wanted to ask him not to go, to stay with me, and help me eviscerate my life as it was. *Don't let me pretend this never happened.* But I just nodded.

Our platter of bacon and thick, golden, buttered toast came a few minutes later, and we tore into it. I couldn't remember the last time I was so hungry. The salted meat splintered in my mouth as soon as I bit down, and it tasted so good I closed my eyes while I chewed until John spoke.

"Where are you going after university to get your dream DJ job?" he asked.

"That's just a pipe dream," I said. "I'd have to go somewhere that has the kind of station I want to be at, and that means some big city. I'm more of a country bumpkin than I'd like to admit. Wouldn't last a week in a city, probably. And getting a job in radio is a one-in-a-million chance, anyway."

He rubbed my fingers with his thumb. "You're talking yourself out of it before you've even tried. What if you're the one in a million?"

I laughed. "Right."

John glanced behind me, and I felt a hand on my shoulder. I turned around, and it was Lenny. Just yesterday I'd told him I was engaged to Ade.

Fuck fuck fuck. "Oh! Lenny!" I stood and we hugged.

Lenny had his coffee in a to-go cup, and so had definitely been in the diner long enough to have seen some amount of mooning. In the time it took to wish for the floorboards under me to fall away and the bowels of the Earth to have pity and swallow me whole, Lenny looked over at John, who had stood and was smiling politely.

Lenny flashed his warm, gap-toothed grin that made everyone around him feel happy to be seen, and extended his hand to shake John's.

"Hey, it's been too long. I'm Lenny, a friend of Viv's from the radio station. You must be the lucky guy."

John shook his hand. "Uh, yeah. Yeah, I guess I am."

"Sorry I don't remember your name – I know we met once before, but my memory isn't all that great."

John looked at me, and then all at once the glint of understanding settled in his eyes while his facial expression remained otherwise neutral. "No problem," he said. "I'm John."

Lenny nodded. "Right. Congratulations, John. She's a great girl. I'm sure you'll be very happy together."

"Thank – thank you," John said.

I shoved my hands in my pockets and looked down at my feet.

John gave a polite goodbye, nice to meet you, and excused himself to the restroom. I slowly raised my face to look at Lenny.

He squinted. "I fucked up, huh? That's not your fiancé, is it?"

"Nope."

"Shit, Viv. Sorry. *Really* sorry. My lips are sealed, promise."

"It's not *your* fault. I can't get away with this kind of thing. I don't know what I was thinking."

He ruffled my hair like I was a toddler. "Whoever he is, he looks pretty smitten."

"I'm sure that's all over," I said. "Seeing as I'm a goddamn liar and a fake."

"Well, it's not like you cheated on *him*. I bet he has nothing to complain about."

I sighed. "I don't know what I'm doing, Lenny."

"Don't be so hard on yourself," he said. "He's on his way back, so I'm gonna go, but if you feel like talking later, come up during my show. I'm gonna have Satan's Switchblade live in the studio in the second hour. An acoustic set! They're classically trained. Should be pretty wild."

"Thanks, Lenny. Maybe I'll see you."

He hugged me and left. I dropped with a thud back into the booth and put my head in my hands. I felt him walk by and sit back down across from me.

"I'm so sorry," I whispered. "I should have said something."

I felt his hand, gentle, on my arm. "Viv, please. It's all right, honest."

I looked up, startled at not only his words, but the kind tone of his voice. "I'm sorry I didn't tell you the truth."

He tilted his head and smiled. "You don't need to be sorry. I was hoping there wasn't already someone, but then again, I didn't ask."

I managed a weak smile.

"It's not even *really* your fault," he said. "Look, I know that girls can't help themselves when they hear the seductive sounds of Joy Division; it must be the spine-tingling vocals about isolation and profound loneliness, which, as you know, chicks *dig*. It's the oldest trick in the book, really. You can't be blamed."

I couldn't help but laugh.

He added, "Besides, you don't have to see or hear from me ever again. If that's what you want."

I shook my head.

A woman in black pants, white shirt, and an Esmerelda's apron stood over us with a coffee pot. We nodded. She filled our mugs and dropped more creamers on the table.

"You sure?" he said.

"Yes," I said.

"OK, good," he said. "So… This actual 'lucky guy'?"

I looked across the table at him. I hated to let that world intrude on this one. They couldn't both survive alongside each other, and right now, I just wanted this one.

He looked down into his coffee. Stirred it a couple more times. "Is he good to you?"

"Yeah. He is."

"OK," he said. "Good."

This was the first time our conversation stalled. I wanted to give him something, some explanation. I stammered, "It's just that every time I think about getting married, instead of being happy and excited, I just feel... mad, kind of. Like this is the inevitable end of something. There's so much I haven't seen or done."

He nodded. "So why don't you?" he asked.

"Why don't I what?"

"Why don't you and whoever *he* is, go see and do those things?"

"He thinks maybe when we're older and he's established somewhere, maybe then we can travel some."

John sat up straight and his voice got low as he goofed on a terrible American accent, drawing out the "e" sound. "That sounds very responsible."

I groaned and dropped my head down to the table.

"And *very* fucking boring," he said, returning to his own voice. He reached across the table and lifted my head up by my forehead. "And not at all like the girl I've been getting to know."

I leaned back against the booth. God, how I wanted that to be true. We ate more bacon. God damn it, the toast was also so good it made my eyes water.

After a couple minutes of silence, he grabbed my hands. "Fuck it," he said. "Come to England. We'll go to London. I'm sick to fuckin' death of the Midlands anyway."

I didn't think I could possibly have understood him. "Huh?"

"Let's drop everything that's not working," he said. "We can live as friends if you like, no strings – just help each other figure it out."

I stammered. Tried to say something coherent. Couldn't.

"We'll go to every Joy Division show there is. You *want* to come to England, I can tell. Why not try, see what happens?"

"I can't – I can't just up and leave. I still have to finish school, and my family's here, and he..." I couldn't think of anything else to say.

He held my gaze. We were holding greasy, buttered hands.

"Fuck university, fuck *getting established,* fuck mortgages, fuck offices, fuck not trying to do something fucking *interesting.* Fuck being held back. Come on, come to England today, we'll go to London tomorrow."

All I could do was stare. He stared back, unflinching.

"Why not? Do you have a passport?" he asked.

"Yeah. I just..."

I pictured myself wrapped in a tattered black trench coat, walking along rain-swept streets that had more history than anything I'd ever seen in real life before, passing small, multi-colored row houses, into the city with lights and shadows and art and life and music swirling all around it.

He tucked a piece of hair behind my ear and held his hand against my cheek. He searched my face and his perfect eyes widened. "You're thinking about it. You are!"

"I... Maybe."

He took his hand back and grabbed another piece of bacon. As he bit off half the piece and chewed, his gaze didn't waver, and his smile got bigger. My desire for him gave me goosebumps.

No one would forgive me, and I could never come back. Going would *really* break everything.

Finally, he sighed, and said, "OK. All right. Fine. But I'm giving you my phone number and address. Just in case you change your mind."

I nodded and said, "OK."

The rain had backed off again to a light drizzle. We walked along a sidewalk through the Main Street of

Marblewell. When we reached the top of a hill, I stopped and pointed at a patch of ocean barely visible through the trees.

"You'll be flying over that today," I said.

"Yeah," he said. "England's not really *that* far."

We continued walking. The leaves on the trees lining the walk were mostly still green, though a few were turning orange or yellow, and some littered the sidewalk like confetti after everyone's left the party. The breeze was a little warmer now.

He told me he'd like to be walking with an arm around me but didn't want to risk getting me in "hot water." I nodded, and stuck my arm through his, a slightly less intimate way of touching, or so I hoped it appeared.

We got to Noel's dorm, and found his room, but John didn't knock. "Will you keep in touch?"

"I'll try," I said. "I'm just not sure what will happen."

"You don't have to be."

He looked around, whispered that no one else was there, wrapped his arms around me, and we kissed. We stood with our torsos and thighs pressed tight to each other. I squeezed my eyelids shut to squelch the gathering hot tears.

Then the door opened. I let go, but John kept an arm around my shoulders. We exchanged good mornings.

Noel said he had to find his wallet and he closed the door, giving us one last moment.

John turned back to me, touched my cheek, and held his hand there. As he looked into my eyes, the bridge of his nose creased, and his gaze went watery.

If you cry, I'm leaving with you.

I held his hand that hung at his side, and he gripped mine so hard that it almost hurt, had it not felt so warm and grounding. He winced as if he were in pain, opened his mouth and said, "I – "

Noel's door opened. He set John's bag down in the hallway.

"Ready, John? They'll be waiting."

John turned toward his brother, then back to me. He did such a small headshake that I almost wasn't sure I saw it.

I'm not ready, either.

"Yeah," he said, and rubbed his eyes. "Right. Bye, Viv."

Fuck. Fuck. Fuck. "Safe travels," I said.

We squeezed each other's hands, then I pulled away. I turned and scurried down to a stairwell at the far end of the hall. I sat just inside, on the top step, collecting my breath and wits, and tried to stop crying. *You've made the right decision. You've made the right decision. You've made the right decision. You've made...*

#

I found myself on a sandy bench at the beach, staring at the waves. The day was overcast and drizzly, so I had it almost all to myself. I stayed there for so many hours, trying to figure out what I was going to do, that I lost track.

I cheated on Ade. My god, I really did. Does it only count as once because it was one night? Or does it count as three times, because...

Eventually, I got cold and walked back to my room. The whole walk back, I imagined John changing his mind at the airport, hailing a taxi, and speeding back. The vision seemed so real that when I got to my room and he wasn't sitting there next to my door, I hung my head and wiped away the tears with my sleeve. There was a note from Izzy saying to call her.

I dried off, changed into sweatpants and John's t-shirt, inhaling his smell that lingered, not caring if it was a little creepy to do so. I walked down the hall to the payphone with my tube sock full of change and dialed her number.

"Just checking in," she said. "You weren't at lunch today."

"Sorry about that. I spaced it."

"Did the English guys stick around?"

I wasn't ready to tell anyone what I'd done. But Izzy always knew if I tried to hide anything from her.

"The younger one had a date or something, and John – the older one – didn't have anything else to do. So, yeah. He stuck around."

"Man, he was *gorgeous*," she said. "Dean thought so, too."

"Oh yeah?"

Izzy put Dean on. "Listen," he said, "I can admit when another man is striking, handsome, beautiful, etcetera. That guy was all of those things. That dark, tousled Rockstar hair. Those insanely blue eyes. And that accent, Jesus. I bet he plays guitar too – I can tell by the forearms – oh, come on. Izzy's taking the phone back - "

"See?" she said.

"Aw, Dean," I said, laughing. "Yeah, John was... Yeah."

"'John was Yeah.' What does *that* mean?"

I sighed, trying to think of a way out. I couldn't. "He came back to my room. He left this morning."

There was a pause as she took this in. "*Really*?"

"Really."

"This is major."

I squeezed my eyes shut. "I know. I fucked up. I really fucked up."

"Oh, hang on, don't do *that*."

"What?"

She sighed. "Don't go beating the shit out of yourself."

"How can I not, Izzy? This is the worst thing that I could do to him. I don't deserve a moment's peace. There's something wrong with me."

"No. Listen, if you were some lascivious floozy – which I'm sure you've called yourself meaner variations on countless times today – you'd have a long history of this sort of thing. But you don't. What happened is a symptom. Adrian is a good guy, but he's not as flawless as you make him out to be."

"Everyone is going to want to kill me."

"That's a *little* melodramatic," she said. "Viv?"

"Yeah."

"I want details."

"You know I don't do that."

"You're such a New Englander," she said. "Call me if you need anything."

We hung up and I shuffled back to my room.

I put Joy Division on my record player and wrote John a letter.

Saturday, September 8, 1979

Dear John,

It's nighttime on the day you left. I wanted to write to you before everything starts to fade. Before that other life comes crashing back in like the goddamn Frosty-Juice Guy. Do you have the Frosty-Juice Guy in England? He's fucking nightmarish – he's loud and is constantly destroying people's walls as he bursts through them. No remorse. Purple, bulbous body. Dead, hollow eyes. "UH-HUH!" he bellows at anyone who is hot and thirsty and therefore must heed his cries. That's what my other life is like right now, the one I didn't want to talk much about.

I don't know yet if I'll tell him. I want to keep it all to myself like a pretty marble closed in my palm. Also, I guess I'm scared. I've never been in this spot before.

When I was in nursery school, there was this kid who used to take my hand and lead me down to the end of a very long hallway once a week or so. There was nothing at the end of the hallway. The overhead lights had all burned out. He made me sit there, silent, while he rode around on a wood fire truck, screaming at any kids who entered the hallway. I was too scared to move or ask for help. Eventually a teacher came looking for us and he had to let me go. When I'd tell my mom about it, she'd always say the boy was harmless, and that it just meant he liked me. I eventually stopped telling her when it happened again. Since this semester started, this memory keeps coming back to me at random times, sometimes even when I'm sleeping; when it does, I wake up in a sweat. I still have a serious phobia of long, dead-end hallways and isolated places – there has to be a way out, or I'll turn back.

If you didn't grow up in a small, claustrophobic place like Stonewald, it's hard to explain exactly how far away everything seems. It wasn't a place that Rockstars or artists came from – not that I was either of those things, but it would have been neat to know some back then. Mr. Webb at the general store once scoffed at Mick Jagger for "prancing around like a goddamn faggot peacock," if that gives you any indication of my local culture. I loved the Rolling Stones, but I kept quiet about it; didn't want to be accused of being mouthy. Mouthy is a bad thing for girls to be, at least in Stonewald.

In high school, I wasn't a good enough student to hang out with the smart kids. I hated gym class, so team sports couldn't have interested me less. I never figured out how to play an instrument, so I couldn't be a band kid. And I didn't like pot, so I couldn't hang out with the stoners because they thought I was a narc. Those were the options at high school in my authoritatively practical hometown. I sat alone at lunch every day and read the music magazines that my big brother Paul gave me. At home, my mom would say things about when I got older, got married, and had kids, but I couldn't see how that was possible, seeing as I didn't even have any real friends, let alone boyfriends.

In late June after my junior year of high school, my dad had to travel for work, and Mom went with him. I didn't want to be all alone, so went to stay with Paul, his wife, and my two young nephews in a rural northern Vermont town. They lived in an old farmhouse with hardwood floors and lots of windows filled with houseplants. I loved it there. That was the weekend I discovered David Bowie and became a music junkie.

Paul had a new, high-tech stereo system and had built huge, wooden slatted crates to hold his enviable record collection. He even had a cassette deck that could record directly from his albums, and he always sent me home with one or two he'd recorded just for me. They never sounded as good on my little dinky tape player, but the songs still felt like friends. I loved flipping through his hundreds of records and looking at the artwork.

My first morning there on this particular visit, I padded downstairs to the kitchen. My sister-in-law had gone to work, but Paul took the day off to hang out with me and the boys, who were playing in the backyard. He poured me some coffee in a ceramic mug, and I sat down at the glass-topped table.

He asked me how high school was going, and I said I wished abortion had been legal when Mom got pregnant with me so I wouldn't have to go.

"Stonewald is a horrible place to be stuck at 17," he told me. "It has a way of making people crazy – especially young people."

He said that was why he left and backpacked around Europe for a while as soon as he could, not long after I was born. He said it was too small in Stonewald – like slowly being suffocated. I agreed. Then he told me that things would get better as I got older and went away to college.

The thing was, I've never been smart, my grades have always been mediocre at best, and I didn't think any college would want me. At 17, I felt like I'd already blown my chance at any kind of interesting life. I didn't know what to do. I didn't have friends, and the only boys at school who would even look at me were scary guys who smoked, blared KISS from their pickup trucks in the parking lot, and yelled rape threats at girls.

I felt like a loser, and was so sick of being all alone. I wished I *could* fit in. I would have faked anything if I'd had the slightest idea how, but I couldn't even figure that out.

"Listen," my brother said, "I have a record that I want you to hear, ok?"

Later on, he took David Bowie's *The Rise and Fall of Ziggy Stardust and the Spiders from Mars* from his record crate. I'd read a lot about David Bowie, but the radio stations I could pick up didn't play him, so I'd never actually heard him.

I still remember every word my brother said: "This record is the story of a guy who would *hate* Stonewald; Ziggy is androgynous, bisexual, *and* prophecies aliens coming down to Earth to save us from ourselves. And a bunch of other stuff happens that I don't really understand, but people *love* him. It gets kinda freaky – lots of meandering guitar solos – but stick with it. Just know that some of the most interesting people didn't fit in in high school. And the *most* interesting people love David Bowie." He put the needle on the record, ruffled my hair, and went to make the boys lunch.

I took a deep breath, relaxed my shoulders, and sank into the overstuffed couch. Looking out the window just beyond the stereo, my gaze settled on a grove of gleaming, slender birch trees swaying as I was swept into Ziggy's story.

Even though I didn't understand all of the words, I gleaned that his world was glamorous and dangerous. It put me on the rainy, metropolitan streets of London, where everything strange and interesting seemed to happen; *that* was where I wanted to be. I clung to each and every second of that record. I had never heard anything quite like it and got lost in daydreams about faraway places and ethereally beautiful boys. That was also the day I fell in love with London.

During the last song on side two, "Rock 'N' Roll Suicide," I became convinced that David Bowie was howling directly at me, that I was in fact *not* alone. I sobbed so hard that my body shook. But this time, it wasn't because I was sad or hopeless or hating myself; it was because I believed him that I wasn't alone, believed him with every part of my being, and it was the purest, most exquisite sense of connection to something bigger that I'd felt since that first day I really heard the radio when I was four. When side two was done, I turned it over and listened to the whole thing again.

Senior year, things did get better – not because I found any real friends, because I didn't. They got better because Paul mailed me tapes every week or two when I couldn't get over there to see them. He sent me tapes of records by the Velvet Underground, the Kinks, the Sonics, the Mummies, and more Bowie. With each one came a letter about why he loved that record, what it meant to him, and why he picked it out for me. There was a lot of stuff about people not fitting in, and how sometimes it could even be a badge of honor. I never quite got around to feeling any sense of pride about my own inability to fit in, but it helped knowing that others did about theirs.

I related much more to the slow, sad songs about being lonely or the rowdy songs about being mad than I did the ones about kissing and holding hands; I'd never been the pretty, willowy girl in the sundress on the beach that someone turned themselves inside out trying to impress, and I never would be. But that was ok, because Ziggy Stardust wouldn't be caught dead smiling on a sunny beach either, and I wanted to go where he went.

Because of Paul, I glimpsed whole other worlds underneath the satiny surface of the top 40's slick, heavily produced hits; worlds on records where other people felt ugly, alone, pissed off, and scared. Those records became everything to me. And when I finally left home and came here and found the radio station, I found more and more records that made me feel like there was still magic in the world. I know that you know what that's like. It's because of Paul and the radio station that I am who I am now. Or maybe they just drew out the person I was trying to become? I'm not sure.

Have you ever noticed on mail addressed to your parents that it's almost always "Mr. and Mrs. [whatever your dad's first name is. Nigel? Alistair?] Blackwood?" Women who were fully formed people before they got married become a prefix of their husbands' names. It's something you barely notice if you're not paying attention, but I can't stop thinking about it. I'm not going to be "Viv" to people some day; I'm going to be "Mrs. Adrian O'Brien." Even when both people enter into marriage with the best intentions, this absorption just happens while no one's looking. It's only been three years since I've started figuring out who I am, and it feels like that's all I get. I'm staring down the double barrel of a marriage certificate, and I am fucking terrified.

So, dear John, I tell you all this because when I met you last night, I was feeling more than a little crazy, and sad, and sick to death of my own thoughts. And a small, quiet part of me wanted to do something I could never come back from, something that would break apart what I have now, something that would irreparably fuck it all up. Honestly, I didn't think I'd go through with it. But you were sweet and funny, and beautiful, and it sounds so childish, but you like the same things I do, and it was just so easy being with you.

How to wrap up this jumble of thoughts? I guess to simply say: Thank you. Even though we only had a handful of hours together, I feel lucky to have had them. Just knowing you're out there in the world makes me happy at a time when I don't know what the fuck is going to happen here.

And even though I'm sure you were just joking about me going to England this morning, I admit I daydreamed about it for much of my afternoon by the sea.

Your Friend,
Viv Pierce

I put it in an envelope, addressed it, affixed several postage stamps, and dropped it in the mail slot in the lobby. It wouldn't go out till Monday, but was a done deal. I'd been holding so much in lately that it felt good to not do that for a change. It was the longest letter I'd ever written.

I flicked on the radio and lay back down on the bed. The sounds of an all-acoustic Satan's Switchblade swirled around me. They were playing their college radio hit, "Dark Arts Honey (Yeah)." I thought about going to hang out with Lenny but fell asleep before the thought got any further.

Chapter 6

A week and a half went by. I still hadn't had the guts to tell Ade what I'd done. On Tuesday night, after making some other excuse not to spend the night with him, I went back to my room but couldn't sleep. Just after ten o'clock, I got up, threw on some jeans and a sweater, and decided to go to his room across campus and tell him. I couldn't stand being a liar anymore, and it was time to come clean. I started walking.

I looked down at the ring on my left hand; I had put it on, assuming I would need to give it back. There was no way we could stay together after this; I knew that much. I'd never seen any flash of a violent side, but it struck me that being cheated on could make some people do crazy things.

When I was 11, the Crosses lived on our street. Their kids were little and took naps, and Mrs. Cross's other man would go over during their naptime. Everyone knew about the affair, but no one said anything to her, or him, only each other. One day, Mr. Cross came home early from work and caught them having sex in the master bedroom. He grabbed his hunting rifle from the living room and shot them both. People said there were brains and bone everywhere. Neighbors who came over to our house to play cards said things like "Little whore had that coming."

Maybe I should wait till daylight when more people will be around. Just in case.

But I kept walking. As I headed off the main walkway and across Norton Hill, lost in my head, I realized that this part of campus was uncharacteristically silent, which was why I looked up as I stepped on to the paved walkway.

I stopped when I saw the two rows of figures lining the path, inches from me: they were all around six feet tall, dressed like skeletons, with their faces painted in elaborate skull makeup. There must have been ten on each side, evenly spaced. No one said a word or moved. Each one held a small, lit candle.

I knew that I should be afraid, but I wasn't. I wanted to see what would happen. I held my head high and walked down the middle of the skeleton men. Still, no one moved. It was the quietest few moments that I had ever had on campus. I slowed my walk. I thought, *I'm walking through death right now. Maybe I died already, and I didn't realize it, and all this is just...*

I was almost to the end of the line when I heard someone whisper my name. It broke my trance, and as I reached the last two skeleton men on either side of me, someone pulled me away.

"Jesus Christ, Viv," Keaton said. "What are you, rushing a fraternity now?"

"Oh," I said, and looked back. "Is that what that was?"

"Pledges," he whispered, and led me away from them. "*Why* would you walk right through that? You need to be more careful."

I shrugged.

I'd met Keaton when I was a freshman and he was a junior; he was much cooler than anyone I knew, with his cropped, curly red hair, round wire-rimmed glasses, vintage white shirts and dress pants with combat boots. He said I reminded him of his little sister.

***

The first time he'd saved my ass was during a party at one of his friend's house. I'd discovered my mixed drink limit after watching a black and white, unsteady student film the friend was screening; the room spun, and I'm told I fell to my knees after wandering into the kitchen. Keaton said some guy he didn't recognize came over and started talking to me, touching my shoulders and brushing my hair away from my drunk face. The guy helped me up and walked me toward a door that led outside.

"Hang on, friend," Keaton yelled, "I know her about-to-puke face, and she is about to puke." I'm told that I laughed so hard that my face turned red, and I actually did start heaving like throwing up was imminent.

When I woke up the next morning, head pounding, eyes dry as bleached bones, I was on a small futon mattress on the floor of the bathroom and the door was closed. I turned my head, and Keaton was next to me. I gasped, and he jumped. He rubbed his eyes and grabbed his glasses from a small table next to the mattress.

"Calm down," he said. "Nothing happened. You got so sick I thought you'd puke up your spleen. I grabbed the mattress from the guest room and stayed with you to make sure that creepy guy didn't try to carry you off again."

"What creepy guy?"

He sighed. "Don't watch pretentious student films or have more than a couple drinks if I'm not around, ok?"

I nodded and fought a wave of nausea.

He propped himself up on an elbow and said, "I only wish that just before you hurled, you'd yelled 'Art is dead' at the top of your lungs."

***

Once we were away from the pledges and in a better-lit area, Keaton put both his hands on my shoulders and narrowed his eyes at me. "You ok? Are you on something?"

"No, *Dad*. I'm not *on* anything. What are you up to?"

He kept examining my face, tilting it at different angles toward the light. "Headed back to the apartment. Probably drink some beer and record some stupid music with Resource Center."

Resource Center was a loose collective of people who met each other through the radio station or through friends there. It was a band, sort of. I never really knew if they were joking or not, but I erred on the side of joking, because they usually laughed after the stop recording button was pressed. There were about four electric guitar players at any given get-together, along with bass, drums, vocals, and whatever other instruments people brought and marginally knew how to play. They usually practiced/hung out and drank Old Milwaukee tall boys at an apartment just off campus.

"Want to come?" he asked.

"Yeah," I said, "but I can't. I've got to do something that I really don't want to."

He crossed his arms over his chest. "Walk with me," he said, and offered his bent arm, like some sort of Southern gentleman in the movies. "Just for a few."

I took his arm. He started walking us slowly in the direction of the off-campus apartment.

"What's this thing you have to do?" he asked.

"I'm afraid to tell you."

"Why would you be afraid to tell me?"

"Because. It'll change the way you see me."

"Oh, for fuck's sake, no it won't. You've seen *me* do lots of stupid shit."

"Not stupid like this."

"Try me."

I stopped walking and turned toward him. "I cheated on my fiancé a week and a half ago and haven't told him." I closed my eyes.

"Wait a second. When did you get engaged?"

I opened one eye. "What is wrong with me? I didn't tell you, either?"

He shook his head. "To who? When's his shift at the station?"

"No, he's not at the station. He's a newspaper kid." I told him how we met. "That was right after Antoine."

I knew Keaton remembered Antoine because I'd gone up to the station after reading the infamous breakup letter, and Keaton was on the air. It was one of those all-night broadcasts some of us enjoyed punishing ourselves with every now and again, and he saw that I'd been crying. He played a bunch of my favorite songs and we hung out till the sun came up and another DJ came along and took over for him.

Keaton shook his head. "*Antoine*. Fancy fucking asshole."

"Yeah. He's the one who made me swear off radio station guys. Then Ade came along, and the rest has all happened in kind of a blur. And I'm a huge slut, I guess, and now I have to tell him."

"First off, don't be so judgmental: sluts rule. Second: you're not."

"What, so I don't rule?"

"Focus. I'm going to tell you something I've never told anybody. I've cheated on someone too."

My eyes got big.

"Don't give me that look," he said. "It was just one time. This was a few years ago. My girlfriend at the time was a real sweetheart. We'd been together almost a year when I slept with someone I met at a party."

"What? Why?"

He pursed his lips together. "Why did *you*?"

"Because I'm an idiot?"

He shook his head. "Try again."

"Because I'm a horrible person."

He shook his head. "Try again."

"Are you sure it's not because I'm a slut and just never realized it until recently?"

"Had you cheated on him, or anyone else before this?"

"No. You can see, my conscience can't take it."

"Obviously. One more try."

"I mean, this other guy… He was perfect."

"No guy is perfect."

"No, just – he was English, which is hot as hell, and my god, he was so beautiful. He likes all the same music I do, he kept complimenting me on how good I was at DJing, he made me feel like I was the only person worth paying attention to in the world, he asked me all about my life, and what I wanted to do with the rest of it."

Keaton nodded. "And newspaper kid is… Lacking in those areas?"

I looked up at the night sky. I couldn't find anything to focus on because it was all cloudy.

"OK," he said, and tented his fingers over his nose. He always did that when he was trying to not lose patience with someone. "Let's try this: without thinking too much, tell me three words about newspaper kid."

I shook my head and said, "Uh."

"That's not a word. Go."

Fuck. OK. Ade. "Consistent. Motivated. Um… Cute. No, well, yes he is, but – ok, third word for real: Organized."

Keaton nodded. "And now, three words about how you feel when you think of him. Go."

"I'm not good at this, Keaton."

"GO."

"Jesus. OK… Mature. Um… Stable. Safe."

"Those are adjectives more than feelings," he said. "But fine. Now the Brit. Tell me three words about him."

"Artistic. Passionate. Gorgeous."

"Three words about how he makes you feel."

I remembered lying naked with him. "Beautiful. Dreamy. H- Uh…"

"Horny? You were going to say 'horny,' weren't you?"

"Um, hungry," I said, then added quickly, "Before him, I never ate half a platter of bacon in front of any guy I wasn't related to. So anyway – that girl. The one you cheated on. How would you describe her?"

He shrugged. "It's a long story I'll tell you some other time. We were much better as a couple in theory than in practice. I acted before I really understood that, but it ended up being right, however shitty it was of me. With Cassie, though, things are just easier."

"Who's Cassie?"

"My fiancée, pumpkin."

"How did I not know this?"

"You've had your head up your ass, just like me. It's ok. I'll still invite you to the wedding."

We started walking again. "I still have to tell him."

"Maybe not. Maybe just break things off. If things aren't going to work out – if you know this deep down, and *I* think you do – do him a favor. Cut him loose. You could save his feelings a little by not telling him about the other guy. The other guy's almost irrelevant anyway. But those feelings – the ones you said, they're what you want."

I took a deep breath and exhaled. "What have I done?"

He stopped our walking and hugged me. "Come make some noise," he said.

When we got to his apartment on the left side of an old farmhouse that had been converted into a duplex, it was about 10:30, and "practice" had been underway for a while, judging by all the humming amps and beer cans sitting on flat surfaces. Some of my favorite people were there, and I ended up staying, listening to hilariously terrible cover versions of obscure Rolling Stones songs, drinking way too much beer, and laughing until my stomach hurt. I think I wailed on the E string of someone's bass on a few songs. Things wound down late, and I crashed on their couch.

Chapter 7

The only things I wanted in the world the next morning were a shower and a big breakfast, but by the time I got up, all I had time for before my first class was to run back to my room to grab my books, brush my teeth, and deposit Ade's ring safely on the bureau. I knew if I went back to my room after that first class that I'd fall asleep and miss the rest of my classes late in the day and early evening, and my grades couldn't afford that. So I stayed out and about with an evil hangover all day, swearing at the sun.

By the time I got back to my room that night after class, it was almost eight. Adrian was sitting on the floor outside my room. He was reading a textbook about pedagogy.

"Ade?" I said, shoving my left hand with its bare ring finger in my pocket.

He looked up, startled. "Hey. Where've you been? I haven't seen you all day."

"Big day of classes," I said.

He stood and moved to kiss me, but he snapped his head back. "Classes? You smell like a cheap brewery."

"Sorry, Ade. I went over to Keaton's last night and haven't had a chance to shower since."

His smile faded, and he put his book in his bag. "What were you doing there all night? And on a *Tuesday*?"

Ade knew perfectly well that Keaton always had been and always would be my friend, and only my friend. There are just some people you love like that. Yet, he still got territorial and overbearing sometimes. I did not have the energy.

"Celebrating his engagement, Ade." *Close enough.*

"Oh," he said, and relaxed the muscles in his forehead. "Well, that's great. Tell him congratulations from me next time you see him."

He doesn't even remember meeting you. "Will do."

We stood there looking at each other, nodding and half smiling.

He said, "Do you want to open your door?"

"Oh… Yeah." I got my key out of my backpack and unlocked the door. I really hoped he wasn't going to want to stay over. I was exhausted and smelled bad and needed a lot of time to think.

I flicked on the overhead light and dropped my heavy bag on the desk with a thunk. No wonder my neck and shoulders ached so much, carrying around half a library on my back. When Ade wasn't looking, I slipped the ring back on.

"Did you eat?" he asked.

"Had a quick sandwich at lunch just before the dining commons closed."

"You must be starving," he said, and sat on my bed. "Why don't you take a quick shower, we can mess around a little, then go downtown, see what's open?"

I decided to ignore the "mess around" part. "It's already after eight on a Wednesday in New Hampshire. All the restaurants have been closed for hours."

He nodded. "Ah, I guess you're right. Maybe the student center's still open."

My stomach growled. "I think they close at nine. Maybe I should go grab something now."

"What if you shower, I go get you something – a chicken sandwich and fries? – and then we reconvene?"

I hated the chicken sandwiches at the student center. They were always gristly and too greasy. And I always got tater tots there, not their limp, soggy fries.

"No, that's ok," I said. "I'll go." I put my coat back on, and hoped he'd follow suit, causing the evening to reach its natural end.

"I forgot you're a picky eater. I'll just stay here and do some homework."

Jesus. "OK."

At the student center, I ordered my cheeseburger and tater tots, and sat slumped at a table waiting for my number to be called.

How can I get him out of my room? I can't do that tonight. I just can't.

"Viv, right?"

My knee hit the metal post under the table as I realized that Noel was standing across from me.

"Sorry," he said, laughing. "Didn't mean to startle you."

"It's ok," I said. "I'm just tired and apparently very unobservant. How are you, Noel?"

"Good, thanks. I'm still interested in the radio station – I've just been awfully busy settling in, getting used to everything."

"There's a general meeting next Tuesday if you want to come. Think they're starting to pair up trainees with DJs."

I asked how things were going, and as he told me everything was going well, a group of four girls walked in, looking around. He waved, and they giggled.

"Those are my friends, so I should go. But just one more thing – my brother John said to be sure to say hi if I saw you around."

A bolt of energy ran through me, until I realized that Noel would likely report back to John that I was looking haggard and smelling like an old couch and stale beer.

I brought a hand up to smooth my hair. "Oh, yeah? How is he?"

"He's good," he said. "Moved into a new flat with his friend Albert, looking forward to being done with it all next springtime. Said something about maybe switching schools for spring term, maybe moving to London."

"He mentioned that," I said. "I wasn't sure how serious he was."

"Yeah, he's been saying he wants a change. He goes to uni about an hour west of where we grew up, and there's nothing much there to get too excited about. So, I say good for him." He leaned over the table and said quietly, "He really likes you. He'll kill me if he knows I told you that, so mum's the word, yeah?"

I felt my cheeks turning red. "My lips are sealed. Tell him I said hi too, please."

"Will do. See you next week." He went to his friends, who surrounded him like it was choreographed.

'He really likes you.' I replayed those four words in my head again and again, and I was sure I was going to float right up to the cigarette smoke-stained dropped-tile ceiling.

"Number 11. Cheeseburger, tots." Those ones, though, reminded me of the situation at hand. I stood and shuffled over to the pickup counter.

When I got back to the room with my food, Ade was reading again and taking notes. As I ate, he talked about his classes and the school he'd be going to to practice some teaching techniques, and ones he agreed with and ones he didn't and all I could think was: *I'm a monster. I'm a monster. I'm a monster.*

When I was done with the slender but surprisingly tasty burger and perfectly crispy tots, I put the container in my trash can and got my shower stuff together.

Don't think about what Noel said. This is your life. Not that.

"Ade, I'm so tired, and I have classes in the morning. Can we call it a night?"

"Maybe if you hadn't been out all night drinking with your friends, you'd have time for me." I should have felt guilty, but I felt mad instead. *Monster.*

"I'm sorry. It was all completely last minute."

He put his book on my bed. "Viv, you've been extra distant lately. When we're married, you can't just go out all night and put me off and not tell me things."

"It's not like I'll have any friends in Connecticut to go out all night with anyway," I snapped.

"You totally missed my point, but… You'll make new friends. We'll make couple friends, too. And my sister says that having kids in school is one of the best ways to meet new people as an adult."

Please. Not tonight.

"Ade. What if…" *Don't say anything. You don't have the brainpower right now.*

He stood and came over to me. "What if what?"

"What if – just hypothetically – what if I didn't want to have kids?"

He blinked at me, startled. "What?"

"Well. I mean, we've never really talked about it."

He shook his head. "I just *assumed…*" He deflated onto my desk's chair.

Maybe this is good. Maybe if I'm honest – mostly honest – maybe I won't be as scared of our future. Maybe he just never thought that was an option before. Maybe this will be ok after all.

"Ade? Are you all right?"

He was staring at the light switch. "I just… This is a big deal."

"It doesn't have to be."

He shook his head. "I need to lie down. Think about this a bit."

Did I break his brain? "Like… You mean here? Or…"

He looked up at me. "Why don't you go take a shower. I'll crawl into bed and we'll talk more later."

Don't sigh. Don't sigh. "OK, Ade."

I took my time, willing the hot, then warm, then lukewarm water to clear the cobwebs from my brain.

This conversation needs to happen. I don't even know for sure that I don't want kids ever. But I might not. I need to know if he's ok with that and open to the possibility. My method and timing of bringing this up SUCK, but at least something will change. Either he'll be ok with it, and maybe things aren't as bleak as I've been imagining, or he won't be ok with it, and break up with me. Either way, this will be solved.

I turned off the water and grabbed my towel. "OK," I said. "This is good. This is *good.*"

"Who are you talking to?" said a girl's voice from a toilet stall.

I got back to the room, and the lights were all off. I wondered if Ade had left, but his voice said "Hey" from the direction of my bed.

My eyes gradually adjusted to the relative dark, and I could see he was under the covers, extending his hand toward me. I set down my stuff on the desk and toweled off my hair more.

"Just a minute," I said. I had slept over at Ade's room a couple of times since the night I met John, but we hadn't had sex, and he hadn't slept in my room, and this all felt incredibly bizarre and I just wanted my bed to myself.

Eventually, my hair was bone dry and I ran out of stuff to rearrange in the dark, so I went over to the bed and slid in next to Ade. I lay on my side, turned away from him, trying to make myself as small as possible.

He put an arm around me, and the length of his body pressed against the back of mine. I closed my eyes.

He exhaled. "I'm sorry I got all weird."

"It's ok. Are you mad?"

"No."

"OK," I said. "Good."

He kissed my shoulder through my t-shirt. "I remembered something my sister said. She said that she never used to want kids either. But not long after she married my brother-in-law, she got pregnant, and she said everything changed then. It was like it was *real*. You know? It wasn't some *philosophical* thing. And once she got over the shock, she was excited about it. About becoming a mother. Other people – friends, cousins – have told me pretty much the same story. People change their minds about this stuff all the time. They say it's the greatest thing they've ever done."

His sister was two years older than us and had three kids. I'd only met her twice, but she was crabby both times.

He said, "You're cold, huh? You're shivering." He pulled the blankets up around my shoulders and wriggled tighter against me. "I know. You're tired. We don't have to talk about it more tonight."

I was squeezing my eyes shut to try to keep from crying. This wasn't the resolution I'd been hoping for. "OK," I said. I set my jaw and closed my eyes.

Chapter 8

The next morning, Ade had an eight o'clock class, and had to go back to his dorm beforehand, so he was up and out of bed early. I didn't have anything until a little before ten, when Izzy would come to walk to class with me, so I stayed in bed and pretended to be asleep as he got his things together. I tasted blood from biting my tongue and cheeks during the night.

He left, and I got up and got dressed. I didn't feel up to going to breakfast and interacting with the world yet, so around nine-thirty, I got a granola bar and a soda from the vending machine in the lobby downstairs. I sat at my desk and chewed the hard, stale oat and honey brick, occasionally softening it with a mouthful of fizzy, sugary liquid. There was a knock at my door, so I opened it.

No one was there. I looked down and saw two little statues on the grubby, thin carpet. I picked them up: one was a bride with an old-fashioned, high-necked dress. Her clay and paint hair was medium brown and elaborately styled into a high, swept-up bun, and she held what I guess was supposed to be a bouquet of red roses. However much time the artist had spent on the hair and dress, they spent that much less time on her face, which was a cluster of small lines and dots that vaguely resembled eyes, a nose, and a mouth. Her groom was in my other hand, and had a slightly more detailed face, wore a tiny tuxedo, and held a top hat in one hand. They were horrifying.

I saw movement in my peripheral vision, and jumped back, startled, almost dropping them.

It was Ade. "Careful with those," he said, and took them from me. "My mom sent them to me to show you."

"What *are* they?"

"They're the cake toppers she and my dad had when they got married twenty-five years ago. She mailed them to me and wanted me to show you." He wrapped them in bubble wrap and placed them gingerly back in the box. "I know they're pretty old-fashioned, but it's her way of saying she likes you. Isn't that great?"

I wondered about how I had gone 21 years without knowing what cake toppers were and now they were dominating my waking life.

"Hey Viv, are you feeling ok?"

"Yeah. I'm good. I just – Izzy's coming by any minute now. We have class soon."

"Oh. OK. Listen, I didn't want to leave things like we did last night, and you were sound asleep this morning when I left, so..."

Like an angel fallen from Heaven, Izzy came walking down the hall. Per usual, she was put together impeccably: her hair was in a perfect French twist, her skin as dewy as a wildflower in May, and she wore a navy-blue dress with white buttons and Peter Pan collar, frayed just a little to show its age from the previous decade.

"Ready to go?" she said. "Hello, Adrian."

"Hi, Iz." She hated when people shortened her name to one syllable. "Viv, let's meet up for lunch, ok?"

I glanced at Izzy, who could smell my fear.

"Actually, Ade," she said, "I was hoping to borrow her for lunch today, if that's all right. There are some things I really need to talk to her about. You know, *girl stuff*."

"Oh," he said. "Sure. Yeah, of course. I'll see you later, then?"

I smiled and nodded, he kissed me on the cheek and left.

"The fuck just happened? It felt like I was walking into an execution."

"He stopped by to show me the cake toppers his mother sent him."

"Cake toppers?"

"For the wedding cake and wedding day and wedding everything that I'm so fucking excited about. They look like little demons biding their time till they can fly away with my soul to the depths of bourgeois hell."

"'Bourgeois,' huh? Careful, people might think you're one of those anarchists."

"I wish."

"You have *got* to say something. This is killing you, and it's hard to watch."

I put my sweater on, swapped out yesterday's books in my bag for that day's, and grabbed the yellow slip that had been in my mailbox. "I think there's either something really wrong with me, or maybe this is just what they call 'cold feet.' You and Dean talk about getting married all the time, and you're not freaking out and doing things you can't undo."

We started walking down the stairs. "Yeah, but Dean's cool."

"He sure is. Hey, do I have time to stop by the mail window real quick? I guess there's something waiting for me, and they weren't open when I checked last night."

She nodded and said, "Spending the rest of your life with someone shouldn't be scary. You don't have to marry him. You don't have to marry *anyone*."

"If I were smart like you, and had a brilliant career in Marine Biology ahead of me, that'd be one thing. But the way things are, I don't think I have any other real options."

Izzy stopped and turned to me. She screwed up the right side of her mouth and squinted. "Hang on. Do you think that a life with Adrian is the only way you'll be able to not live at home with your parents?"

"I don't know. Maybe. I hear it's tough for women to get decent jobs. Not you, of course, but – "

Izzy shook her head. "Jesus. That's so *bleak.* Was it your mother or your sister who fucked you up this badly?"

I shrugged.

We got to the mail window and I gave them my slip and told them my number. They handed me a slim, rectangular box wrapped in brown paper. John's name was on the return address. He had drawn dancing stick figures and radios all over the paper.

"Oh my god," I said. "Oh my god, it's from him."

Izzy reached into her purse and handed me a pocketknife. I inserted the knife along the seam and cut, careful to not damage the drawings or any of John's writing. I opened the box and slid out something wrapped in foam and bubble wrap. Inside was a letter sitting on top of a picture in a frame.

The picture was an intricate, highly detailed ink drawing. It was me. I was standing behind an extraordinarily accurate depiction of the board at the radio station. The turntables even looked like they were spinning, but not in a cartoonish way with lines around them; they were blurred just enough to show motion. I was wearing the flannel and Johnny Rotten t-shirt I'd worn the night I met John. I was holding the Joy Division record and smiling. It was definitely me, except beautiful. The frame was painted dark red and had all different sizes of silver metal stars glued to it. No one had ever done anything like this for me.

Izzy grabbed the drawing and examined it. "Holy shit. I love him."

I unfolded John's letter.

10 September 1979

Dear Viv,

I drew the enclosed while I was on the plane back home Saturday. I didn't want to forget anything. Thankfully, it was a mostly smooth flight, so I was able to avoid any major disfigurations to your lovely face. I don't know if you'll see this and think I'm a crazy person, but I hope not. I can express things much more accurately through drawing than writing, but I'll try a bit of that as well...

I have no idea where things will be at for you when you receive this. Maybe whatever happened to be in the air that weekend is long gone now, and you prefer to forget everything and get on with your life. And if so, I'll respect your wishes. But since I have your attention now, there are just a few things I want to say. And if I don't hear back from you, I won't be bothering you again.

I know that what happened complicated things for you, and for that I'm genuinely sorry. For me, it was about as straightforward as it gets: I liked you. I expect I'll still like you very much by the time you read this. But you owe me nothing, and I want to be clear about that.

You said that "the lucky guy" is good to you, and that eases my mind. But it's been troubling me that as you explained your situation, that the glint in your eyes and your manic grin faded. And it seemed that your excitement and enthusiasm for all the things we'd talked about quickly turned to self-deprecation and a touch of nihilism. Having dabbled in nihilism myself not long ago, that worries me.

Whatever happens, whatever you decide going forward, please don't let anyone water down the person I saw so clearly during our short time together. What you want isn't stupid, and I'm certain that London would welcome you with open arms (as would I, if you'd let me). If you do come and want me to be on my best behavior, I will. I'll be a perfect gentleman.

Which reminds me – after our talk, I kept thinking about London. And I'm working with my university to see about transferring to a school there for the spring. I have a couple friends there and am thinking of renting a spare room in their flat. I really am sick to fuckin' death of the Midlands. Life feels too short to just stay put.

I'd love to hear from you, but will take the hint and leave you be if not. Most of all, I hope that this drawing lets you see yourself as I did.

Your Friend,
John Blackwood

My eyes misted up, and I felt a warm pressure in the bottom of my feet. I let the memories of that night flood my synapses: the kiss in the record library, his orange and green smell, him in my bed, the rain through the windows, that round, sweet face with the porcelain complexion like a 1930s drawing of the full moon, smiling down. His bare, warm arms encircling me. The talking about things that mattered to me.

I looked up at Izzy. "We have to get to class now," she said, "but you're calling him later if I have to physically force you."

I nodded. With shaking hands, I wrapped the picture and letter in the foam and bubble wrap and placed them back into the box. I put the box into my backpack, and we headed toward the door.

Izzy walked over to the bulletin board near the front door of the lobby and took something off it and handed it to me. It was a flyer from the school: "Get out of here," it said. "Many schools in Spain, Italy, England, and France still accepting

Coastal University of New Hampshire students for Spring 1980!"

Chapter 9

Six and a half of the longest hours of my life later, I was back at my dorm. I had stopped at the library to look up the time difference between New Hampshire and England, and learned that they were five hours ahead. So, in a way, he was in the future, which I found comforting.

I took the paper with his number on it, along with my calling card, and walked down the hall to my floor's only phone. It was a payphone mounted to the wall inside a little alcove. Thankfully, no one had gotten there before me, so I dialed one long string of numbers, and then the next long string of numbers. I heard little clicks and quiet beeps as my call traveled across the wires and ocean.

I had absolutely no idea what I was going to say, or what I hoped he would say, or what the hell I was doing. And what if he wasn't there? Maybe take that as a sign to not needlessly complicate everything further.

A male voice answered. It was hard to tell if it was him with just two syllables.

"Hi," I said, wondering how I'd never noticed how reedy my voice was. "May I speak to John, please?"

"Just one moment."

My knees were shaking, and I sat down in the little metal framed chair with the nubby orange cushion. It was nine-thirty at night there, so he could be in the middle of anything. I could be interrupting something I didn't want to know about. I pressed the earpiece tighter to my ear, straining to hear anything on the other end. All I could hear was footsteps.

"Hello?" *That's him, all right.* I felt it in my skin.

"Hey. John. This is Viv. Viv Pierce from America?" I rolled my eyes at myself.

There was a pause, during which I assumed he was trying to remember the name, or make an excuse to get off the phone immediately, or…

"I am *so* happy to hear your voice, Viv Pierce from America," he said.

I exhaled, finally. "Is this a bad time?"

"No," he said. "This is great. So great. How are you?"

"Oh, good. Fine. You?"

"Yeah. You know. Fine as well. I got your letter yesterday."

"I got your drawing and letter this morning. That's about the coolest thing anyone has ever done for me."

"Yeah? You like it?"

"I love it. It couldn't have come at a better time, too." *Keep it light.* "I kept trying to hide that crook in my nose, but you got it anyway, and you even made it look like it belonged there."

"I kept wanting to hold my finger in that indentation."

I glanced up and down the cinderblock hallway. No one was around.

"That's really… sweet." *Sweet? What am I doing?* "Hey, weren't you going to see Joy Division?"

"That was the plan," he said, "But my friend's car wouldn't start, and we couldn't figure out a way to get there in time."

"Sounds like you need friends with better cars," I said.

"I hear they're playing London next weekend. So I *am* working on finding friends with better cars for that."

"Good. I expect vivid detail so I can live vicariously. Be prepared to take notes."

"Absolutely. Unless…"

"Unless?"

"Unless you think you might want to abandon everything there and come with me? See for yourself?"

My heart thudded like it used to whenever Han Solo came on the screen in *Star Wars*.

"You sure do know how to keep a joke going."

He paused. "Yeah. Yeah, I… guess I do. Could I ask you a favor?"

"Yeah. Of course."

"Could you record your radio shows, and send them to me? I'll pay you back for postage, of course, and - "

"You want tapes of my show?"

"Sorry. Is that strange?"

"It's just –I don't even know if any of my friends listen to my show, and they're right here."

"Silly people, taking that voice of yours for granted."

I was smiling so much it was embarrassing. I was glad no one could see me. "I – yeah. I can. We have a setup at the station."

"That would be brilliant, thanks," he said. "And I've begun recording some John Peel for you, if you're still interested. Wanted to get a couple of tapes' worth before sending. I'm certain you'll be pleased with the bands he's had on recently. I want to tell you who so badly, but don't want to ruin the surprise."

Keeping in touch. Sending tapes to each other. This was dangerous. But the world felt better because he was in it and thinking of me.

"Definitely still interested," I said. "You send me those, I'll send you mine. We'll be like the Columbia record and tape club."

"Only with a hundred percent less roller disco."

I laughed. I saw movement down the hallway and glanced in the direction of it. It was Adrian. He looked up, caught my eye, and waved. He started walking toward me.

"Hey, can you hang on for a second?"

"Of course."

I put my hand over the mouthpiece and tried to look casual. "Hey, Ade."

"Hey. Who are you talking to?"

"Oh. Just… Keaton. Had a question about some of the records that came in. What's up?"

"Can you call him back?"

"I'd like to finish our conversation. It's timely."

"OK. I can wait." He leaned against the wall and picked a piece of lint off his jacket. "Let's go to dinner downtown. My treat."

I looked down at the phone. I took my hand off the mouthpiece and kept an eye on Ade.

"Sorry about that," I said. "I, um, have to get going. I know you still have some questions. About the records. Can we talk later?"

"Is it the Frosty-Juice Guy?"

"Huh?"

"From your letter. The Frosty-Juice Guy busting down your wall?"

"Kind of."

"Right. One more thing, then I promise I'll let you go."

Ade was pacing up and down the hall.

"Yeah sure," I said. "Go ahead." I held up my index finger toward Ade in the universal sign for *one more minute*.

"I wasn't joking that morning," John said, "and I'm not joking now. Come to England. We'll go to London."

"Oh, wow. That's… a really complicated question. Can we talk about it some other time? Maybe this weekend?"

John sighed and said, "Uh-huh."

"Saturday during the day?"

"I'll talk with you then. Can't stop thinking about you. Bye."

He hung up. I sat with the phone in my hand. *'Can't stop thinking about you.'*

"Ready?" asked Ade.

"Almost," I said. I placed the phone back on the cradle and stood. "Let me just throw on a different top."

We walked back to my room together. When I opened my door, I spotted the picture and letter lying on my desk, right out in the open like I had any autonomy over the space in my own room. I closed the door quickly.

"I forgot," I said, "my room is a mess. Can you just give me a minute and I'll be right out?"

"Sure." He kissed me and I tried not to scream. "Hurry back."

I went into my room and opened a desk drawer quietly. I glanced down at the picture; right there in black ink, the version of myself that I wanted to be for real, all the time. Not just for three hours a week on a Friday.

"You still in there?" Ade said from outside the door.

Something in the drawer caught my eye: my passport. My blank, unused passport that was going to stay that way for a long time. Maybe forever. I put the framed picture, John's letter, and the wrapper with his drawings and writing inside the drawer and slid it shut. "Still here," I said.

Maybe it wasn't too late with Ade. Maybe I just had to really start telling him what I did want.

I changed out of my threadbare sweater, put on a newer one and put my ring on. I had to try to act the part until I could figure out what the hell I was doing.

Chapter 10

At dinner, Ade talked about how his mom's birthday was coming up in a few weeks, and how she really wanted me there for her party. I couldn't figure out why; I was positive she didn't like me, cake toppers or no.

I stabbed three tortellini onto my fork and began eating them one at a time. Ade took a sip of wine.

"I need to talk to you about something," he said.

I stopped eating and looked up at him. "Sure."

"I know this week's been rough and everything. But we really need to start talking about a date."

"Aren't we on a date right now?"

"A date for *our wedding*, Viv. God, you're a million miles away."

"Sorry."

"My family has been after me about it. I'm thinking June. We'll have May to decompress from school and graduation, and then - "

"Ade," I said. "What if we…" *Shit shit shit. What if we what?* "Kind of… Postpone the wedding?"

He set his knife and fork down on his plate. "What?"

"I'm *not* saying cancel," I said. "Just… Postpone. For like a year?"

He shook his head. "What – why? Where is this coming from?"

I stammered, "It's like I've told you, Ade. I've never really been anywhere outside of New England except Canada and like twice to New York. I want to travel, see some stuff." As I said the words, I realized they were completely true. That was what I wanted.

"But…" He raised his hands in disbelief. "I told you. We can do that – we *can* travel. After I get through grad school and get a good teaching job where the Principal is looking at retiring in a few years – once all that's underway, we can travel." He took another sip of wine.

Think think think. "What about summers? Teachers get summers off. We could travel then."

He cut a meatball into quarters. "That's a myth, unfortunately. There are a ton of conferences and professional development in the summer, in addition to holding at least a part-time job to keep being able to pay bills." He twirled his spaghetti around his fork, using a spoon to keep it neat and orderly. "I'll be able to take *some* time during the summer in a few years, but you have to really hustle and work constantly while you're young, especially if you've got your eye on bigger career plans like me."

Stay strong. You have an idea. A plan. Say it.

"But Ade, by then we'll probably be close to thirty, and have – " I swallowed hard, "kids, and all of that. Traveling won't be as easy. And I know, it's kind of my thing, something I feel like I have to do before I – " I swallowed again, and tasted pepper at the back of my throat. "Before I settle down. So maybe you do grad school and teach for that first year, I live with Izzy and Dean in New York, get a job and travel some? That way, I get it out of my system, and you can focus completely on school and work stuff."

I got increasingly more excited as I pulled this plan out of thin air, because I realized that was what I'd wanted all along, and I just didn't know it till just then. Maybe I wasn't a horrible person. I made a mistake, but if this happened, I'd forget I ever cheated on Ade and I'd appreciate him and us more. I realized I was grinning.

"Viv. That's crazy. When would we see each other?"

"No, no, it's not crazy. We'd see each other on weekends. This solves everything."

"I didn't realize that there were things to solve. What is going on?"

"I told you," I said. "I need more time, Ade. I need to see a little more of the world."

He shook his head again. "Viv. You're not listening. I'm on a timeline. The kind of career I want is time sensitive. The first years after college are crucial."

"But I'm not asking you to postpone your career," I said. "I wouldn't do that. I'm just saying we don't have to get married right after college. Not everyone does that anymore."

"But I *do* want to get married right out of college," he said. "I want a wife and kids and you probably think that's really square, but it's what I want. You're blindsiding me here."

I was quiet and looked down at my tortellini.

"I just think you're being very short-sighted and selfish," he said.

I looked up. "*I'm* being selfish? Are you serious?"

"Yeah. I am serious. You don't want college to end. You just want to hang out with your precious *friends* and act like you're too cool for everything."

I felt a coil of anger rising. "If I'm so horrible and immature and *selfish*, then why do you want to marry me at all?"

He looked around to see if anyone was looking at us. They weren't. "You're completely overreacting. You're the one bringing this up out of nowhere."

I leaned in closer and said through clenched teeth, "Why do you want to marry me at all, Ade?"

He leaned in closer too. "Because I love you. You have no direction, but it's ok. I see your *potential*, Viv, and it's amazing. You could go so far."

"How far, Ade? The suburbs? The kitchen? The nursery? PTA meetings?"

"Where the *hell* is this coming from?"

He wasn't willing to budge. And finally, neither was I. I felt the tears rising. I didn't want to hurt him. But I'd wasted nearly a year and a half of his life and he deserved better.

"Ade," I said. "I can't do this. I'm sorry. I just can't."

"Can't do *what*?" he said.

The tears spilled out and I tried to wipe them away, but they kept coming. "I can't marry you. I'm sorry."

I wiped my eyes again, took the ring off, and placed it gently on the table. I reached into my jacket pocket, got a twenty-dollar bill, and put it by my water glass.

"Why are you doing this?" he whispered, which made me cry more.

I put on my coat. "I'm sorry," I said again.

I got up and walked out into the cold night with no direction in mind. I walked back to campus, and started heading back toward my dorm, but the thought of being alone right then was too much. I would brood and obsess and second-guess myself and what if Ade came to see me? Then what?

I kept walking and found myself at the radio station. Thursday nights were a lot of people's rehearsal for Friday nights, so I was sure someone would be around. I wiped my eyes as best I could before opening the door to the station's hallway.

As I opened the door, a yellow plastic bowling ball whizzed past me and went ricocheting down the stairs.

I looked up to see Brian and Matt from the fraternity we at CNH affectionately called Beta Beta Omega; BBO was the non-asshole frat. I'd met Izzy at one of their parties, and we'd been best friends since; I'd always love BBO for that.

Sometimes a BBO brother would stumble his way into a radio show, as both Brian and Matt had.

They had set up a kids' toy bowling set in the hallway, with the big pins and plastic balls. They saw the ball go flying past me, down the stairs, and said, "Oh *shit,*" and then "Hey Viv," simultaneously. They were a little drunk and debated which one of them was going to go retrieve the ball. Finally, they decided to abandon it because they had two more and you didn't need more balls than that anyway. Then of course they giggled.

The big studio door swung open and Keaton stuck his head out. His face turned pink as he hissed, "Can you *please* do this somewhere else? You're really fucking loud, and I'm about to go on the air."

"Come on," said Brian. "You used to do this with us. Remember? Come on, bowl one. It'll be fun."

"I can't bowl, dummy, I'm on the air."

They pouted. Keaton's face softened when he saw me and nodded.

"Sorry," he said. "Some other time, ok fellas?"

I helped them clear away the pins and put them back in their little retro 50s-style fake bowling bag.

"Guess so," said Brian and Matt in unison. They grabbed their jackets and headed out.

"Got a minute?" I asked Keaton.

"Get in here." He swung the door closed and locked it behind us. "Just in case they come back."

A Tom Waits song grumbled its last few notes and Keaton went on the air to read the news. I sat in the spooky Windsor chair.

When he finished reading the news, playing a short PSA, and starting his next song, he turned to me and leaned on the counter. "You don't usually come up till later on Thursdays."

"Neither do you."

"I'm filling in for Gary for another half hour. Then I'll come back at ten for my regularly scheduled programming."

I held up my left hand. "I did it. I broke it off."

My feelings must have shown on my face because he came around the counter, kneeled down, and wrapped me in a bear hug. "Doesn't feel better yet, huh?"

I went limp against him and let the tears roll. "No. I feel like my insides have been scraped with a rusty fork."

"Sounds about right. You did the right thing, though. For both of you."

"So why do I hate myself more than ever?"

"Because you've got a heart. You're going to be ok."

"But I don't care if I'm ok. I want *him* to be ok. He looked so sad."

Keaton put his hands on my shoulders and looked into my eyes. "He's not your responsibility anymore."

"I am such an asshole."

"Stop. Let's go out for pizza when Gary gets here."

I wiped my eyes with the back of my jacket sleeve and nodded.

Chapter 11

After a late breakfast with Keaton and his housemates and my two classes for the day, I reluctantly headed back to my room to clean up and change clothes, expecting an angry letter or dead flowers or gum in my lock. As I walked, I started building my playlist for that night in my head to keep all the other stuff at bay.

When I got to my room, there was nothing unusual; no notes, messages, dead organic matter. I put my key in the lock, but paused when I heard the phone down the hall ringing. I decided to let it keep ringing.

When I got back from the shower there was a note on my door saying that Adrian had called. I went quickly back into my room and proceeded to be very quiet in case he decided to follow up with a visit. I just couldn't face him yet. Adrian was a master at poking holes in logic if he didn't agree with it, and I was a pushover who didn't like confrontation; I figured we'd have to talk about things more at some point, but I needed a little more time to let this decision firm up before I could subject myself to being told how wrong I was. Or worse, how badly I'd hurt him when he didn't know exactly *how* badly I'd hurt him.

I decided to head to the place no one knew I went on the rare occasion I needed absolute solitude after the weather got cold: the beach downtown. I always pulled up the hood of my sweatshirt, put on a plain jacket over that, put on sunglasses, and tucked my chin into the little head cocoon the sweatshirt made when I tied it up. I could have been a movie star or a homeless person as far as anyone knew when I was covered like that, and people left me alone.

Mercifully, my mind eventually emptied itself, and it was just me and the sea. One thing about this ritual that calmed me was being in the presence of something that had a clear and powerful purpose: be the sea. Just be this thing that you are and don't doubt it, and you can fuck things up in good ways and bad. Good or bad, not yours to decide; leave that judgment to others and just be this. I craved that confidence, and each time I sat by the sea, I drew it into me just a little more. I didn't grow up near the ocean, and I soaked it in like a person gasping for breath, especially since I'd been back at school this time.

When it started getting dark, I glanced at my watch and realized it was time to go to the station to pull records. I got up, shook my blanket out, folded it, and put it back in the bag. I walked to the radio station.

I climbed the old, rutted stairs up to the second floor, walked past the student newspaper offices down the hall, and continued on to the CNH hallway. Some people were talking and smoking in the lounge, but I didn't stop to see who.

Kelly was in the studio, with about a half hour to go on her show, playing some kind of medieval choral music. Kelly was one of those exotic Goth girls: delicate and slender, cheekbones of chiseled alabaster perfection, her shiny black hair streaked with a little indigo, the shimmer of which matched her eyes. She wore velvet dresses in the darkest of jewel tones and was the object of much stammering male affection. She always smelled like a sacred temple of something. She had started DJ-ing last spring, but she was now sick of New Hampshire, and told me that she was transferring after this semester to art school in Providence. She was smart and really funny, despite her gorgeously glum appearance, and I liked her a lot, but even on a good day, standing next to her made me feel as cutting edge and stylish as Archie Bunker. And this was not a good day. We exchanged hellos and I dove into the record library.

It was a comfort listening kind of night: The Jam, The Clash, Wire, Blondie, Ramones, and a full four song block of Joy Division to end things, alternating between the EP and the full-length. Except for my show, I'd barely listened to music for the past two weeks. I purposely hadn't listened to any Joy Division since the John weekend because it would have just opened everything up all over again. But everything was kind of opened up now anyway.

Just before it was time to go on, I put a tape in the radio/tape unit in the lounge. It was 45-minutes each side, and I had another one ready to go once I filled this one.

During my shift, a few people dropped in and left, on their way to somewhere else, mostly parties. Someone flipped over the tape after 45 minutes and then I put in the next tape after that.

In my last hour, Izzy and Dean came up and hung out. I told them about the night before.

"I guess it's really over," I said.

Izzy put her arms around me and said, "You did the right thing."

"Then why does it feel like the world hates me right now?"

"Who hates you?" she asked.

"Everyone but you guys and Keaton, I assume. Maybe Lenny."

They informed me that after my shift, they were taking me out to the campus pub, where we would drink and dance to a ska band from Boston.

"You guys," I said. "You should be doing couple things, not wrecking your weekend with me."

"Sorry kid," said Dean. "We like you. Let's have some fun later."

#

When my shift was winding down, I went back on the air just before the four-song block of Joy Division, not knowing what I would say, but feeling a certain weird significance that I wanted to document and put in the mail to John the next day.

"I have just four more songs tonight before DJ Darrell comes along to treat your ears to three hours of Reggae and Dance Hall. Unfortunately, my last songs won't make an easy segue, but hey, that's the unique charm of college radio.

"Listeners, have you ever loved some song or band with every inch of your mind, heart, and soul instantly, so much that it makes you actually happy to be alive at *that* very moment in time because any other moment in time, you might not have stumbled on something so perfect, beautiful, and strange if your life had gone just a little to one side or the other? And then, made a new friend who also loved that particular song or band like you do? You're immediately connected through that; that sound from another world that lifted you out of the depths of despair or the mundane parts of life. Sometimes, just knowing you're not the only freak going through something rough is all you need to change course. And even if they're not next to you anymore, listening to this music brings them closer – not nearly close enough, especially if they're on another continent – but still, closer. The next four songs are that music for me.

"So, like Casey Kasem doing those long-distance dedications of Eagles songs or whatever, I dedicate this little block to my friend on another continent who loves this band as much as I do, the friend who made me glad to be alive, and glad that I didn't fade away before that. Here's a bunch of Joy Division. Happy Friday night, Marblewell."

When my shift was done, I put away the records and collected the two tapes from the lounge and put them in my bag.

"That's cool that you're recording your shows now," Dean said as we were about to head out. "You made me tear up there."

"Aw, Dean. John asked if I'd send him tapes of my show for some reason."

He and Izzy exchanged a glance.

"It's not like that," I said.

"Whatever you say, darlin'," Dean said.

#

Later, after the band finished playing, Dean and Izzy walked me back to my dorm. I assured them I could make it to my room just fine. I was exhausted and ready to go comatose for several hours.

I got up to my floor and started down the hallway but stopped when I saw Ade sitting next to my door. He took a big swig off a green wine bottle. The hair on the back of my neck stood up and I decided to run before he saw me, but he saw me before I could.

"You sure are gone a lot."

I froze. "What are you doing here?"

"I waited for you here last night, too." He took another swallow of wine. "We need to talk."

I didn't move. *Maybe he found out...* "Maybe we should go downstairs to the lounge. We can find a quiet couch."

"Why?" He squinted. "Are you *afraid* of me?"

"Why are you here?" I asked again.

"I told you," he said and stood. "We *need* to talk."

"I think we already did."

He stood and took two steps toward me. His face had grown an uncharacteristic stubble and he had dark circles under his eyes. "You can't just drop a bomb on me like that and not give me the dignity of a response."

I stepped back, acutely aware of how empty the hallways were. "It's for the best, Ade. For both of us."

He set the wine bottle down and ran his hands through his hair, causing it to stick up in the longer spots. It made him look wilder than I'd ever seen him.

"You don't get to decide that by yourself, Viv. We've been together too long."

"Ade, I've tried telling you. I want to travel. I probably don't want kids. And I hate Connecticut. And none of that works with your plans. So what else is there to talk about?"

He looked down, took a deep breath and muttered "OK" to himself. He always did that when he was readying himself for something difficult. He looked back up.

"I don't accept the breakup," he said.

"What?"

He relaxed his shoulders and tried to look affable with a pasted-on smile. "You've had something on your mind ever since we got back here. It's clearly causing you stress. Just tell me what it is so we can move past it and get on with our lives."

My neck muscles were on high alert. My body was screaming, *RUN*. I *had* told him what was on my mind. It had taken me a while, but I did. I folded my arms across my chest.

He narrowed his eyes and that smile vanished for just long enough to remind me that he was trying a little too hard to put me at ease. "You know what, Viv? I'm not going to let you fuck this up."

He almost never said "fuck," and it made my back teeth go cold. "What are you talking about?"

"You have this pattern of not finishing what you start. Of not doing what's best for you. My father calls it 'self-sabotage.'"

I shook my head. My eyes burned from being awake way too long.

Adrian straightened his posture. He nodded. "That's exactly what this is," he said. "You think you're not good enough for me, and you won't let me help you."

"*Help me*? Help me what?"

He put his hands into his blazer pockets. "Help you have some kind of meaningful life. Viv, it's ok that you don't fit in with my family or where I live. You asked me last night why I want to marry you. I *like* that you're different from the other girlfriends I've had. And I've never told you this before, but I think it's kind of hot that I'm marrying a surly bad girl. I only ever dated goody two-shoes before."

All I could do was stare. This was supposed to be over.

Adrian took something out of his pocket and walked toward me. "Let's just pretend last night never happened. I forgive you."

I backed up slowly, not wanting to startle him. "Forgive me? For what?"

He appeared much more relaxed now. Jovial, even. "For making such a rash decision. You obviously hadn't thought it through. That's *so* you. People get cold feet. It's ok."

He took my left hand in his, and my spine stiffened to the point I thought it would snap. With his other hand, he slipped the goddamned ring back on my left finger. I looked down at it, willing it to be someone else's hand, then looked back up at Ade.

"The ring belongs to you," he said. "You can't give it back."

I thought I might throw up.

Ade kissed me on the cheek, leaving a trace of spit I was sure would burn clear through to my skull. “Come on. Let’s go celebrate.” He raised his eyebrows.

He put an arm around my shoulders and began leading me to my room. *Where the hell is everyone? Why is it so fucking quiet up here?*

We reached my door. The gold circle with the ostentatious stone constricted on my finger like a blood pressure cuff.

Say something. You don’t have to let this happen. “Ade. I… I’m so tired. Please…”

“You’re always tired. Let’s get you to bed, bad girl.” He tucked my hair behind my ear and started kissing my neck.

No. “I slept with someone else, Ade.”

He stopped kissing my neck. He kept his hand on my hair. He brought his face up to mine. Red wine had dyed the creases in and around his lips. His breath was sour.

“You *what*?”

Air stuck in a bubble in my chest. His brows knit into a V. His grip on my hair tightened and pulled at the roots.

I swallowed. “That weekend you went away for Steff’s bachelor party.”

Under the flickering fluorescent light overhead, Ade’s eyes looked like black saucers. His mouth flattened into a hard line. He still wasn’t letting go of my hair.

“You … *cheated* on me?”

My jaw clenched into spasms. I nodded.

He let go of my hair and turned away. He began pacing. His breath came faster. He rubbed his eyes with his palms.

Finally, he stopped moving and stood facing me. I braced myself. If he hit me, it would only hurt for a little while. And it was really over now. Even he couldn’t bring us back from this.

Just get it over with.

"And then you *lied* to me. For *two weeks*." He shook his head.

"I'm sorry," I whispered.

He wiped at his eyes. He was crying. "I can't fucking *believe* this."

The hardened shell that had sprung up around me cracked. I'd prepared myself for fury and maybe even violence. Not this. He was hurting and I wanted to help him. No one should have to cry because of *me*.

"Ade," I said, and reached out for his shoulder.

He jerked away and swatted my hand. "Don't you fucking touch me."

I folded my hands together and looked down at the ground. *Shit. How am I going to give the ring back without making this even worse?*

Ade sucked in a breath. "Who is he?"

I looked back up at him. "It doesn't matter. He's long gone. It was just one night."

"You don't get to tell me what does and doesn't matter. *Who is he?*"

I rubbed my eyes. I didn't want to tell him.

"Who's this 'friend on another continent'? The one who likes the same weird, shitty music you do? Huh? The one you talked about on your show tonight."

I stammered, "You never listened to my show."

"Did tonight, though. Man alive, but you can talk. That's the guy, isn't it?"

Keep it to yourself. "It's a friend who likes the same weird, shitty music as I do, Ade. Like you just said."

"That's why you're so hot to travel all of a sudden. You want to fuck this guy some more."

"Me wanting to travel is not a new thing, Ade. I've been telling you this all along. Remember last year when you talked me out of going abroad for a semester?"

"Oh, fuck you. Everything you did or didn't do was my fault or your family's."

We stared at each other. My fear subsided, and I just wanted to be done.

"We're done talking tonight," I said.

"No," he said. "We're not."

I got out my key.

"Hey," he said. "I'm not finished."

I faced him. "If there's a particular name you want to call me, Ade, just fucking do it. If you want to hit me, just fucking do that. Get it over with."

The muscles in his neck flexed as he stared me down, and he breathed hard.

I turned and put my key in the door. "Goodbye, Ade."

The air got knocked out of me and I realized I was pinned against my door. Ade's body pressed against the back of me. I tried to break free, but he was too strong. He twisted my left arm so it was behind me and yanked the ring off my finger, taking a little skin with it.

He brought his mouth to my ear. "My parents were right. You *are* trash." He shoved me so my cheek bounced off the door, then picked up his bottle, flipped me off, and turned to go.

I exhaled, unlocked the door, turned the knob, then flicked the key so it would lock again, swung the door shut, and fell against it inside. My knees gave out and I slid down to the ground.

My door shuddered in its frame as I heard a thunk and a smash. From the other side, Adrian growled, "You bitch. I'm the best thing that ever happened to you."

I heard his footsteps going down the hallway, getting fainter. I whispered, "I fucking hope not."

When my legs stopped shaking enough to stand and I was sure it was quiet, I cracked my door open. Adrian's wine bottle lay in shattered fragments in the hall. I looked both ways. He was gone. I went to the kitchenette, got the broom and dustpan, and cleaned it up.

#

Sept. 22, 1979

John –

As requested, here's tape one of the Pierce Sessions, a.k.a., "This Song Could Save Your Life," recorded on September 21, 1979. I'm writing this in the wee hours of September 22. I'm keeping this short because it's been a hell of a day, and we'll probably talk before this reaches you.

Anyway, the last twenty-five-ish minutes should be of particular interest to you. Hope you're doing great.

Wish I Was There,

Viv

I collapsed on my bed and screamed as loud as I could into my pillow.

Chapter 12

After a ragged night's sleep, I was up early at my stereo with my headphones on, listening to an old tape that Paul had made me, when there was a knock at my door. I jumped and asked who it was.

"Joyce from down the hall," a sleepy voice said. "Phone for you."

I opened the door to a visibly hungover girl in bright pink sweatpants and a Fonzie t-shirt, rubbing her bloodshot eyes. "Thanks, Joyce."

"You do know it's way too early for this."

I glanced at the clock to see that it was only 7:30. "Sorry, Joyce."

She craned her neck and squinted at me. "What happened to your face?"

I glanced in the mirror over my dresser. There was a purple oval on my cheekbone just under my eye where I'd hit the door. "Just a wild Friday night."

She yawned. I followed her down to the phone, and she slipped into her room.

My throat hurt from the primal screaming and my cheek throbbed. My left ring finger's knuckle was pink and hurt to bend. The payphone dangled from its thick silver cord, and I eyed it with suspicion. *Please don't be Ade. Please please please.* I sighed, slumped into the little chair in the cramped phone alcove and answered.

"I'm so sorry, the time difference slipped my mind."

John! "Oh, thank god it's you."

"This is far too early on a Saturday, isn't it?"

I stretched my stiff neck. "I was up already listening to music. Too early for poor, hungover Joyce, who has the misfortune of her room being near this loud phone. But not me."

"Are you sick? You sound hoarse."

"No, not sick. The ol' dulcet tones should be back in no time."

"Do you have a little time to talk?"

"All the time in the world." I glanced up and down the hallway, but saw no one.

"The Frosty-Juice Guy isn't there, then?"

I didn't want to be evasive, but making the conversation this weighty right off the bat was not how I wanted this to go. "The Frosty-Juice Guy is a metaphor. The Frosty-Juice Guy will always be there, just out of sight, for all of us."

"Right. That was Plato who said that originally, yeah?"

"Sure. I'm always quoting him. I don't even realize it anymore."

I asked what he'd been up to. He said he'd been settling in, going to classes. Standard. Only with that accent, it sounded much more elegant.

He cleared his throat. "My brother said he saw you this week."

"Yeah," I said. "That's right, on Wednesday. I'd stayed out too late the night before and still hadn't quite recovered. He said you might be transferring to school in London in the spring?"

"Seems more and more likely by the day. A little stupid to not finish out things here, but… Talking with you inspired me."

"Inspired you to do something you might regret for the rest of your life?"

"The rest of my life? I doubt that. It's just university. Hang on. Are we talking about something else?"

"What else would we be talking about?"

He paused. "I mean… What happened – with us. Do you regret it?"

I made some stupid noise I always made when I thought hard about how to word something. "No. But I do wish that I'd switched the order of things." *Ok, sure, that's a start.*

"Let me puzzle through this," he said. "So, if I understand correctly, the order of things such as they are: at some point in ancient history, as far as I'm concerned, you agreed to marry someone. Not the aforementioned wall-busting nightmare man, but a human man. Then, you met me. Then, I swept you off your feet with the first, all-too-short Joy Division record. Then I accidentally found out you were engaged. Then it didn't make me like you any less, though I wish I'd met you first. Then you… What? I'm missing some pieces of the narrative."

"You're really good at this."

"What's that?"

"At making me laugh when I feel like hell. I would have broken off said engagement before the point at which I met you, instead of after. It would have been easier for everyone."

"Ah. There's the piece I was missing."

"Yeah. I would have still… I wouldn't have changed anything about that night itself. Except I would probably have put on a different musical selection in my room, because that was… Challenging."

He laughed. "I think we made it work. I'll never listen to The Fall in quite the same way. So… you're no longer betrothed, then?"

I looked up. A brown spider wove a web where the ceiling met the wall. "Correct."

I took a deep breath and told him about the dinner after I'd talked to him on Thursday, and how quickly everything had crumbled.

"Are you all right?" he asked.

"I don't think I get to feel anything but bad and guilty right now."

"Why are you so fucking hard on yourself? Were you raised Catholic?"

"Only culturally. I just - should have talked to him about all this stuff a long time ago."

"You were still figuring it out. God, Viv. If we weren't ever allowed to fuck up without constant self-flagellation, life would be unbearable."

I leaned back in the chair and my head rested against the cool wall. "He knows. I told him last night."

John was quiet.

I added, "I didn't tell him who you were or anything. And he doesn't know Noel exists, so he's safe, I'm sure of it."

"I'm not worried about Noel. I'm worried about you."

"Don't be. My dad taught me how to throw a mean punch if I need to. I'm not some delicate little flower."

"Sorry. Didn't mean to imply that. I just – he didn't *hurt* you, did he?"

I rubbed my cheek. "Not on purpose." *God, shut up.*

"'Not on purpose?' Wait, what's that mean?"

"It's not a big deal. He came to my room last night to talk me out of the breakup. He kept saying that he wasn't going to let me self-sabotage and a bunch of other stuff, and then put the ring back on me. I panicked and blurted out what I'd done. Of course he got upset."

"But he has no right - "

"It's not like he hit me. It was just a little push."

"He *pushed* you?"

"This is not your problem, John. And it could have been a lot worse."

He took a deep breath. "I need you to understand something: no one has the right to hurt you or push you. No matter what."

I buried my face in my hands. "It's not that simple," I said.

"Viv. It is."

I needed for us to talk about something else. This was too much to lay on someone I wanted to like me. "I'm fine. Can we *please* talk about you now?"

He exhaled. "We're not done with this, you know. But fine, I'll give you a break. For now. What do you want to know?"

"Have you ever been in love?"

He didn't answer right away. I was about to apologize for crossing a line when he said, "Yes."

Curious as to what kind of girl could capture a guy like him, and half hoping to learn she was a lot like me, only not as funny or accidentally charming, I asked him what she was like.

He shifted in his seat. I let myself remember what he looked like when he was thinking; he'd cast his eyes up, exposing the perfect L of his jawline with a light coating of dark stubble, bobbing his head as if trying to shake the thought out like a toy in a plastic globe when it got stuck in one of those machines outside the grocery store. "She was a self-taught Witch, one with the elements and all that. She was nearly as tall as me, with long, wavy red hair, emerald eyes, always smelling of sandalwood and sparkling with amber, draped in soft fabrics with batik patterns or something. She had this whole mystical thing about her."

"Oh." *A wavy, drapey, willowy, magic redhead. Great.* I looked down at my navy-blue sweatpants and white gym socks that were thin at the toes, and frowned. “Is she still around?”

“No. We were together for about a year. Lorelei said she loved me, but I could tell she was getting restless. She began going up to Scotland on weekends to meet up with a coven she’d been hearing about; some big shot Priestess heading it, and lots of people using magic passed down through their Grannies. One Sunday night she didn’t come back. Nor Monday morning. A week or so went by, and she called me to tell me she was staying there. That was the end.”

“That seems sudden,” I said.

“It *felt* sudden. I was devastated. It was close enough to the end of term that I made it through, thanks to a few compassionate professors. I took the following year off to get my head back on straight. That was when I began to re-emerge. Started liking things again, spending time with my friends, drawing again, that sort of thing.”

The very idea of him being that heartbroken triggered a protective instinct in me that I hadn’t been aware of; *how dare she?* But what I’d done to Ade wasn’t any better than what Lorelei had done to John. It was even worse.

“Have you seen her since?”

He cleared his throat. “We have several mutual friends, so yeah, sometimes when she’s around this way or in London. We don’t talk about anything that happened, just exchange pleasantries and go to opposite ends of the pub. I don’t want to make a scene, and she seems to have nothing to say to me, so I just let it go. Or pretend to let it go, technically.”

“That sounds hard. Has there been anyone else since her?”

“Nothing serious. Haven’t been up to cracking my heart open and handing it to someone again just yet.”

“I don’t blame you,” I said.

“I need to ask you something. This guy…”

"Ade?"

"Yeah. What was it about him?"

Ade was the last thing I wanted to talk about, but seeing as John had told me about his big love… "I had known him for a couple of years before we ever went out. He had this vibe about him that was confident, but not cocky or gross. He always seemed to be in one serious relationship or another, and I was usually – um, 'dating' someone at the radio station. He was way more clean-cut than the guys I usually went for. But when we started going out, it was kind of a kick to feel his attention on me, instead of his usual girlfriends who were way prettier and more stylish than me." *Like a surly bad girl.* There was a sharp taste at the back of my throat.

John was quiet for almost too long for my nerves, then said, "I assume he has a similar sensibility for music as you?"

"Not at all. He said the stuff I listen to is 'too weird' and 'upsetting.'"

"So, the two of you didn't listen to Joy Division together, I take it?"

"No way," I said. "If he listened to anything, it was whatever was on the oldies station. You know what it's like to listen to the most incredible record with someone, and talk about the lyrics, or the bass line, or the vocals? To sit with someone at two in the morning and bond completely over something as ethereal as why a song touched your soul?"

He took a deep breath. "Yeah."

"I guess it should have been a red flag that Ade didn't. But the guys that did, the ones before him, they just weren't interested in sticking with me for very long. Ade treated me the way I'd seen him treat those other girls before me; like someone who he could see himself with for a long time. He seemed like my best shot at a normal life. But by the time I admitted to myself that maybe I didn't want a normal life, I was in way too deep. Then I met you."

"I'm not clear if that's a good thing or a bad thing."

"A good thing. It probably all would have fallen apart eventually. Better now than a few years down the line, not recognizing myself in Connecticut."

"Is Connecticut another metaphor?"

"No. Connecticut is very real."

I told John about the weekend I'd gone to Adrian's parents' house last spring to meet them. I'd been putting off seeing them again since.

Of course, I'd been nervous; I'd never really liked anyone's parents besides my own (and even then, it was spotty), but with these people, I had to make an effort. Both his mom and dad were tan and athletic, thanks to "a nasty tennis and golf addiction," his mom had giggled. The large Colonial house was immaculate and dust-free, with tasteful antiques placed just so, but I noticed this sharp, hovering scent that was what I imagined formaldehyde smelled like.

"My first morning there, I'm about to head to the shower. Ade stops me and says, 'Hey, I just wanted to mention that my mom is kind of a nut about keeping the shower clean and streak-free. So, when you're done, please be sure to wipe it all down with a towel.'" I paused, but John was quiet. "Please tell me that you think that's weird."

He laughed. "Obviously."

"OK, good. So, I'm done showering. I scan the tub and the floor, make sure I haven't left any hair of any sort lying around. My towel is wrapped around me, so I look for another one to wipe the stupid shower with, and I find a medium-sized pink hand towel. I do a good job wiping my shower water off – the whole time, I'm rolling my eyes – and I carefully hang the towel on the shower curtain rod to dry."

"So you're all set for a nice, relaxing weekend at this point. Very hospitable people."

"*Exactly*. Later that afternoon, Ade and I get back from going out, and his mom says she needs his help in the kitchen, and I continue on to my room. A few minutes later, he comes in, he's all pale, and looks really shaken. I asked him if he was ok, thinking a grandparent must have died or something. He goes, 'When you wiped down the shower earlier, did you use a pink hand towel?' I said, 'Yeah. Why?' He goes on to tell me that his mom is furious, because you just don't *do* that with a hand towel, and that one in particular was special somehow, and to please come find her if I had trouble finding a suitable towel after my next shower."

"A suitable towel?"

"*Yes!* It was awful. I was stuck there till the next day, with this terrifying woman giving me the stink eye while she smiled to my face, and shook her head at her son when she thought I wasn't looking. I opted out of showering again until I got back to my dorm Sunday night. Apparently, she didn't think much of *that* either. Ade heard about it for weeks." *Trash.*

"Wow," he said. "So you're firmly anti-Connecticut."

"It's where dreams go to die and then get shit-talked about behind their backs by their boyfriends' mothers."

He was laughing. Then he said, "Can I ask you a serious question?"

"Of course."

"Do you think we'll ever see each other again?"

"I hope so."

"Me too. But *how*, do you think?"

It hadn't occurred to me that we *wouldn't* ever see each other again, but now that I thought about it, I wasn't sure how we could. Then I remembered the "Get away now" flyer in my room.

"Let me look into it," I said.

"*Really*?" he said.

"If you're serious, I will look into it for next semester."

"I am. I truly am."

"Then I will."

"OK," he said. "This is good. *Really* good."

The soles of my feet felt like they had springs on them, and I thought if I stood, the adrenaline would propel me straight up through the ceiling.

"OK, so," he said, "I'm excited and afraid of saying something embarrassing, so I'm going to hang up before that happens. And I'm going to call you at a day and time that you tell me. And you can let me know what you find out?"

I wished that he would say whatever he thought might be embarrassing, seeing as I was unable to stop myself, but I didn't push it. We decided he'd call me in the music directors' office the following Friday before my show.

I'm not sure how long I sat there staring at the phone, thinking about everything we'd just said, and what might happen. Before this, there were four people in the world who could draw the real me out, even when I wasn't sure who that was. Now there were five. I was terrified.

Chapter 13

Monday afternoon, I climbed the stairs to the radio station, but went up another floor, to the international exchange office. By the time I got up there, I'd practically talked myself out of thinking I could pull this off. Studying abroad would take months to prepare for: it was already the middle of September, tipping over toward the end, really, and I'd probably need shots and more paperwork and how long were passports good for, anyway? Well it all seemed absurd at this point, but I went. I clutched the flyer that Izzy had handed me the previous week – the one that proclaimed that there might still be a chance to go overseas, like some kind of proof that I wasn't just a spaceshot trying to do something so major at the last minute. *See?* I would say, if pressed. *This was your office's idea, not mine. I thought it seemed crazy, too. I'm just here because I told my friend I would ask.*

Though their offices were only a floor above WCNH, it seemed like a different place altogether; their windows were cleaner, they had colorful little Guatemalan rugs placed throughout the main reception area, their couches didn't bow in the middle and didn't even have any stains or cigarette burns. All around the waiting area were posters of faraway places: Paris, Barcelona, Edinburgh, Berlin... London.

The London poster's background was evening blue, with a silhouette of a city skyline. In the foreground stood a Buckingham Palace guard with the iconic towering, fuzzy black hat and a neutral expression. A brightly colorized British flag filled out the rest of the space. My eyes were drawn to that evening blue sky, with the old buildings of London jabbing at it like crooked teeth; I pictured lights blinking on in the buildings as dusk got darker, and people emerged from flats or shops or pubs, not apartments or stores or bars like we had here; their words were even more fun to say – not as many r's.

"Hi! Hello!" chirped a voice from behind me. "Can I help you?"

She was a small woman with glasses and a blazer, and had emerged from an office off the main area. She looked like she had answers.

I held up the flyer.

"Hi," I said. "I saw this on a bulletin board, and I was just curious: are people really still signing up to go abroad next semester?"

She smiled. "Oh, yes! They sure are. Many of our cooperating schools are having trouble getting their typical American numbers, so they're sweetening their deals: dropping tuition, offering nicer rooms, public transportation passes for nothing extra, those sorts of things."

"Why are they having trouble getting Americans?" I asked.

She lowered her voice. "All this crazy stuff, escalating tension between us and Iran. Parents are convinced their kids will get taken hostage or their planes hijacked, even though they're not going anywhere near Iran. It's just paranoia, nothing based in reality."

I hadn't even thought about non-IRA terrorists, who I was also afraid of, but refused to say it out loud. She could see me hedging.

"Where are you thinking you'd like to go?"

"England? I think?"

She clapped her hands together in excited approval. "That's a great choice! You don't have to worry about the language, there's so much history to explore, and it's a beautiful country. Whereabouts are you thinking?"

"London? I guess?"

"Come on into my office, and we'll see what we can find out."

She flipped through catalogs, cross-referenced them with charts, and listed off three universities that were still accepting students.

"Do any of those have a student-run radio station? Like we do here?"

She tilted her head. "We have a radio station here?"

"Yeah, it's the next floor down from this office."

"Oh, that's real? I've seen the signs, but just assumed it was some kind of weird joke or something. I don't really listen to music unless it's classical. Anyway, let's see."

She consulted the thick catalog with the tiny print, hoisting her reading glasses up on her nose. One of them did have a radio station, she said.

"Can we find out if I could get a shift there?"

She smiled and said she would look into it. She took down my information and said she should have an answer by the end of the week, and to check my mail and stop by Thursday or Friday if I hadn't heard from her. She gave me a plastic bag with UCNH's logo on it, and filled it with pamphlets and checklists. She said it had everything I would need to prepare and acquire if this worked out. I nodded, thanked her, and wandered down to the radio station, lost in a rabbit hole of thoughts.

"Are you high, or something?"

I was leaning against the doorframe of the station's hallway. Kelly waited for an answer. "It's like 11:30 in the morning. No, I'm not high."

She shrugged. "I don't know what you're into. I'd be high all the time if I thought I'd have to stay here after this semester."

I might not be, though.

"Yeah, I know, Kelly," I said. "You're too exquisite for New Hampshire. I get it."

She picked a loose piece of crimson shawl fringe from her velvet top and let it flutter to the floor. "I just need to be with more of my own kind."

I nodded.

Ronnie, a former, short-lived makeout partner from sophomore year, stepped out of the lounge and stood next to Kelly. He was still pretty cute, I hated to admit. He'd been following Kelly around for a while, eagerly snapping up any morsel of attention she threw him.

"Hey Kelly, ready to go get coffee?" He then added, "Oh. Hi, Viv."

I gave him a single nod and an obligatory partial smile.

He held his arm out, which she looped hers through, looked back at me, rolled her eyes, and they went out through the other door.

All three office doors in the hallway were open, and I was glad not to be alone. I went to the Music Directors' office I shared with Keaton, and found him on the phone. He waved. I looked through our mail, opened up the boxes of new records, and set them in the to-be-reviewed stack. Keaton hung up.

"That was Lou from Tisket Tasket Records," he said.

"Jesus. Again?"

"I'm not sure how else either of us can re-state the fact that we do *not* have a children's music show, we never *had* a children's music show, nor will we ever, *therefore*, we do not have a *need* for children's music, and we do not have room for records that we have no need for. And how fucking creepy is it to have kids' records lying around a college radio station?"

"You listen to me, Keaton," I said in my best wheeling-dealing, condescending Lou voice, "You don't need a specialty show, Keaton, to play top quality music like this! Slip in some of this stuff between your gloom and doom bullshit, Keaton, those college kids will think it's hilarious. They'll eat it up, Keaton!"

"God, I wish there was a way to just never take his calls again." He lit a cigarette and opened the window.

"Who's on the air right now?" I asked.

"Lenny. But get this," he said. "Remember Rebecca?"

"That lady 'from the community'? Kinda weird, right?"

He nodded. "She's no lady. Turns out, Rebecca's got a bit of a *potty mouth*. She's supposed to be on the air now, but earlier, she was dedicating a song to someone – I presume her boyfriend or whatever – and over the air, said something about his effect on her... Uh... C word. Only she didn't say 'c word.'"

My jaw dropped. "*What?*"

He continued, "Lenny and I were talking when she said it, and I just froze. So Lenny jumped in there and made some smooth excuse as to why he was interrupting her on the air. Then he told her he'd take over her shift today, and that he'd be reporting her to Andy."

The number of penalties we could get slapped with for something like that would shut us down. Hopefully, per usual, not enough people had been listening to notice.

Keaton had to get to class, so I got the desk. As I was leafing through the newest *NME*, Lenny poked his head in.

"I heard you had an exciting morning," I said.

He shook his head. “What a wacko,” he said. “Rebecca and her cunt give those of us ‘from the community’ a bad name.”

I tried to act unflustered, but that word always startled me, and I must have flinched, because Lenny apologized. I said it was fine.

“This is a real long shot,” I said, “but in all those books about broadcasting that you have, do you think you might have anything about DJ-ing in England?”

He thought about it, moving his eyes and pointing his finger like he was going through his bookshelf at home. He had a memory unlike anyone I’d ever known, and if anyone had a question about radio or music, he almost always knew the answer, even the most obscure stuff.

“Yes,” he said. “I believe I do. Are you talking student, or professional?”

“Student to start with,” I said.

“Really?” he asked, a small smirk poking through. “This wouldn’t have anything to do with the guy at the diner, would it?”

“Only kind of,” I said.

“Uh huh.”

“Don’t you have to get back on the air?”

“No,” he said. “Andy’s covering the rest of the shift for me. I have to get to work soon. But not yet. So... What? You’re going to England?”

“I’m not sure yet,” I said. “Maybe.”

He nodded. “I think it’s a great idea.”

“You do? Why?”

“Because England is fucking *cool*,” he said. “And I love Marblewell – all my family’s around here – but going somewhere like England changes people, usually for the better. Except those twits who come back with shitty fake

British accents after a semester, acting surprised that you'd mention it, because they 'hadn't even thought about it, ha ha.' Don't do that."

"I won't. Promise. But I doubt I'd be coming back to Marblewell anyway. I'll be done with school after that, so I probably wouldn't have a reason to."

And that's how it hit me that if I did this, my life in Marblewell, and at WCNH, would be over within three months. I wasn't ready to think about that, and neither was Lenny, apparently – either that, or it didn't bother him – so he continued his thought.

"You've *got* to go to London; it has so much more history than anything we have here. It's a fantastic combination of a long past and a bunch of cutting-edge music and art scenes that'll blow your mind. Is the dreamboat from the diner meeting you there?"

"I'm not sure yet. I'm not going for him, anyway."

Lenny laughed. "That's what you're telling yourself? OK."

"What the fuck, Lenny."

"Why are you so mad?"

It pissed me off whenever Lenny turned his sarcasm on me. It made me feel stupid, like I wasn't part of the club.

"Because. I'm not some air-headed bimbo who only does stuff because of *dreamboats*. I like to think I'm a little smarter than that. At least, I'd like to think that *you* think I'm a little smarter than that."

He tapped his fingertips on the doorframe and looked down at the floor. Then he said, "Think about it: how many amazing things in history and music and books happened because someone fell in love, and decided to go somewhere or do something because of their beloved? Like, *everything*. People falling in love is what makes *everything* happen. I just don't understand what's wrong with going somewhere for a guy – or a girl, whatever."

"I don't think you understand," I said. "I barely know this guy. I don't *love* him."

He shook his head. "You're too young to have so many rules. You can't go to England for a guy. You can't love someone unless you've known them for... How long exactly?"

"At least six months. Preferably longer."

"Jesus, Viv – you've heard of love at first sight."

"That's just in stupid movies."

"Is it?"

"You're too sarcastic to be a romantic, Lenny."

"More romantic than you think," he said. "Let's just say there's a gorgeous, brilliant girl in Boston who loves me and makes me feel like anything's possible. And I might be moving there soon. But anyway, we're not talking about me."

"Wait, you're moving to Boston?"

"Look, if it doesn't work out, you'll still be in England, which would still be nifty, right? But I know what I saw in the diner. Please don't overthink this."

Sure, I'd been thinking about John almost constantly, especially since talking to him over the weekend. And he seemed to think I was special somehow, and I knew *he* was, so the very idea that someone as funny and smart and my god, he set my nerve endings on fire. Yeah, the very idea that someone like that would even notice me, let alone want to see me again – I had to admit, that did make me wonder if maybe I was something sort of special, or at least, maybe I *could* be.

There would be no typewriters or Connecticut or the threat of future children hanging over me like that big boulder falling toward Wile E. Coyote in the canyon, and no one else's goddamn to-do lists.

I grabbed the mangy Cookie Monster puppet that had inexplicably been on this desk since before I got to Marblewell, and made its mouth open and close as I said "OH – kay. You give me cookie?"

Lenny reached into his backpack and threw me a Saran-wrapped chocolate chip cookie. "My mom made that. I gotta go to work now, but I'll get you that book about broadcasting in England. See ya."

And then he left, like a fucking magician exiting the stage in a puff of smoke.

Chapter 14

All that week, I was uncharacteristically chipper, sincere, even bouncy. Izzy gave me more side-eye than ever, but eventually grumbled, "It's good to see you this type of annoying for a change."

Despite the certain verbal assault my mother and sister would definitely lay on me when word made it back home, for the first time in ages, I was excited and looking forward to something. My passport would be all set till I turned thirty. It barely even bothered me that I kept finding balled-up food wrappers and soda cans near my door. People could be so gross, but who cared, because I was going to see *London*, and the very thought of it made me lightheaded, as did the barrage of vaccinations I got on Wednesday in preparation for travel. I was ready for this trip early. I'd never made early happen before.

I started several letters to John, but wound up abandoning so many of them that they eventually filled the remainder of a notebook I'd originally bought for a Victorian Literature class the previous year.

Dear John,

I fucking can't wait to see you!

<u>Abandoned:</u> *Hi!!! I'm 13 and love ABBA and Unicorns!!! AND BOYS!!!*

Dear John,

I was just listening to Joy Division (again!), and thought I'd do some stream-of-consciousness writing

Abandoned: *Oh, I'm soooooo deep. Look at me cracking open my subconscious and listening to music. How fucking tedious.*

Dear John,

Just back from a general meeting for the radio station. Nothing too exciting, but I saw Noel there, which was nice.

Those meetings used to be more eventful and fun until last March, when the general manager's birthday fell on the same day as the general meeting. We (the station's directors, coordinators, etc.) were all at a raucous party at said general manager's just-off-campus house, drinking and dancing, and assumed that there was no meeting that night. Turns out, no one had thought to actually cancel it. So, we got a phone call at his house from someone saying a bunch of members had been waiting for the meeting to start. We all had an "Oh shit" moment, and walked as fast as we could to the science building, where the meeting was. We were laughing and making jokes, but started the meeting after saying we were sorry for being late. This lady named Serenity (I'm not clear if she's a DJ or just hangs out with Blaze, her – boyfriend? Husband? Friend? I honestly don't know – who is.) who's sitting dead center in the way back row stands up and puts her hands on her hips. She didn't say anything, just stood and glowered. Blaze slowly got up and stood with her. The whole room got quiet. Blaze looked at Serenity, who still said nothing. He turned to us and said, "We find this extremely unprofessional. You're all drunk. You should be ashamed." Serenity nodded.

I was still feeling a bit more bold than usual, shall we say, from an earlier whiskey shot, so I whispered to my friend Keaton, "Folk music fans hate fun." At least I meant to whisper.

Abandoned: *This story isn't as funny as it used to be. I sound like an alcoholic frat boy. That's exactly the kind of American they don't want any more of in England.*

Dear John,

Just back from lunch. I'm so excited to see what lunches are like at a university in England. I bet they're

Abandoned: *Lunch? I'm writing about lunch? Wondering about lunch? Fuck.*

When Friday finally came, I went up to the exchange office on the third floor. Madge was there, her reading glasses pushed down on her nose, rust and gold blazer thrown over the back of her chair as she clacked away at her typewriter, looking back and forth between the paper and a large book splayed open beside her on the desk.

"Hi," I said. "I'm Viv. We talked earlier this week about me maybe going to London next semester?"

Madge looked up at me and frowned. She looked unnatural with a frown. "Oh, right. I hate to be the bearer of bad news, but... I may have been a little optimistic when we first spoke. It doesn't look good. I'm sorry."

"What do you mean 'It doesn't look good?' What can I do to change it so it *does* look good?"

She tried to smile reassuringly, but it just made her look sad. I felt like the floor was going to drop out from under me. She shook her head.

"Unfortunately, your grade point average is just a little too low to be eligible for this program. Plus, none of the London schools' courses match up with the ones you need next semester in order to graduate, so even if you get all A's this semester and raise that GPA, you still couldn't be done by May. And I'm sure you don't want to put off graduation."

I looked down at my hands folded in my lap, and my vision blurred with tears. How fucking stupid could I have been to think someone like me could just jet away for my last bit of school? If I was smarter, and gotten better grades, or if I had just gone last year when I'd had the chance...

Madge patted my hands and passed me a tissue. "I'm sorry, dear," she said. "But just think: you can travel after you graduate, and you won't have to worry about homework, or classes, or anything. You can go wherever you want, free as a bird!"

I wanted to make her feel better, and to get out of there so I could sob in private. I nodded, grabbed my backpack, thanked her for trying, and went downstairs to the station, hoping that no one would be milling around the hall.

But there was Kelly, hovering in the hallway like a scowling hummingbird. "You look awful," she said.

"I know. Don't you have any classes to get to?"

"Don't *you*?"

I sighed, and made my way past her, aiming for the office's cinderblock solitude.

"Not in the mood, Kelly. Sorry."

I unlocked the door.

"What's the matter? Did someone die, or something?"

"Just the last of my hopes and dreams," I said. "No big deal."

She picked at the hem of her tiny, dark, vintage cardigan. "Sorry."

What a jerk I was. I seemed to always be snapping at her. "Thanks. So you really like Rhode Island, huh?"

"It's ok," she said. "Providence is like any New England city. It's good for college students, and there's a pretty good arts scene. I thought Marblewell was more promising than it actually is. Sorry to say anything bad about it. I know you love it here."

"I do, but all I've ever really known is here and where I grew up. This is a bustling city compared to my hometown."

"I know what you mean," she said. "The place I grew up was Hicksville. I had to pretend I was normal for eighteen years, and it about murdered me. I feel like I become more myself each new place I live, you know?"

"I thought you were younger than me. How many places have you lived?"

She laughed – the first time I'd ever seen her laugh – and said, "A bunch. I'm 23. My grandmother left me some money for college and grad school when she died, so I've been dabbling. I like seeing different places, so this is one way to do that. I'll probably head to New York City after Providence when I feel restless again. Anyway, I've got to go. But whatever your setback is, just remember that a gruesome death's right around the corner, so don't wait to move on when you feel like it."

"Thanks, Kelly."

It was lunchtime, but I wasn't hungry. I went back to my room and napped for a few hours. When I woke up, there was just enough time to put on clean clothes and get back to the radio station for the call at six.

#

I got to the music office at quarter of six to be sure not to miss his call, and waited. Six o'clock came and went, as did 6:10, 6:20, 6:30… I thought about calling him, but I didn't want to seem desperate. And it wasn't like I had good news anyway.

Still, I wanted to hear his voice and maybe even find something funny about this with him. He'd say something to make me feel better, and I really needed to feel better. I picked up the phone twice, or maybe ten times, just long enough to confirm that it was still working – dial tone, check. At five minutes of seven, I realized I should pull some records for my shift, and just hoped he would call during the next three hours.

Two and a half hours passed. By that point, I was convinced that he'd never call me again because as soon as I'd let on that I might call his bluff and go over there, he realized he didn't actually want me to. I couldn't blame him, either. Then, the phone in the studio rang.

"Hello! This Song Could Save Your Life!" I answered.

"Hey hey," said the voice. "I just wanted to see if you found out some good news today." It was Izzy. She had taken time from her weekend in the city with Dean to call me, and all I could muster was disappointment.

"Oh, yeah. That. I uh... I can't go. My GPA tipped them off that I'm too stupid. And none of the schools have the last batch of classes I need anyway, so. That's that."

I heard someone's guitar tuning loudly in the background before screaming feedback took over.

"Jesus," Izzy said. "I'm sorry to do this, but Dean's band is about to go on, so I should get back out there. We'll have a pizza date Sunday afternoon, ok?"

We hung up, and I hit the turntable just in time to avoid dead air. I got my next record ready. I looked at the light connected to the phone. It still wasn't flashing, and my office phone hadn't rung all night either. Tears prickled my eyelids.

The next DJ came in, all good vibes and smiles, and readied his reggae records like little vinyl suns getting ready to light up the night. I dragged my big sad clouds back to the record library and put my records away.

I grabbed my bag and coat, said goodbye to Darrell and wished him a good show. The air was so cold, I felt it through my clothes and under my skin. I wished I'd brought a hat.

Most Friday nights I took the back and side paths to avoid the throngs of loud, drunk students, but I was still shaken up and a little scared from Ade's visit the previous weekend, so I took the main, busy walkway back to my dorm.

There were large groups of students sitting on benches, others standing. Many drank from innocent-looking soda bottles with strong whiffs of rum when I passed them. I turned down to the path to my dorm, and as I approached the long, stone steps leading up to the front door, a guy and a girl with long yellow hair were making out on the half-wall. I rolled my eyes and must have audibly scoffed, because the boy glanced up in my direction. It was Adrian. He grinned, grabbed her ass, and went back to kissing her while looking me in the eye. It was weird to see him doing that with someone else, but also a relief. I forced myself to look at the front door, not him, not them, and focus on going inside.

I reminded myself that I had this coming, climbed the steps, and put my key in the front door. When I got to my room, it looked like someone had emptied a whole trashcan in front of my door; there were used sandwich wrappers, and empty soda cans, chip bags, and candy bar foil. The pile rose against my door, tall as it could get before toppling halfway to the opposite wall. I smelled grease and decaying lettuce.

"What the fuck?" I whispered.

The phone down the hall started ringing.

I noticed a piece of lined paper with the jagged edge of what had once tethered it to a spiral-bound notebook. It had been stuck to my door with cement-grey chewing gum, and on it was scrawled "Trash for trash."

Oh, come on.

The phone was still ringing.

I went to unlock my door, but the key stuck partway in. When I pulled it back out, strings of that same chewing gum stretched like spittled mozzarella from the key to the thing that had once been a lock.

Fuck fuck fuck. I hung my head and went to stop the incessant ringing.

"May I please speak to Viv Pierce in room 213, please?"

"John?"

"Yeah! I'm so sorry I couldn't call earlier. My train broke down on the way back to the flat, then on the long walk home, my infuriating, confrontational friend visiting from London got into a row with some much bigger guy who'd been hassling some girls. My friend won, I *think*, but still got the piss beat out of him. I had to take him to hospital, and once he was finally checked out and released, I got home as quick as I could."

"There was a *fight*? Are you ok?" I glanced at the clock and did the time conversion in my head. "Isn't it past three in the morning there?"

"I'm fine," he said through a yawn. "A bit tired is all, but knowing I might get to talk with you has kept me going. I don't really fight, just keep an eye on my friend when he does."

"I was afraid I wouldn't hear from you again."

"I promise you something: if we're scheduled to talk, the only thing that could keep me from it is some kind of unpredictable disaster. Or a daft friend with a hair-trigger temper who's pissed off so many other friends that I'm the only one around to make sure he gets tended to."

That made me smile for the first time that day. But at the same exact time, the hot bubble that had been stuck in my chest since I'd gone to see Madge earlier rocketed to the surface, and a sob came barreling out so involuntarily, I wasn't even sure it was me. I put my forearm over my mouth and tried to calm my breathing.

"My god, are you all right?" he said. "What's happening? Viv? Hey…"

"I'm sorry," I said. "I'm ok, I'm ok."

"What happened? Why are you crying?"

I took a deep breath. "I can't come in January. Even though I've been trying really hard, my grades aren't good enough. I'm too dumb to go to England."

"Hey, no – there's nothing dumb about you. Tell me what they said?"

Sniveling and wiping my nose on my shirt sleeve, I told him what Madge had told me. "And everyone keeps saying I can go next May, but I've been waiting for so long already, and all I want is to get there and see it and see you, and I just…" I stomped my feet like the pissy little toddler that I was. "I don't want to *wait* any longer. Even when I try to do things the right way, like this, it doesn't work."

"I wish I was there with you," he said. "I would put my arms around you, and tell you every single lovely thing about you that I know. And then I'd dry your eyes, help you pack your things, and bring you to the airport. Tonight."

"I would really like that," I said. "All of that."

"But if our reunion has to wait until May, then all of that can wait until then, too."

I thought about a plan for May, calculating the money I'd saved working at the bookstore in the summers, plus the bi-weekly pittance for my Music Director stuff. I could probably find a part-time job in Marblewell too, and just put everything in an England fund.

I wiped my eyes with my jacket sleeve. "Why are you so nice to me?"

He exhaled. “Because I like you so much, and I can’t wait to get to know you better. I want to see you someplace that draws you out completely, far away from everything that makes you doubt yourself.”

He said he’d gotten my tape in the mail. “You talked about connecting with someone, and how it made you glad to be alive in that moment?”

“Yeah.”

“It moved me. I feel the same.”

“I wish I could’ve met you at a different time. Like sometime in the distant future when I’m hopefully not such a fucking mess.”

“Well, I’m glad I met you when I did. You’re a fucking mess that makes sense to me. Besides, everyone’s a mess. Some just keep it hidden better.”

“You’re not.”

“That’s hilarious. Is that what you think?”

“Compared to me? Yeah. That’s what I think.”

“Apparently, I’m one of the ones who hides it well.”

“Yeah? Were you engaged when we met, too? Or are you now, or something?”

“No. I mean, not *exactly*.”

“What do you mean, not exactly?”

He sighed. “Remember the Lorelei I mentioned?”

“Red-headed witch, super sexy, magic this and sparkling that?” At least, that was how I pictured her.

“Right. It wasn’t just that I was in love with her. I was going to ask her to marry me on the night she was supposed to return from Scotland. Had the ring and everything.”

“Oh my... Wow.”

“Yeah. Oh my wow, too. I still get this stabbing pain when I say it out loud.”

“Aw, John...”

"So if you really want to know what my mess looks like... I told you I was devastated. What I didn't tell you is that after about a month or so of jumping at the phone every time it rang, and running to the mailbox every time the postman came, and sprinting to the door whenever there was a knock, and scanning the places we used to go for her face, or a glimpse of her hair, and getting absolutely nothing – no word, no glimpse, not even a second-hand 'hello' through mutual friends – I just... broke."

"What do you mean 'broke'?" I was afraid that I already knew the answer.

He took a deep breath. "One night I simply couldn't take it anymore; the constant, dull throb of it all, the complete hopelessness. The constant feeling of fucking… aloneness. I couldn't see an end to it. I took a bunch of pills my friend had given me for recreational purposes one time, and laid down."

No no no…

"The next thing I remember is waking up under excruciatingly bright lights with tubes going into my arms. My throat felt like it was on fire, and my stomach felt like it had been ripped out. They'd brought me to hospital and pumped my stomach. My roommate at the time, Sammy, was there. He'd found me. I thought he'd left for the weekend, but he had to come back to the room for something."

I squeezed my eyes shut, trying not to picture it, but the image was already there. "My god..."

"Pretty fucking dramatic, yeah?" he said. "Anyway, that's why I took a year off university. Lots of head doctors, and workbooks, and talking. It took some time, but I started feeling better, and was able to get off the awful medications I was taking. Sorry to get so heavy. I blame the late hour and lack of sleep."

"It's ok. Honest. Did you ever get to tell her anything?"

"No. Never did."

His Lorelei left him when he thought they'd be together for the rest of their lives. I left Adrian when he thought we'd be together for the rest of ours. I really *was* a monster.

"I know what you're thinking," he said. "Your situation is *not* the same."

"It kind of is, though."

"No. You didn't vanish with no answers. You told him what it was you needed, and he wouldn't compromise. His response was that he had a plan that was very, very grown-up and that your silly desire to see more of the world would interfere with that. He called you 'selfish,' for fuck's sake. I mean, he essentially said 'no,' as if you were asking his permission."

"You make me sound so *reasonable*. I think that's a first."

He paused. Then said, "I hate that you don't think of yourself as reasonable."

He was right. I didn't think my dreams were realistic, and everything I loved was unimportant. How was it that I could think the world of John – who wanted to be an *artist* for a *job*, whose current main ambition was to live in London, and who loved music as irrationally as I did – and yet think so little of myself?

"You still there?" he said.

I shook my head. "Yeah. I'm just… Rethinking some things."

"I just think it's important you give yourself credit for trying to make it work. If Lorelei would've told me what she needed, what she wanted, I would have done anything, followed her anywhere."

"I can't stand that you almost died," I said.

He took a deep breath. "Me either. Now, anyway. I'd gotten tunnel vision, and when things didn't go the way I wanted, I didn't think there was any other way. Coming back from that, having the goodness of my friends, meeting interesting new people like you, letting the things I love sink into my skin – I just want all of that, all the time. I want to see new places. I want to find a place that feels like *home*, not simply the place I live or the place I'm from. Not only do I not want to die anymore, I have this relentless urgency to make my life the way I want it."

"That's a relief," I said. "So how *do* you want it?"

"It's a bit vague at the moment – more of a sketch than a detailed, vivid picture."

"Try me."

"Let's see… Art. Music. City. Friends. Maybe love again someday, but only time will tell."

"Friends give you love," I said.

"True."

"You showed your friend love earlier by making sure he was safe and taken care of, even if he started it. And you don't ask for anything in return. That's real love. Being in a relationship with someone is nothing like that – that has conditions."

"I suppose it depends on the people?"

"I guess," I said. "I don't know. You must be losing it from lack of sleep. I should let you go to bed."

He yawned. "It would probably get expensive to ask you to stay on the phone until I fall asleep."

"Probably. I'm really sorry I can't be there next semester."

"We'll just have to keep talking and keep each other's spirits up till you can get here, yeah?"

I smiled. "OK. John?"

"Yeah?"

"I just want to be sure I say this: I'm really glad that you're still here. Promise me you won't do anything like that again."

"I promise. You promise me one thing, too."

"OK."

"Stop beating yourself up so ruthlessly."

"What am I supposed to do with all my spare time?"

"Write me letters. Read the ones I'll be sending you. Listen to as much incredible music as you can. Be with your friends who love you as you are. Think about the things you want to see once you're over here. Promise."

"I promise that I will try really hard."

John cleared his throat.

"OK. I promise."

After we hung up, I dragged myself to the kitchenette, got a trash bag from under the sink, collected the note and souvenirs that Adrian had left for me as a reminder of my worth, and brought them to the dumpster in back of the dorm.

Then I called campus safety to ask if they could help me with the lock. Thankfully, I guess, this happened far more frequently on campus than I ever knew, and they brought over a kit. I was back in my room about seven minutes after they'd arrived.

When it was finally time for bed, I took the picture of me that John had drawn, and stood it up on my nightstand so it was facing me. I lay my head on my pillow and stared at the picture. *That's the real me.*

Chapter 15

John and I talked on the weekends and wrote each other letters. I learned that during lunch breaks at work or school, he liked to go to a nearby park to eat his cheese and tomato sandwiches and draw whatever dogs happened to be playing, and that his stepmother hand copied recipes from magazines and sent them in the mail to him mid-week so he could have a couple to try on the weekends. And he actually *made* them. He wanted to make me Chicken Curry in May. I didn't know what Chicken Curry was, but I couldn't wait. No guy had ever made food for me.

I started getting the promised Peel Sessions tapes from him and listened voraciously. John Peel seemed to know everything about music, at least all the music I loved, but the way he talked about it was so personal he felt like a friend; he talked about certain bands hitting him hard, and certain songs making him have to pull over while driving because the emotions they made him feel were that overwhelming. He quickly became my role model, to the point where I had Resource Center on my show to play four songs live, like Mr. Peel would have done.

As it turned out, that was a terrible idea that culminated in the outing of a love triangle in the band, via an improvised song, and a prompt breakup:

Tom:

"But Amy, sweet Amy, I think you should know,
Sam kissed Jen last March when he threw her in the snow.
They're still hot and heavy like a couple of jerks,
Having sex in your apartment when you go to work.
I'm here for you, Amy, and your sweet crimson pout,

When you're ready to kick his sorry ass out."

Amy: "What? Sam?"

Sam: "Tom, you *promised.* I hate you."

Jen kept drumming.

Amy: "I hate you all. You suck, Sam."

A door slammed.

At least no one swore on the air. I didn't have a live band on my show again.

Izzy and Keaton kept me going to places in addition to the radio station or my room, which was probably good. I felt better and lighter than I had in a long time.

My mother called me on a Saturday in October. "I shouldn't have to remind you that you're still our daughter," she said. "You haven't been home since you left for school. We need to start figuring out some wedding things."

It had been just over three weeks since I'd broken up with Ade. Two weeks since I'd started trying to fulfill the promise I'd made to John. The prospect of going home put a knot in my stomach; I was afraid that going back to the town that had never liked me would convince me it was right all along. I tried to play my radio shift card to my mother, reminding her that it was a responsibility that I took seriously, and that others depended on me, but she told me that I would find someone to fill in and that I would be home the following weekend to start the planning.

Gripping that phone so hard that my palm cramped, my brain kept screaming *Tell her now, tell her now, tell her now.* But I chickened out. After the call I ran to the bathroom and threw up.

#

That following Friday, I'd been home for about two hours when my mom asked me to set the table, which I did. There hadn't been time yet for fake-scouring Bridal magazines or for me to come clean about my recent major decision.

She seemed relaxed and smiled more easily than I'd seen in a very long time. She barely even said anything mean about my haircut, just had a stricken facial expression. She was even humming some tune as she chopped carrots and stirred the beef stew cooking away on the stove. This maternal bliss version of her made me very uneasy. I placed the last butter knife in its place next to the blue and white toile-patterned plates and made an excuse to go up to my room.

I lay on my bed, staring up at the greyish white ceiling with the glow-in-the-dark stickers of stars and planets, nearly invisible in the slanting light of the October sky. Paul had gotten the set for me for my birthday one year when I was having a hard time in school, and he helped me put them up correctly, following the chart of the solar system that came with them. He had told me, "I got these for you so that every night, even after a shitty day of being a kid here, all you have to do is open your eyes and you'll be reminded that there's a big, limitless, beautiful world out there. I didn't want to make a big deal out of this in front of Mom and Dad because they'd say I was just trying to make you think like me and put big ideas in your head." He brushed off some dust and stuck Saturn up there. "But you're already like me, and some big ideas are already forming. I can see it." I idolized Paul, so it was one of the nicest things anyone could ever say to me.

I had to figure out how and when I was going to tell my parents about Adrian. I thought maybe I should tell Mom alone because she cared about the whole thing way more than my Dad did, and she should be the first to know. But if Dad was there too, she wouldn't be as mean as she would if it were just her and me.

The last time I'd had news this big to break was when I told my parents I wanted to go to college and that I would get a job to pay for as much of it as I could, and that I would pay back the rest after I graduated and got a better job. Mom said that some people weren't cut out for college.

"Your grades are mediocre at best now," she'd said. "You think you're going to get smarter by going clear across the state and *paying* for school?"

My dad had turned to her and said, "And some people do great in college, even if they didn't do all that great in high school. It's a different kind of learning. Think of it as an investment."

Dad was usually my buffer, and I'd need to take advantage of that this time, too.

I heard a car pull into the driveway, and then voices downstairs. I padded down and cautiously approached the kitchen. An unsteady toddler came careening into the living room and tripped over the corner of the area rug, landing on his bulbous little nose. I kneeled down to help him at the precise moment he started to wail and cry.

"Hey, Ricky," I said, patting his little shoulder, "You ok?"

More wailing. Nothing was bleeding. My sister Sherry came running in and as soon as she saw me leaning over her son, said, "What did you do to him?"

"Nothing," I said. "He came tearing in here and tripped. I was trying – "

"Jesus. What did you do to your hair?"

I ran my hand over my bare neck and looked down at my socks. "Just a haircut."

She scooped up her son. "Looks like a friggin' helmet." She brushed his downy hair away from his face and examined his nose and forehead. He stopped crying. "You're fine, buddy." He buried his face in her neck.

"I didn't know you guys were coming this weekend."

"Mom wanted my help with wedding things. She said you've been a real spaceshot about it. Sorry, I was supposed to say, 'Mom and I wanted to surprise you with a girls' night!'" She said her husband, Jason, and their two kids were just staying for dinner, then he'd take them home and she'd stay overnight with us. "I can't even drink because I'm pregnant again. So we'll all stay up late drinking cocoa, eating popcorn, and giggling over bridal magazines and shit." She rolled her eyes.

In addition to this being the first I'd heard of another baby on the way, I was stunned by the realization that this evening would turn out worse than I'd even thought possible. Plus, I had never giggled in the presence of my sister in my life and knew that tonight would not be the night.

"Wow," I said. "Another baby. That's great. Congratulations. I'd better go add some more place settings."

"Yeah, this'll be my last. Then it's your turn. I'm done."

I turned and went to the kitchen.

#

During dinner, all attention and eyes were mercifully on my clumsy two-year-old nephew, and mild-mannered four-year-old niece Jenny. My mom or dad would ask a question and Ricky would act out some version of an answer with his hands and loud bellows. Everyone would laugh. Then Jason would ask, "And what about you, Jenny?" And she would reply with short sentences and a polite smile. Then everyone would say, "Awww."

Later on, when my sister came back inside after seeing Jason and the kids off, the air felt darker, like when a summer thunderstorm snuck up over a hill when you weren't paying attention, and wasn't storming yet, but the booms and strikes and rainy sheets were imminent.

"Well, I'll be in the living room reading the paper," my dad said.

My mother stood at the sink, facing yet another formidable pile of dirty dishes. "I'll wash, Sherry, you rinse, and Viv, you dry." I hung my head and slunk over to the sink, readying myself for the rain to start its drenching.

"What's your damage?" Sherry asked.

I shrugged and focused on the darkness eavesdropping right outside the window above the sink. "Nothing."

"She doesn't have to do dishes at college," my mom said. "She just sets them on a conveyor belt and poof, they're whisked away. What a life, huh?"

My sister laughed with a bit of a catch. "She'll learn soon enough that a household doesn't work like that. Nothing gets done unless the woman does it."

My mother nodded. "Gospel truth," she said. She'd picked that phrase up on a week-long trip down South when she was volunteering with the Girl Scouts when Sherry was a member. I had dropped out a month into Brownies because I could never memorize the words to the song and some girls made fun of me. Sherry had earned every badge there was.

"Speaking of," Sherry said, and handed me a plate to dry. "What's the plan? You've picked a date, I assume?"

I dried and placed it in the drainer to my right. I ground my back teeth together. "There's," I said, and closed my eyes, "not going to be a wedding."

The sink shut off. "What are you talking about?" my mother asked.

I heard Sherry put down a plate, and her shirt rustled. My eyes were still closed, but I could feel her stare giving the left side of my face a burn.

"Vivian Lucille Pierce," my mother said. "*What* are you *talking* about?" I could hear that she spoke through clenched teeth. My sister's silence scared me more; she was eight years older than I was, and blamed me for every imperfect childhood memory she had, even the ones before I was born.

I opened my eyes and slowly turned to their furrowed brows and scowls. Sherry's jaw twitched.

"I – I – broke… Um. Broke off the – the engagement. A cou- " I cleared my throat, "a few weeks ago."

My mother set down the casserole dish she'd been steel-wooling and rinsed her hands. "Why?"

I turned to them. *Don't tell them everything. Just stick to the basics. It's safer that way and they don't need to know the other thing.*

"Adrian and I – we just didn't…" Izzy had given me a pep talk the day before that included the words I now used: "Our priorities were very different, and I didn't want to hold him back."

Sherry said, "Your *priorities* were *different*? Really. What 'priorities,' exactly?"

I felt like I would split in two and implode. I looked up at the overhead light above the sink. "I – I wan – want to, to travel. And – and see things. I – I've always wanted to see London. Or I have for a few years, anyway, and – "

My mother rubbed her forehead with her palm and said, "This again."

Sherry shook her head and said, "So you threw away the rest of your life because – what? – you want to backpack around Europe?"

"No, not necessarily backpack, but – well, Paul did, and he was only eighteen."

"It's different for men," Sherry said. "And you get lost in Boston, for Christ's sake. You'd never make it out of Europe alive if you went by yourself."

"Did he hit you?" my mother asked.

"What?"

"Was Adrian abusive?"

"No."

"Did he cheat on you?"

"No, Mom. I – " *No. Don't tell them. Not even if they torture you.* I took two steps back. *Stick to the script.* "Adrian's career was the most important thing to him. It was more important to him than – "

"Well of course it's important, Vivian," Sherry said. "He has to be able to support a family. At least he was aiming high. What else wasn't good enough for you?"

"No, it's not that anything wasn't good enough for me – I'm the thing that's never good enough."

"Oh boo-hoo," she said.

"Everything ok out there?" my dad called from the other room.

"No, Bill," my mother said. "Nothing is ok out here."

"What the hell's going on?" he asked as he stuck his head into the kitchen.

My mother turned to him and said, "She broke off her engagement."

He tilted his head. "Oh. Is… that it?"

My mother sighed. "I'm going to bed. You two take care of the dishes."

"It's only seven o'clock," he said. She left the room without another word. Dad looked after her and shook his head. He turned to me and Sherry. "Did I miss something?"

Sherry shot me a death glare. "I'll go talk to her," she said and followed where Mom had gone.

My dad turned back to me. "You ok, sweetie?"

"You're not mad at me too?"

He laughed. "Course not. I never liked that little twerp anyway."

"Really?"

"He was a brown-noser. I can't stand brown-nosers." He walked over and hugged me. "Don't let your mother and sister beat you up too bad."

I wrapped my arms around him. "I have a feeling this is just the beginning."

"Probably is," he said. "But you're a grown-up. You don't have to stand for it."

I always had. "I wish it was that simple."

"You're twenty-one. You make your own decisions. You could even leave right now without saying another word to anyone else, and I wouldn't blame you."

"I'm sure that would go over really well."

"Well, you *would* be abandoning me here with a couple of grumps."

"I won't do that to you, Dad."

He patted my back and kissed my forehead. "Well, I'd best go check on your mother."

I started on the dishes. Sherry came down a few minutes later and started drying without saying anything, but glaring at me.

Finally, she said, "By the way, not that you'd remember, but Mom was worried sick the whole time Paul was gone."

"You're right. I don't remember. Because I was an actual baby."

Her jaw twitched again as she clenched her teeth. "Do you have any idea how bad you screwed up this time?"

I set the pot I was scrubbing down and turned to her. "Why do you care about this so much?"

She squinted and put her mostly dry dish down in the drainer. "Because Mom does. You don't understand what it's like to worry about your kid, no matter how much of a loser they are."

I took a deep breath. "I'm not – "

"What are you going to do once you're out of college? Huh?"

"I… I have a friend in England I want to go see."

"'Friend,' huh?" She eyed me with suspicion. I didn't elaborate. "So then what?"

I turned back to the sink and started scrubbing again. "I don't know. Did you always know what you wanted to do?"

She crossed her arms over her chest. "You're overcomplicating it. You get married, you have kids, and when they leave the house, *then* you get to do things like travel if you're still young enough. The kids aren't supposed to come back."

"I won't move back home. But I don't know if – I'm not sure I want kids. I'm not even sure if I want to get married ever."

She scoffed. "So, what? You're going to support yourself as a radio DJ? Is that your great life plan?"

"I don't know yet."

"You really do think you're too good for the kind of life Mom and I have."

"No, I really don't."

She rolled her eyes. "Right. Boy do you have a rude awakening coming." She took the elastic off her wrist and pulled her long, light brown hair back in a ponytail. "News flash, little sister: guys are the ones who have choices. It's different for us. You think you're going to graduate college and places will be falling all over themselves to offer you some 'cool' job and all you have to decide is which one? Even if you can find a job you don't hate, you'll never make as much as a man. You think you're so above everything, but you're a shitty student. Always have been. And you never learned anything practical. You can't even get that pot clean."

I scrubbed harder and tried to not cry. I couldn't let her know I knew she was mostly right. Everything Izzy said, everything John said… They didn't know me like my family did. Izzy and John had options that someone like me didn't.

"What?" she said. "Cat got your tongue? Ok, I'll go on. You know what's going to happen when you get out of school? I do. You'll stay in Marblewell for a while. You'll either work in a bookstore there if you're lucky, or end up waiting tables – which is really hard, by the way. Your rent will eat up most of what you make. Everyone you know there will move away, and you won't have anyone left. You think you're smarter than everyone, so no guy's going to want you. And you'll end up back here 'just for a little while' while you work and save up some money. And years will go by and you'll still be Mom and Dad's problem. Meanwhile, Adrian will definitely find someone else, marry her, start a family with her, and hold down a job. Which is more than I can say for Jason right now. He's out of work *again*. Anyway, if you have two brain cells to rub together, you'll patch things up with Adrian and beg him to take you back. Grow up."

I threw the sponge in the sink and walked away, feeling the hotness in my cheeks and the tears start to flood my eyes.

"Yep," she called after me. "Typical. Run away from your responsibility. Let me pick up your slack *again*."

I took the stairs two at a time and closed my door without turning on a light. I turned on the radio, closed my eyes, and fell back on my bed. My heart pounded and my breath came faster and faster until I was afraid I might suffocate because I couldn't draw in a full breath. I turned my focus to the radio. The DJ talked about the unseasonably warm temperatures that were coming over the weekend, and what great news that was for all the hunters out there, and by the time he played the inevitable "Heat Wave," by Martha Reeves and the Vandellas, I could almost breathe again.

I didn't want to be a burden on anyone, certainly not my parents. Sherry was right about a lot of things, mean as she was. And I hated to admit it, but there was a small, quiet voice in my head somewhere that had started convincing me that maybe there *were* some special things about me. John seemed to think so, or at least he said he did. Maybe he was just being nice.

I changed into my t-shirt and sweats and drifted into a patchy, twitchy sleep. I kept waking up on my stomach saying, "No no no," but couldn't remember what I'd just been dreaming. Later, I heard my radio switch off and the floorboard near it creak.

I shot up to a sitting position. "Who's there?"

"I kept hearing voices while I was trying to sleep. It was your radio." It was my mother.

"Sorry," I said. "I didn't think it was that loud."

I heard her walk a few steps toward the door then stop. "What really happened with you and Adrian?"

I rubbed my eyes. They were itchy. I wondered when the big light in the driveway had stopped working. It was so dark I couldn't see anything except the barely glowing Big Ben alarm clock saying it was midnight.

"We weren't right for each other, Mom. We just weren't."

I heard her sniff. "Life isn't a fairytale, Vivian. Nothing's ever perfect. But he was special. You were lucky, and you threw it away. I've never been this disappointed in you." She took a few more steps and I heard my door click shut.

I sat staring in the direction of my door. I had let her down again. I pulled my knees up to my chest and tried to curl into myself and get small enough to disappear. I felt something in my very center disintegrate, fall to pieces, and vanish like a shooting star. I wondered if I'd never actually left Stonewald and had dreamed all the other stuff.

My legs and back cramped. As I lay back on my bed and stretched, I opened my eyes. In total darkness, the stars and planets and galaxies on the ceiling were glowing brighter than I ever remembered.

...even after a shitty day of being a kid here, all you have to do is open your eyes at night and you'll be reminded that there's a big, limitless, beautiful world out there.

Think about the things you want to see once you're over here. Promise.

I walked quietly to my door and opened it. It was still pitch black, but I knew that it was three steps to the stairs, then six stairs down to the landing, a half turn to the right, then seven steps down to the living room. My dad was fully reclined in his chair and snoring softly. The tv played the hissing static of the end of the broadcast day. I turned the knob until it clicked off. There was a little light coming in from the kitchen. Dad snorted and I heard him sit up.

"Elizabeth?" he whispered.

"No. It's Viv, Dad."

"Couldn't sleep?"

I walked over to his chair and kneeled beside him. "Dad, I'm gonna go. I'm sorry to leave you here like this."

He yawned. “That’s ok, sweetie. It’ll all blow over sometime. Drive safe.”

“I will,” I said.

“Got enough gas?”

“Filled up on the way here.”

He cleared his throat. “Good. Ok. Where you headed?”

“Not sure.” I kissed his cheek and he kissed mine. “I love you.”

“Love you too,” he said. “Your mother hid your keys in the cabinet with the cornflakes. I’m going back to sleep now.”

“Thanks, Dad.”

His soft snores started up again. I went to the kitchen and glanced at the clock: 12:50 a.m. I got my coat, purse, shoes, hidden keys, and exited silently.

Everything was broken now. Good.

Chapter 16

I got to UCNH sometime after three. I parked in the lot of the building with the radio station. My Ziggy Stardust tape had ended long ago, and I hadn't even noticed. I stared at my dashboard. I was shaking.

I turned the radio on to WCNH, assuming I'd hear the static indicating no one was there. Instead, I heard Hank Williams singing "I'll Never Get Out of This World Alive." I went to the back door and pushed the button labeled "WCNH" on one of those bumpy plastic label-maker strips that had been there for as long as anyone could remember. It was unnatural how much weather that thing had survived.

I heard the familiar thunk-thunk-thunk down the stairs, the push and release of the bar lock on the door, and looked into the confused face of Lenny. I realized I was still in my sleeping clothes.

"Can I come up?" I asked.

"Of course," he said. He put his arm around my shoulders and guided me up the two flights of stairs. He kicked out the old cracked *Norton Anthology of English Literature* propping the door to the hallway open, checked how much of the song he had left, queued up another record, and asked if I wanted some coffee.

"Yes, please. Unless you happen to have anything stronger."

"There's the emergency whiskey in the record library."

I nodded. He rinsed out a purple Tisket Tasket Records coffee mug, filled it from the coffee maker in the lounge, went into the record library, got the whiskey, and poured in a healthy glug. He walked me to the couch in the lounge, and I sat and sipped. Finally, I exhaled.

"You look terrible," he said.

I looked up at him, his unwavering stare trying to parse what he was seeing. I said, "I think I have to go."

"Where?"

"Away. Really far away."

"OK. What the fuck happened?"

"I'm not even sure, really," I said. "I was home, and just… years of things that made me feel stupid and worthless and alone came flooding back and I got this feeling I haven't had in *so long*. Not since high school."

He sat beside me on the couch, wrapped his arms around my shoulders, and rested his head against mine. "You did good coming here," he said.

The song playing through the radio stopped. "Dead air," I said.

Lenny jumped up and ran to the studio. I went to the office. Took out my keys, unlocked the door. I went in, sat down, and looked at the Elvis clock on the wall. 3:30am. 8:30am John's time. Perfectly reasonable. Except maybe not on a Saturday morning.

Fuck it. I dialed the extensive string of numbers to reach him, and the next string of numbers that paid for it. The double gurgle sounded nicer than our single, aggressive ring. I wasn't paying attention to how many times it rang. But eventually, I realized it had probably been too long, and was about to hang up.

A sleepy voice croaked, "Hello?"

"Hi," I said. "I'm sorry to bother you so early. I really am. But, is John there?"

"Viv? Is that you?"

I hadn't recognized his voice. But now it enveloped me like my flannel sleeping bag used to as a kid.

"You all right? Isn't it like three in the morning there?"

"Something like that," I said. "Did I wake you?"

"Yeah, but that's ok. I like waking up to your voice." I heard him yawn. "How's your trip home?"

"Not great. I'm actually back at the radio station now. It's a long story, but I ended up leaving in the middle of the night."

"What happened? Are you all right?"

"No," I said. "I mean, I'm not hurt or anything, I just... can't stay here anymore. I feel like I'll suffocate if I do."

"Then don't," he said.

I looked down at my hands. They were shaking. The oversized desk calendar grew soggy with my tears. I hadn't realized I was crying.

"Remember when you said how stuff built up and built up? To the point where you felt something in you break?"

"Yeah," he said quietly. "Viv – "

"I remembered my promise to you," I said. "Can I..." *Fuck. I can't. It's too much.*

"Yes," he said. "Fly into Heathrow. Get the earliest flight you can. I'll be there any time you tell me."

I shook my head. "Are you sure?"

"Of course I'm sure," he said. "Call me from the airport when you know something. Putting on some coffee now. I'll be right here until I hear from you again."

"You know it would be perfectly reasonable for you to say no. Right?"

"What fun would that be?" he asked. "I fucking can't wait to see you. I'll talk with you soon."

We hung up. Lenny hovered out in the hall. I went out to see him.

"Want to hang on to my car for a while?" I asked.

"I have my own car. It's nicer than yours. But my niece could use one. Does this involve a ride to Boston?"

I nodded.

"You got it. Let me just hit the sign off and lock up."

As Lenny played the sign-off, I watched him and mouthed the words silently. *You've been listening to WCNH in Marblewell...* I wandered around the halls of my most sacred place, the one that had given me sanctuary at a time I needed it most. It was everything I had ever wanted, and it had given and given to me, and now... Just like that, this might be the last time I ever saw it, smelled it, felt its pockmarked bulletin boards under my fingers as I slid them along it. I grabbed an old band flyer, turned it over, found a thick black magic marker, and wrote:

DEAR WCNH:

I love you from the bottom of my ridiculous, fucked up little heart. I don't want to leave you, but I have to go. See Lenny for details. Someone needs to take my shift on Fridays, at least for a little while. And Keaton, sorry to bail on music director stuff. I will be in touch soon. I'll miss you all so much.

All my love,

Viv

PS: Blaze and Serenity: I'm sorry I was such a dick to you both. You didn't deserve that. And Serenity was right – I think my aura was all weird.

The fumes from the marker stung my nose. I pinned the note to the center of the bulletin board. I went into the studio, taking in every little detail of the board, the stained vinyl chairs, the haunted Windsor chair, the record bins, the dim, first-date-level lighting.

"Ready?" Lenny said.

"I think so."

A few minutes later, we were in my dorm room. I located my passport, changed into actual clothing while Lenny waited outside in the hall, and threw a bunch of stuff into a suitcase and a duffel bag. I consolidated my albums and tapes into two yellow milk crates and asked Lenny to take care of them.

"How long you going for?" Lenny asked when he came back in.

"I don't know. Maybe not long. Maybe as long as they'll let me stay. This is crazy, right? I should absolutely not do this."

He nodded. "Of course not. I'm so fucking excited for you."

I taped a note to my door that read: GONE TO FIND ZIGGY STARDUST. WILL BE IN TOUCH.

Lenny helped me carry my things to his car in the parking lot. We put my bags in his back seat, the milk crates in the trunk, and we got in the front. Lenny's car always smelled like Vanilla. He started the engine and adjusted the temperature.

"I'm scared," I said. "I've never been out of the country, except once to Canada."

He turned toward me, took my left hand in his, and rubbed my palm with his thumb. He'd started doing that when I was nervous about my on-air audition tape freshman year, and it always calmed me down.

"You'll be fine. People do it all the time," he said. "Can I ask you something?"

"Sure."

He tapped my wrist. "I noticed that scar the first week I met you."

I groaned. It was barely a scar anymore.

He said, "Was it... intentional?"

"It was a stupid thing in high school," I said. "I don't like to talk about it."

"You don't have to tell me anything if you don't want to," he said. "But I've always wondered. I figured we were close, and you'd tell me about it someday, but it never came up."

"It was a tough time. But things are better now."

He moved closer and put an arm around me. I leaned my head on his shoulder. "So you *did* try?"

I couldn't look him in the eye. All the shame, the loneliness, the hopelessness, had gotten too heavy for me at 17. I'd never told anyone before, and it had healed up so much since then that no one noticed, or at least no one said they did. But I might never see Lenny again, and I owed it to him to be honest. "I *started* to try. But it hurt too much, and I stopped…" I shivered, remembering the gush of blood and sharp sear of the razor.

He wrapped both his arms around me. He sniffled, then cleared his throat, which made *me* feel like crying. "I'm so glad you're still here."

"Me too."

#

There was no traffic, so we made it to Logan in an hour – Lenny said he'd never gotten there that fast before. It was six by then. I'm not sure how many ticket counters I went to before I finally found one that offered a nonstop flight to London; stalling in America just wasn't anything I could stand, now that I'd made up my mind. But I didn't have enough cash on me for the ticket.

"Guess I'll have to wait till Monday when I can get to the bank," I said to Lenny.

"You'll talk yourself out of it by then," he said, and gave a credit card to the woman at the desk before I could object. He turned to me and said, "Keep your cash. My treat. You're going."

I threw my arms around him while they printed my ticket. "I love you, Lenny."

"Love you too. Now let go. You're embarrassing me."

It happened faster than I'd assumed it would: present my passport, check my bags, leave Boston at 7:30am, arrive in London six and a half or seven hours later. I didn't have time to rethink anything. They would let me go, I'd go.

I grabbed a payphone and dialed John's number, in quick succession with my cumbersome calling card number. He answered after the first ring.

"Viv?"

He really had been waiting.

"Yeah," I said. "I'm leaving soon. I think I'll be there around seven-ish tonight your time." I told him my flight number and so on. "Is this really ok?"

"Are you joking? This is better than ok. I'll leave Lonsdale soon, and shore up a place to stay in the city by the time you're there."

I rubbed my dry, tired eyes. "This doesn't seem real. This is insane. Thank you."

"Really can't wait to see you. You should go – don't miss your flight."

I got everything ready to go through my gate, and I told Lenny he should go see his Boston girl and spend the day with her. He said he'd already called her, and she was expecting him.

"Maybe bring her some croissants from one of those little bakeries on Newbury Street," I said. "And some kind of milky, Italian coffee. Jesus, maybe that's just what I want right now, but I bet she'd love it, too."

"Call during my shift later, if you can. Just to let me know you got there."

"I will. Play some Motorhead for me?"

Lenny nodded. We hugged, and he said, "I am so proud of you."

That bolstered me enough to get on the plane.

Chapter 17

"Ladies and gentlemen, welcome to Heathrow International Airport in London. For our guests visiting from abroad, local date is the twentieth of October, time is 7:20pm, and the temperature is 13 degrees Celsius, about 55 degrees Fahrenheit."

The cabin was thick with the cigarette smoke of my fellow passengers, and my throat hurt from having steeped in it for hours. While I waited for people to unbuckle, stand, stretch, and shuffle, I glanced out my little window and let my eyes adjust to the darker parts outside. Lights on other planes flashed on and off, runway guides beckoned travelers to them, and tall lights lit up parts of the tarmac.

But beyond all that were the lights of my new city, at least for a little while. I could just make out the shapes of some stocky buildings standing guard between the sprawling airport and the moving headlights of cars winding along roads I wasn't familiar with. I thought about where I might be able to fit into it all. And I was just minutes away from seeing John – he was so close. Goosebumps sprang up all over me. I had no idea how things would turn out – we may very well be just friends this time around. Which was good – it would be safer. And at the moment, safer was better.

"Miss?" said a flight attendant.

My row mates, and apparently, most of the rest of the plane, had left while I was lost in the twinkling lights outside and in my own head. I put on my jacket, got my bag from under the seat in front of me, and made my way off the plane.

The terminal bustled with people and conversations. Everyone else seemed to know exactly where they were going.

Some ran to loved ones waiting for them just beyond the gate. And behind it all was a gleaming, expansive labyrinth of walkways, newsstands, escalators, blinking digital flight schedules, and billboards. Pleasant English voices boomed information over the speakers. I couldn't quite understand what they said, though I did catch something about keeping an eye out for abandoned luggage and trash cans inside the building having been moved outside because of a bomb threat earlier that week, but that everything would be back to normal soon. Enjoy your time in London, they said.

I let the wave of other passengers carry me along as I scanned for John's face. I spotted him off to the right, and he waved. He was wearing faded jeans and a black, woolly-looking jacket with pewter buttons up the front. The rest of the airport fell away.

Easy does it. Stay in control. I snaked my way toward him through the perpetual motion of the crowd.

When I reached him, we stood facing each other, almost afraid to touch in case it would make this impossible moment evaporate into a taunting, cruel dream. Being this close to him gave me a stinging awareness of my skin and his effect on it: it sprouted invisible tendrils that floated up and forward toward him, and if I hadn't looked down at my feet on the floor, I would have sworn I was levitating.

He grabbed my shoulders and every nerve in them sprang to life under his fingers. "You're really here," he said.

Much to my horror, I started to cry; not with any kind of sadness, but with the relief that marathon runners break down with when they reach the finish line.

Fuck it; I had enough friends already, and nothing with other humans was ever safe anyway.

I dropped my carry-on bag, wrapped my arms around his neck and pressed against him. The tension in my body released to the point where I thought I might fall backward and take him with me. His hands found their way under all my clothing layers, onto my tailbone, and ignited a warmth in me I'd almost forgotten was still there. He kissed me, and I tasted the salt of my tears and his minty, sweet tongue.

When we paused for breath, which I couldn't quite catch, my mouth said, "I want you," without my brain's permission.

He blinked and said "What?"

I shook my head, trying to disperse the hormone-drenched stupor that his closeness had brought on. "Sorry. Got a little carried away there."

He raised the left corner of his lips. "Want to?"

I scratched a nonexistent itch on my forehead, looked down, and nodded. John picked up my bag, flung it over his shoulder, took my hand, and guided me out of the terminal, toward some restrooms on the perimeter.

There was a line of three single, wheelchair-accessible restrooms. Seeing no one in a wheelchair nearby, we ducked into one and locked the door. The cold-toned overhead fluorescent tube lights were not going to do me any favors. Yet John looked even more perfect in a flickering blue sepia that darkened his short, jagged hair and threw a cinematic contrast on the shadows of the contours of his face. He took his coat off, and he was wearing my Mission of Burma t-shirt. It clung and hung different on him than it did on me.

I don't know how to have sex in a bathroom. I'm not light enough to be picked up like those teeny girls in the movies, and I can't lay on a public bathroom floor – gross – and what if I smell bad...

He hung my bag on the coat hook, pulled me against him, and kissed me.

"The shirt looks good on you," I breathed. "I, um, haven't showered since yesterday morning."

He brought his mouth to my ear, and whispered, "Don't care." He bit my earlobe and ran his soft lips down the length of my neck. My eyes rolled back in my head.

We fumbled with our clothes until they were all balled together on a patch of paper towels that John had thrown down in the corner nearest the door. I ran my hands up through his hair, making it stand on end, and stepped back to take in every freckle and scar, every cowlick in his chest and pubic hair on his strong, sinewy body.

He reached out and tucked my hair behind each of my ears, then traced my eyebrows with his thumbs. He let his gaze wander down me; he'd see the darkening bruises on the fronts of my thighs from where I'd bumped into chairs getting on and off the plane, and the prickly hair on my shins that I'd neglected shaving for too long, and the shadow under my belly that was far from flat. Instead of shrinking or wanting to turn off the light, I stood up straight.

I took a couple of steps toward him, stretched on tiptoes, and kissed him. I backed up against the cold tile wall, pulled him against me, and blood whooshed in my ears.

#

When we emerged, the terminal had emptied out. I was high and stupid from our encounter, and it occurred to me that I should get my bags.

We made our way to the baggage claim arm in arm. My bags were the last two spinning around the silver carousel. I grabbed one, and John the other.

"Can we get some whiskey?" I asked.

He wrapped his free arm around me. "Right this way," he said.

We stepped up to the cramped, dark, woody bar just off the main walkway, and John asked what kind I wanted. I remembered that I didn't know fuck all about whiskey, though I knew enough that whatever I'd drank at the radio station earlier was poison.

"Something Irish?" I said. "I don't know. I want it to burn."

The bartender came over and John ordered two Bushmills. The bartender set two small, green glasses in front of us. We clinked. I took a small sip and recoiled. But the warmth going down felt good. John put his arm around me as we sipped.

I looked around this airport bar, this gathering place for transients, and saw all manner of different faces; some thin-lipped Brits, some laughing Irishmen, some darker-skinned men and women whose ethnicities I was too small-town to identify from a glance, and I was in love with all of them. I wanted to know everything about them, to hear all of their stories that had brought them to this place.

John said he had some friends who lived in London, and were out of town for a few days, and that we could stay at their place. "Is that all right? You can have your own room, if you prefer."

The whiskey blazed a trail of fire down my esophagus and bloomed when it hit my stomach, making me warm from the inside out. "No way. I want to fall asleep next to you," I said, and rested my head on his shoulder.

"If you insist." He kissed the top of my head. "I couldn't be more ecstatic that you're here, but I have to ask you something. You sounded awfully shaken up when you called last night. Tell me what happened?"

My eyes fixed on a cocktail napkin with gold lettering on the bar. Once again, I hated for that world to intrude on this one. But, I told him everything. I kept my head on his shoulder while recounting every delightful word I hadn't blocked out yet; I couldn't look him in the eye because I was embarrassed at how childish and unsophisticated the whole thing must seem. There's nothing punk about wishing your sister would stop calling you a loser or that your mom would just like you for who you were for once.

When I was done, John was quiet and still. *He's probably regretting inviting a tantrum-throwing baby into his life.*

I raised my head. His eyebrows were knit together. He started to speak, but then brought a hand to his mouth. Finally, he said, "You've been hearing those sorts of things your whole life?"

"To varying degrees. I'm probably making it sound worse than it was."

"No." He shook his head and wiped his eyes with the back of a palm. "I'm certain you're not. A friend of mine from university committed suicide after a lifetime of being told he wasn't enough. Not just by his dad, but by his schoolmates, cousins, everyone in his backwoods little hometown. It got into his head and had wrapped itself 'round his brain. I could always tell when he'd been home on the weekend, because he'd look deflated and pasty, with dark circles under his eyes. Otherwise, he was this hilarious, generous, compassionate kid who'd always befriend the people around him who didn't belong to groups, and he'd orchestrate them into their own group. One time he couldn't stop those voices from home pecking at his psyche, and he jumped from a tower at school."

I held one of his hands. "I'm sorry."

He said, "I hope you got away without it all wrapping 'round your brain."

I hoped so, too.

After we finished our drinks, we made our way to the subway, which I learned was called the Tube, and squeezed ourselves into a packed train that was bright and clean. The people surrounding us didn't appreciate my bulky bags, and even though they scowled at me, I grinned at each and every one of them, beside myself with gratitude to be there, with my arm looped through John's. It was about twenty minutes to our stop, and a fifteen-minute walk from there.

"Are you sure this isn't too much of an imposition?" I asked on the walk to the apartment. "I mean, I just yanked you out of your life today. You're not obligated to do anything for me. You know that, right?"

He stopped walking and turned. "You know what I'd be doing right now if you hadn't come here? I'd be in Lonsdale, at my flat or the pub down the road, wishing the months until May away, hoping you wouldn't forget about me before then."

"Not a chance," I said.

I held on to his arm tighter as we walked. We got to his friends' place a few minutes later. It was one half of a small duplex, with a set of concrete stairs leading up to the front door. The houses were all pretty close together, like they tended to be in city housing anywhere. John unlocked the door, and we stepped inside. A small hallway with a deep green tiled floor led to a staircase to the left, and what looked to be a kitchen straight ahead. Black iron hooks lined the wall, and he took my coat and hung it on one.

"You must be starving," he said. "Did you eat anything?"

"I had coffee and a scone on the plane earlier. Never had a scone before."

"Let me guess: your mouth is still dry, and you're slightly dehydrated?"

I forced my tongue away from the roof of my mouth. "Actually, yes. So, nothing since this morning, and yes, I'm starving. But fair warning: I don't really cook. And all I have is useless American money until I can get to a bank."

"Do you like curry?"

I remembered that curry was the thing he'd written about his stepmom sending him recipes for, but I still didn't know what it was. I tried to play it nonchalant and said, "Oh, yeah. Curry is great. I love it. That has... uh, chicken in it, right? Why are you laughing?"

"It's just Indian food. I haven't perfected a recipe yet, but know several places that have."

I sighed. "I don't know what Indian food is like. I've never had it. If you like it, though, I'm sure I will, too."

"OK, right. Something with chicken in it? Sauce and rice and vegetables ok?"

"Some of my favorites right there."

"There's a takeaway place just down the road. I can go pick it up if you want to wash up or rest for a few."

As tired as I was, I didn't want to sit inside and miss out on a chance to see a piece of London. I told him I'd go with him, he called the place, I set my bags against the wall in the hall, and we set out.

We stopped at a small, square, painfully lit store that carried beer, wine, and snacks. All of the candy bars were unfamiliar, and I wanted to try every single one, especially the ones touting "biscuits" on indigo wrappers. I scooped up five, and turned to see John looking at me, amused.

"Your candy is prettier than ours."

"If you say so. What would you like to drink with your first night of probably many curry takeaways? You like ale? Cider? Wine? I think there's more whiskey at the flat."

"Anything but wine please," I said.

We walked to the small beer cooler in back of the store, and got some cans of lager I didn't recognize, and some

Guinness, which I'd only ever heard of. Out of habit, I pulled a twenty out of my bag. The man behind the counter said something I couldn't understand. He and John looked at me, waiting for an answer. My eyes went wide, and I'm sure I turned the color of a radish.

The man behind the counter laughed and spoke slower. "Not used to the accent yet, then? I was just asking if you're American. The money there."

"Oh, God, I'm sorry," I said. "Yeah. Very American, apparently."

"Just arrived tonight," said John, putting an arm around my shoulder and smiling.

"Whereabouts you from?"

"New Hampshire."

"Yeah, yeah," he said, thinking as he made change for John's correctly British money. "That nearer to New York, or Boston?"

"Boston," I said.

"Nice city, that," he said. "My brother went over there for a girl not too long ago. Said he may not come back."

"My friend is probably moving there soon," I said, reminding myself to call Lenny later. "Also for a girl. I guess it's where they keep the good ones."

He glanced at John. "Not *all* the good ones, aye mate?"

John gave a nervous laugh, and then looked down at his shoes. The man put the cans in a paper bag, looked back at me, and said, "Your man there is blushing. You two have a nice night."

We thanked him and left, making our way to the restaurant a couple of blocks over.

"I most certainly was not *blushing*," he said.

"Whatever you say, cool guy. I'll pay you back when I can get to a bank and exchange this useless paper in my pockets."

"I'm not worried about it."

As we walked, I looked at the buildings around us; some towered, with stone faces that looked like corrugated cardboard, while others that housed people, hunkered in tones of deep red, blue, and the occasional muted yellow. There were elegant, black iron streetlights that swept the shadows back, and metal and wood benches hosted the occasional sleeping person with a bottle in a bag. We crossed a small, arched bridge over a narrow river, and the sheer freedom I felt at that moment seized me in its manic grip. A light drizzle, not quite rain, hung in the air around us. I stopped in the middle of the bridge, and so did John. I stood on tiptoes, wrapped my arms around his neck, pulled him close, and kissed him.

"Can you feel that?" he said. In the cold October air, his words made a ghost the size of a breath, which then vanished.

"Yeah, but I wasn't going to mention it."

He laughed and took a small step back. "Sorry, no, not that. I meant... I can't explain it any better than I just felt the strangest sensation in the air."

"I think so. I keep thinking I'm going to wake up."

He grinned, tilted his head, and pinched my left cheek. Hard.

"Hey! That hurt, motherfucker."

He laughed. "Looks like you're awake. I think we're safe."

We walked arm in arm the rest of the way to pick up our dinner, and brought it back to his friends' place. We spooned some of everything on to sturdy white plates. A thick, comforting, earthy smell wafted up, and I breathed it in like medicine. Forkful after forkful of chickpeas, chicken, spinach, and cubed cheese over yellow rice in a warm, tangy, Cumin and yogurt sauce got me feeling full and smiley and grateful.

We talked and drank cans of lager and stout. John leaned back in the dark, spindled chair and patted his nonexistent belly, smiling. "That was good."

"I can't believe I've gone 21 years without this food," I said. "How did I think I was even living?"

He leaned toward me, still smiling, and touched my left cheek with his long, elegant fingers. It seemed like he wanted to say something, and so did I, but the unintelligible words hung briefly in the air between us before evaporating.

We brought the plates and silverware to the sink and put the cartons of leftovers in the refrigerator. As John started washing the dishes, he said, "You think you're here for a while?"

I found a small towel and stood next to him, drying the dishes before placing them in the drainer next to the sink.

"I'm not sure. There are quite a few pissed off people at home right now. I'm in no hurry to get back to that. I didn't tell anyone but my friend Lenny. He drove me to the airport."

I couldn't stop thinking just then of how John had a life elsewhere – I had no idea what to do when he inevitably returned to it. He examined my face, and apparently the panic of having no plan had seeped through. "You all right?"

"Yeah. I just... Realized I seriously have no idea what I'm doing. Or where to go. After here, like when your friends want their apartment back, I mean."

"You can stay with me, if you like. I was sort of assuming I'd go back to Lonsdale, but then again... I don't know. You've inspired me."

"Oh, no. Don't go getting inspired. That's a terrible idea, whatever's happening in your brain right now."

He laughed and put his arms around me. "All right, all right. But, please come with me. It's terribly boring compared to the city, but you're welcome if you want to."

"You're sure it wouldn't be too big an imposition? What about your roommate?"

"Albert works odd hours, and isn't really there much when I am. I'm certain he won't mind. Don't worry about it. In the meantime, let me show you a good time in the big city. Do you want to go out tonight? We can probably still grab a couple pints somewhere."

A day of traveling and time change and trying not to think too much about the fallout back home was catching up with me. I kissed him and slid my hands under his shirt, feeling his warm skin sprout goosebumps over wiry muscles. My eyes got heavy. I slumped against him.

"Hey," his quiet voice brought me back from, apparently, a brief nap.

"I'm awake."

He laughed, and led me upstairs to a small, yellow room with no decorations or excess furniture aside from a full-size bed heaped with blankets and quilts, with a wood, slatted headboard painted a creamy off-white, and a small dresser with four drawers. He drew the shades in the two windows.

"Their previous flat mate moved out not long ago. This is the guest room for now. It's slated to be my room in January. Again, I must offer you the chance to have the room to yourself if you like. I don't mind sleeping elsewhere."

I shook my head. "Please stay here with me. I don't want you to vanish."

"I won't vanish," he said.

He showed me the bathroom, where I brushed my teeth and intended to shower, but failed because I just wanted to crawl into bed.

Later, in the quiet glow from the streetlights outside, we listened to people talking and laughing on the street below, making their way home from somewhere. His arms were around me, and my head rested on his chest.

"It's so loud here," he said, his deep voice reverberating in my skull. "Nothing like the peaceful quiet of a New Hampshire night, is it?"

"I like hearing all that life out there. I can go to sleep and not worry that the rest of the world has fallen away."

"Fallen away? Like a zombie apocalypse?"

"Sure. Like a zombie apocalypse. Weirdo."

He laughed. "Well, I don't know. Help me understand."

"I just mean that my life has always been quiet. So quiet that sometimes it felt like the world had forgotten I was there, and no one was ever going to come look for me. I've dreamed of coming here for years, and tonight it's right outside that window, talking to me. I never thought I'd get here."

He ran a thumb over my left wrist and held it there. I held my breath. "Promise me one more thing."

I looked up at him, his long eyelashes making spidery shadows across the tops of his cheeks. "OK."

"Never again," he said, and kissed the pale scar tissue.

"If I'd had any idea then…" I started. "I promise."

He squeezed me and put my hand over his heart, fingers spread. From outside, a woman yelled something about someone being a sodding cunt. Finally, exhaustion won.

#

I woke up around two in the morning, and remembered I'd told Lenny I would call him. I rolled on to my side and looked at John lying there in the warm glow of the streetlights through the drawn shades. I tried not to wake him as I slipped out of bed, but he stirred.

"You ok?" he asked.

"Yeah, I'm good. I just remembered I promised to call my friend and let him know I got here ok. I have my calling card – I won't stick your friends with the bill."

"That's the last thing on my mind."

I went back over to the bed and kissed him. He cupped my face in his hands.

"I can't believe you're really here."

I couldn't believe... Well, any of it. "Be right back," I said, and went downstairs to the phone in the kitchen.

"WCNH, Heavy Metal Knock Out Show."

"Lenny - I made it. I'm in London. Can't believe it yet, but it seems real enough."

"Good girl," he said. "And the dreamboat?"

"Still a goddamn dreamboat."

We promised to write, said goodbye, and hung up. I remembered that I hadn't told Izzy. She was at Dean's this weekend, so I dialed his number and left a message when his machine picked up.

I went back to bed and found that John was awake, but just barely. He turned on his side and smiled at me in the pale glow bleeding through the shades. "Hey," he whispered. His eyes fluttered shut. I wrapped an arm around him, clinging tight. As I drifted off, the city sighed on the windows.

Chapter 18

The next morning, it was grey and drizzling again, or probably still. The gas fireplace on the wall in the kitchen took the chill off, and the pot of tea that John made helped with that too.

"We'll have to pick up some coffee from the shops later," he said. "What would you like to do today?"

"I would like to go find Ian Curtis and give him a hug."

He sipped his tea, thinking, and then went upstairs.

"Did I say something bad?" I yelled.

He came back down, holding a piece of paper with some dates and places written on it. "Seems a bit heartless to leave me for a Rockstar already, but like I said all along – no strings."

"I just said 'give him a *hug*.' Although... He *is* breath-taking. Thanks for being cool about it."

He pulled a chair next to mine and put an arm around me. "Sorry, love, I'm afraid he's spoken for – wife, baby, all of that."

"Oh."

"So sorry. But these are some Joy Division shows coming up. A friend of mine works in a record shop here in London and gets all sorts of show dates – he let me know about these, and I copied them down."

I looked at the paper and shook my head. "I don't know where anything is."

He pointed at the 22 October line – the next day. "Assembly Rooms, Derby - that's right next to Lonsdale, where I'm living now."

I couldn't believe what I was hearing. I just stared at the paper, wondering when my eyes were going to pop out of my head. "Oh my god," was all I could say.

I looked over at John, who was beaming. "Think you'll still be around?"

I nodded.

"Oh, and they're opening for the Buzzcocks on this stretch, hope that's ok."

I threw my arms around his neck and kissed him.

We headed out for a walk around noon. The neighborhood had a tidy line of trees between the houses and the street, and every so often there was a small cart with steam rising from it offering Indian, Pakistani, Thai, and Jamaican foods. I wanted to get a bowl from each one, but remembered that I had nothing to pay with. I needed to get to a bank first thing in the morning to exchange my cash so I wouldn't have to keep sponging off John. Then I'd need to find a way to get some of my savings from home transferred over; maybe Dad would help me. Of course, I'd need to tell him where I'd ended up first…

"You all right in there?" John said.

"Just working out some logistics, which is not a strength of mine."

We held hands as we let the slope of the hill lead us toward a bustling central square paved with cobblestones that I kept tripping over. There were more food carts, one of which filled my nose with the scent of warm coconut. My stomach grumbled.

A man around my age with long, wavy, dark hair and big, green eyes stood off to the side playing an electric guitar through a small, squat amp plugged into an electrical outlet sticking up out of the ground. Just as he started singing, his eyes got wide and he turned sideways, barely missing being barreled into by a tall guy with a shaved head, wearing an olive bomber jacket and jeans rolled up to expose the highest leather tie-up boots I'd ever seen in person. He fell backward, but just as soon as he hit the ground, he sprang back up and drew a fist back at two similarly built guys, also with shaved heads, who were running straight at him.

"Fuck off back to where *you* came from, you cunts," he yelled as he punched one of the runners square in the nose with a crack and spray of red.

"Fucking hell," John said, and took off toward the fight.

I watched in horror as John approached the one in the olive jacket at almost the same rate as the second runner, who I noticed had a swastika on a sleeve of his black bomber jacket. *What the fuck, what the fuck, what the fuck?*

The man in olive glanced in John's direction, and smiled big, revealing two rows of crooked teeth with one missing just left of center on the top. "John, mate!"

Swastika reached him just before John did, and the man in olive turned forty-five degrees to his right and slammed into swastika with his shoulder, taking him off balance and knocking him to the ground.

The guitarist had moved out of the way with his amp, and sipped some water, waiting to resume his set.

John was saying something I couldn't make out and throwing his hands in the air, while his friend laughed and patted him on the back. The one with the gory nose was getting to his feet and spitting ribbons of stringy blood. John's friend held up his index finger, indicating that John should step aside and wait, which he did. John's friend then went toward the one whose nose he'd bloodied.

John looked over at me, waved, and mouthed "Sorry."

The swastika guy, meanwhile, had gotten up and was moving quickly toward John, who was unaware that he was about to be ambushed.

No.

I took off running toward John before either of us realized what I was doing.

My dad's instructions were simple: "Make a fist, but be sure that your thumb isn't curled up inside the fingers, because if you land a good one, it'll break."

Swastika guy was getting closer, and glaring at John, oblivious to me hurtling toward him.

As John realized what might be about to happen, his eyebrows shot up and he shook his head at me.

Swastika guy pulled a fist back to throw at John.

"When you throw the punch, give it everything you've got," my dad had told me. "But Jesus Christ, don't hyperextend your elbow, because you'll lose your balance and give the other guy control. Just *jab*, take your fist back. *Jab*, *jab*, take it back."

My punch landed on the right side of the guy's face, which sent him stumbling. I readied my fists again. John's mouth hung open as he stared at me.

Swastika guy regained his composure and strode toward me, his nose and mouth and eyes all scrunched up in a twisted mask of fury.

I'd practiced this so many times on the heavy bag at home that it was pure muscle memory: *jab*, *jab*. Only this time, bone and cartilage shifted under my knuckles instead of the unyielding fabric of the bag. Swastika guy's nose rained blood and snot into his shocked-open mouth.

John and his friend ran to stand in between me and swastika guy, who then slouched and walked fast toward his friend, who was waving for him to leave with him. As they turned their backs to us, John's friend said, "Crack a fuckin' history book: the Nazis lost. Nazis *always* fuckin' lose."

John grabbed onto my shoulders with shaking hands. He examined my face with wide, unblinking eyes. "Are you all right?"

My fists were still in fight mode, and when I released them, the adrenaline evaporated, and my right knuckles throbbed. I had a hard time catching my breath, but said I was fine. I realized I was bouncing up and down on the balls of my feet.

He pulled me against him, squeezing so hard I felt his heart hammering against me. "Please don't do that again. You could have been killed."

"*You* could have been killed too," I said.

He let out a long exhale. "You weren't kidding about knowing how to throw a punch."

I glanced over his shoulder, and his friend was beaming with those Halloween teeth. His eyes were gold, like he was lit up from inside. "Nice one, love. Let's find you a pint and some ice for your hand, yeah?"

I nodded. I held out my sore hand to examine it; the skin between the first and second knuckles was bright pink, and some blood peeked through on my middle knuckle where a layer of skin had ripped off.

John loosened his grip on me to look at my hand. "That looks painful. Viv, this is my friend Bruce – the one who works at the record store. Also the bastard who got into a late-night row that caused me to miss our phone call that time."

Bruce shoved his hands into his pockets and looked down at the ground. "Sorry 'bout that. In my defense, that guy was an anti-Semite piece of rubbish. Deserved what he got." He looked up at John, then at me, then back at John. "Hold up, this is the girl you were talking about that night."

John's cheeks flashed pink. He mumbled, "Maybe."

"Yeah, yeah – she was American, you met at a... Where was that? A radio station, yeah?"

John was blushing hard now. I raised my eyebrows at him.

"I meet loads of girls at radio stations, Bruce, I can't be expected to keep them all straight."

Bruce rolled his eyes and kissed my good hand. "Pleased to meet you, Viv."

We walked a few paces behind Bruce. Everything was pulsing: my heart in my chest, the soles of my feet, my knuckles where I'd nailed the guy who was going to hurt John.

John and Bruce talked about some mutual friends, though I couldn't understand a lot of what they said; he talked a bit faster with Bruce, and his accent was thicker than when it was just him and me. I wondered if I'd acclimate and be able to understand people better the longer I stayed, and that inevitably brought me to the question of how long that would be. I wasn't even sure if I'd unofficially quit college by coming here.

We arrived at a brick building with a bright blue and yellow sign that read "The Bull and Compass," and went in. Everything inside was dark and woody. The bar in the middle of the room gleamed like a beacon, and the bartenders behind it wore white shirts with dark green plaid vests, and poured pints.

Bruce ordered us a round of beers and got menus.

"Drinking here starts a bit early on the weekend," John said. "You don't have to drink it if you don't want to, I'm certain Bruce'll take it for you."

"Oh, I want to," I said. "I'm celebrating."

"Yeah?" John asked. "Anything in particular?"

"Fucking everything."

He took my hand, and I winced. He apologized and held my good hand in his.

Bruce came back, handed us our beers and then put a white towel with ice in it on my right hand. We headed for a table toward the back, away from the group of people watching soccer on tv and shouting at the players on the field.

"Hell of a jab you've got there," Bruce said. "Done that a lot?"

"Never on a face before." I told them about the heavy bag at home.

John adjusted the towel so the ice was hitting all four of the fingers involved. It began to numb the heat, and my breathing finally returned to a typical rhythm.

"So," John said to Bruce, "what exactly happened back there?"

Bruce took a swallow of his beer. "Those gits were hassling some Hindu people just going about their business. Calling them all kinds of horrible names."

John rubbed his eyes with the palms of his hands. "You told me that you'd be sure to have at least one or two other blokes with you the next time you tried to break something like that up."

Bruce dipped a cocktail napkin in his beer and daubed at a small cut on his cheek. "I said I would *try*. White supremacists don't wait for people to have their friends with them, do they? Am I supposed to just do nothing?"

"I know," said John. "And I admire the hell out of you, you know that. But I also worry about you."

Bruce cocked his head to the side and patted John on the cheek. "I'll be fine. It's not like it's America, with guns blazing everywhere." They both glanced at me, and Bruce's cheeks turned pink. "Sorry, love."

I shrugged, and thought about poor Mrs. Cross. "Don't be. You're not wrong."

I looked at the menu and pretended to read it as John and Bruce talked, but I couldn't quite focus on any words. I'd never hit anyone before. And while it wasn't fun, it made me a little more confident knowing that I could handle myself in a scary situation this far from home. John asked if I knew what I wanted.

"What's good here?" I asked.

"It's all pretty much a variation on potatoes with meat, or potatoes with fish," he said.

"Sometimes there'll be cabbage, too," Bruce added. "Probably a bit blander menu than what you have in America."

"You guys are really selling me on your country," I said.

Bruce laughed. "Plenty to love in Merry Old England. Especially if you love potatoes."

We placed our orders at the bar, and returned to our seats.

"How long you staying?" Bruce asked me.

I looked at John. "I don't exactly know."

John said, "As long as you like."

The door opened and a group of five people came in, talking and laughing as they made their way to the bar. Bruce eyed them all, and excused himself to go talk to a friend.

After eating lunch, and meeting Bruce's other friends, who turned out to also know John, he and I ended up at the dart board.

"We can head off on our own any time, if you like," he said. "You must be shaken by what happened earlier, yeah?"

"I'm ok. I like seeing you with your friends – I can only understand about every fourth or fifth word you say, but you're adorable."

"Adorable, eh?" he threw his dart. It did not land where he wanted. He frowned.

"Awful dart player, though." I threw mine. It hit just outside the bullseye. "Maybe this is fucked up, but I feel fine. I felt less threatened when that guy was running at me than when he was running at you. And I know that you and Bruce wouldn't have let him get to me, anyway."

He turned and wrapped his arms around me. His neck smelled of shaving cream and lime.

"Do you really want to come with me when I go back to Lonsdale tomorrow? Because you don't need to if you'd rather not. I'm sure Sammy and Claire would let you stay as long as you like. Lonsdale's dreadfully dull compared to here – bit safer, of course, but I'm afraid you'll get bored there during the week."

"Is this the same Sammy who... Found you?"

"Yeah. He finished university on time and moved here last spring with his girlfriend."

I pulled back to look at him. "Are there buses and trains and stuff in Lonsdale?"

He nodded.

"Then I can explore while you're going to classes or doing homework or whatever. I'm sure it all seems dull to you, but it's all new to me. Plus, Joy Division. I'm not missing that."

He smoothed my hair, and the way his face softened when he did that made me certain that nothing bad could ever touch me again. "We can come to London on the weekends if you'd like," he said. "Claire and Sam go to her parents' home in the country most weekends, and I bet they wouldn't mind."

"If you're really ok with an American hayseed tagging along with you, cramping your style, then I'm game."

He smiled. "I think there's a Kinks song about something like that."

"That's a hillbilly. I'm just a hayseed."

We abandoned the game of darts and rejoined the rowdy group, my hand in John's.

Chapter 19

Monday morning, I got to a bank near the train station and exchanged all the cash I had on me; it was enough that I'd be able to pay for some food and drinks for a few days if I was careful, and my Joy Division ticket later, and I'd need to call my dad to see if he could work with my bank to get more funds transferred later this week. As long as I could access some of what I had in my checking, and maybe some from savings, I'd be ok for a while. That was all the thinking about banking I could handle for the day.

We got to the train station, which was immense; inside, there were four separate counters at opposite ends of the expansive building of concrete, glass, and stainless steel. Business people in suits and belted trench coats and students in jeans and leather jackets ricocheted from one point to another, exiting out the back with bursts of cold air. A group of about ten Hare Krishnas with mostly shaved heads and flowing robes danced in a circle off to one side, clanging finger cymbals and chanting something I couldn't understand, but sounded joyful. I'd only ever seen them on tv, so I let myself stare. No one else paid them any mind.

Like in the airport, there were constant announcements booming over the speakers, and I couldn't understand any of them, either because it was an accent I wasn't used to, or the volume of it all, or that I was trying to believe that I was really there, and about to ride a train from London with John.

I felt someone pulling on my arm. "Excuse me, Miss, did you see who left this backpack?"

"I'm sorry, what?"

A man of about 40, I guessed, in a uniform of grey and blue, pointed toward a red backpack sitting on the ground about ten feet away. "Did you see the person who left that bag there?"

"No, I didn't. I'm sorry."

He spoke a string of numbers and words – one of which was "abandoned" – into a radio. I looked around for John, and my breathing got faster when I didn't see him. I felt a hand on my shoulder and whipped around. *Oh, thank God.*

"Got the tickets," he said. "Ready?"

A group of four men in the same uniform as the one who'd been asking about the backpack came running from around all sides of us, and I clung to John. Two of the men waved black, humming things with red and green blinking lights over and around the bag. Another announced, "Everyone stand back, please."

John pulled me to the exit. When we got outside and away from the building, I noticed that he was paler than usual.

"What just happened?"

"Abandoned backpack – security was checking it for explosives," he said, trying to catch his breath. "You're ok?"

I nodded, but my knees felt like they'd buckle. I'd read stories off the news printer back at the radio station about the Irish Republican Army setting off bombs in London, but hadn't put it together yet that, *Oh yeah, this is where that happens. Right here, where we are now.*

"Is there somewhere to sit down?" I asked.

John put an arm around me and steered me toward a metal bench, where we both sat. "That's one advantage of Lonsdale; don't have many bomb scares."

We both listened, but didn't hear any explosions.

"Hopefully it was nothing," he said.

I'd been looking forward to the train ride, but now my palms were sweaty as I thought about being in an enclosed space with people we didn't know, going however fast it is trains go. *We'll be ok. We'll be ok.*

I had to check my two big bags, which were searched and scanned with one of the black wand-looking things, as were my purse and carry-on bag. We found seats with a little table between them near the back by a window. It wasn't as crowded as I was afraid it might be, and we were able to keep the four seats to ourselves and stretch out.

"Well," he said, and held my hands across the table. "Another very London moment there."

"Do you get used to it?"

He squinted his eyes, thinking. "Guess I haven't. Not yet."

The train got rolling a few minutes later. The station and platform we'd been waiting on turned to a grey blur as we gained speed. John moved to the seat next to me and we stretched our legs so that our feet rested on the seats opposite. John took a sketchbook from his bag and slashed some lines on the page with a black pen.

I leaned my forehead against the window. Soon, the brick, smokestacks, and graffiti of the city gave way to verdant, rolling hills dotted with sprawling barns, cows, and sheep. I wondered if some girl in a small town with a small life would hear our train from her house and wish she were on it. I imagined the sheep with little bowler hats and the cows with large monocles, their bahs and moos accented with the British niceties I was getting accustomed to already.

"What you laughing at?" John said.

I hadn't realized I was. I turned, and he was looking out the window, trying to see what was so funny. I glanced at his sketchbook and realized I had been absorbed in my goofy imagination for long enough that he'd drawn a detailed sketch;

it was me, leaning against the window with my eyes half open and a dreamy expression.

"How do you do that? It really seems like magic, the way you see something and then recreate it with a pen. It doesn't make any sense, and you're so good at it."

He blinked and looked down. "It's not magic."

I wanted to know that part of his brain, or at least glimpse it. "Tell me. How do you see something and know it's something you want to draw?"

He looked back up at me. He put his pen to his mouth and bit the cap. "I've never tried to put it into words. So bear with me."

I nodded and stretched my neck.

"Usually, I make a drawing when there's something in particular I want to remember. Some people take a photo. Some people write it down. I want the image to run down through the top of my head, through my brain, down my throat and shoulders and out through my arms and fingers so that it's only the essence – the most crystalline feeling of a moment – that remains. So whatever it is I'm seeing that I want to remember becomes a part of me, a part of my blood and bones, and I can't forget."

I looked again at the sketch; it was a me I didn't see when I looked in the mirror or at a photograph. In both this sketch and the drawing he'd sent was a me like I wished I was. I wondered if I was deceiving him without meaning to.

"But how do you even start?" I asked. "How do you pick out what's going to be in the drawing out of all the things you see in a day, or even in just one place? There's so much to take in here."

He tilted his head and scratched his chin. "It all starts with lines. See, like here," he pointed at the window in the sketch, then the window next to me. "A window's an easy frame.

Straight lines are where I start. So, after the window, I went to your hair; horizontal line across your forehead, straight line down to where it stops on your jawline, angling up and back toward the delicious nape of your neck. Sorry, then the curved ones – like your nose, cheek, chin, the earlobe I keep wanting to bite more – I just approximate them with like S shapes and crescents. Then just connect them all with small slashes."

I kissed him and leaned against his shoulder. *You see something plain and turn it into something so beautiful it's worth framing and protecting with glass.* "So, like I said. Magic. Alchemy. The dark arts."

I watched two older nuns in full black and white habits a few rows up playing cards with two Hare Krishna guys in orange robes and bare heads. The Nuns giggled and slapped their cards down on the table when they appeared to win the game, and the Hare Krishnas roared with delight.

John took an indigo wrapper from his pocket and produced one of the candy bars I'd grabbed my first night there. He tore it open and snapped it in half.

"This is the one with a chocolate-covered biscuit," he said, handing me half. "Or as you'd call it, a *cookie*."

The word "cookie" sounded slippery and awkward coming out of his mouth, and the hilarity of the sound made me laugh as I bit into the thick, sweet bar.

#

When we got to John's place around one, his roommate, Albert, wasn't home. A green glass bong sat on the kitchen counter. He mumbled something and carried it into Albert's room.

The kitchen wasn't big, but large enough to hold a small table and four chairs. The sink, on the opposite side from the door, was stark porcelain, wide and deep, with a few chips missing. The refrigerator was to its right; it was slightly smaller than the ones at home. The green tile counter space between the sink and stove had a short stack of mail on it. On the walls were two large watercolor paintings of a gorgeous, pixie-like black man with short dreadlocks; in one, he looked up at the sky in front of grey, hulking buildings, a long dark coat blowing out behind him, and in the other, he looked directly at the viewer with a creased forehead and an expression that said, "And you are?"

John came back into the kitchen.

"Who's this?" I asked, pointing at the paintings.

He smiled. "Jean-Michel Basquiat. Aren't they great?"

I nodded and kept staring at them. "Are they yours?"

He put his hands in his pockets. "I wish. My roommate painted those after meeting him on a trip to New York City last year. Albert's a genius with watercolor, and is obsessed with Basquiat."

I hadn't heard of the subject, and was too embarrassed to say so. John told me he was an American artist.

"He's young, not even quite twenty, but he's got a certain energy about his work that leaps off his canvases. Much like Albert's work."

"I have so much to learn about art."

"It's almost all I think about, so consider me at your service." John picked up my suitcase and duffel bag. "Want to put your things in my room?"

I nodded and he brought me through the living room to his bedroom. There was a full-size bed in the corner, under a slanted ceiling. It looked so inviting and cozy, heaped with blankets and a couple of cushy-looking pillows, I wanted to crawl in. Two small windows above a large, square desk allowed in plenty of the cloudy light I was quickly becoming accustomed to; two pieces that John was working on took up most of the space, and I made a note to look at them in detail later when he wasn't right next to me so I could focus on them and not him and his skin and mine.

A trunk and a dresser occupied the wall to my right just as I walked in. Above those were several framed drawings, each a different style and color palette.

"Those are drawings from friends," he said. "We do an exchange at the end of each term to keep up on what we're all working on." He put my bag and suitcase down next to his black trunk.

There was one of a man with a microphone, and I stood in front of it to see if I recognized him. He was drawn in blue ink on a plain piece of white paper; his face was almost round, but like it had been squashed just a little, making it sort of horizontally oval. His hair was in a deep part, swooping over his forehead, and his cheeks stood up like small apples, like mine did whenever I made pretty much any facial expression. His mouth was frozen in a howl, and his eyes were closed. The hand that didn't grip the mic was a fist pointed straight up. I couldn't take my eyes off it.

"Recognize him?" John said, wrapping his arms around my middle.

I shook my head.

"That's Mark Smith from The Fall," he said. "After my trip to the States, and our – *listening party* of their first record, I was particularly interested in them, so a friend at uni gave me this drawing he'd done of the singer after one of their gigs he saw. Isn't it magnetic?"

"Incredible," I whispered. I'd only seen posters with prints of famous paintings tacked up on someone's wall. The amount of original art I'd seen in the last couple of hours made the world seem more inspiring, changeable, wonderful, than it had ever been before.

I spun around and kissed him. He put his hands under my t-shirt and pulled me hard against him. I pulled him over to his bed, and we fell to the soft mattress.

#

When I'd made myself presentable a little while later, John had The Jam playing on the stereo in the living room. He turned when he heard me come in.

"Are you hungry?"

"Very," I said, and looked at the clock – it was just after two. "But it's a little early for dinner, isn't it?"

"Or late for lunch. Who cares? We're on our own schedule, yeah? There's a fish and chips stand down the road just a bit. I can go get us some and bring it back if you want to get settled."

"That sounds great. Would you mind if I made a phone call? I should probably just get calling home over with so I don't have to keep dreading it."

He showed me the phone on the wall in the kitchen and left to get us some food.

I dialed the number to my dad's office, hoping to catch him before he went out to a job site.

A woman answered. "Bill Pierce's office."

I paused. He must have just stepped out. "May I speak to Dad – I mean, Bill, please?"

"Vivian?"

Oh my God. "Hi, Mom." *Shit shit shit...* "Yeah, it's me."

She said she'd been trying to get ahold of me all weekend, that she didn't appreciate me "running away" in the middle of the night and asked if my dad had known I was leaving. I said he was sleeping when I left, which was technically true.

"So? Where the hell have you been?"

I told her. She didn't believe me. "Where is Dad?"

"He's at a job site. I'm going through his filing cabinets looking for the deed to our house. Stop fooling around. Where have you been?"

"I told you. England."

"When did you turn into such a wiseass? Do you think this is funny?" she asked.

"I don't think this is funny," I said.

"Sure." She lit a cigarette and exhaled. "So, guess who I talked to."

I looked out the big picture window and noticed that it had gotten overcast again. John hadn't brought an umbrella. I hoped he didn't get rained on. He got chilled easily. "I have no idea."

"Adrian," she said.

I froze, trying to avoid detection. *Maybe if I pretend it was a bad connection, and then just don't call back...*

"Vivian. I know you're still there. I can hear you breathing."

"Why did you talk to him?"

She said she'd called him to tell him how upset she and the whole family were. How much they "adored" him. And on and on. My mother was the Queen of minutiae, dramatic pauses, and the and-do-you-know-what-she-saids when she was telling a story. She even said she'd asked Adrian if he'd give me another chance.

She was quiet for a moment, then added, "And do you know what he said?"

I closed my eyes and lay my head down on the table. *God, no. God, please.*

"He said that you… *slept* with someone else." She sucked in air through her teeth. "Well, I about *died* of embarrassment. How could you *do* such a thing?"

I rolled my forehead back and forth on the cool Formica table. I heard the kitchen door click open and shut and paper bags rustling.

"We did not raise you to go gallivanting around acting like a common," she lowered her voice, "*whore*."

My torso felt like one of those medicine balls had been fired into it, knocking the breath out of me. I sat up, but couldn't bear to look at John just then. I dropped my head back, pressed my lips together, and squeezed my eyes closed. Warm tears slid down my cheeks.

She was emboldened by my silence. "Adrian said he thought it was someone from another country, but wasn't sure who. While we were on the phone, Adrian *cried*. A man *crying*… And it's not like I could *defend* your actions. You make me so *mad*. When you were home, had I had any idea you'd acted like that," she lowered her voice again, "like the town tramp, for God's sake…"

She paused to take a breath and a drag off her cigarette. John had pulled up a chair next to me. His left temple rested against my right one, and he had heard every word in the last tirade.

He touched my cheek and I let him take the phone from me. "Mrs. Pierce, hi. I'm Viv's friend, John."

I covered my mouth with a hand, pleading with the Universe to not let her say anything too horrifying to him. I opened my eyes and watched him.

"That's correct," he said. "England, ma'am. Right, England… No, she wasn't joking." He glanced at me and winked. Then his nose crinkled, and he shook his head. "Sorry, what difference does that make? Listen please, ma'am, your daughter is my friend, and a guest in my home. I won't tolerate anyone speaking to her as you have, so… Yes, I understand who you are. But I won't have part of her memory of being here include sitting by while you spew horrible insults at her. So, this is goodbye… No… She will be in touch if and when she wants… We're hanging up now. Bye, ma'am."

He hung the phone back on its cradle and turned. I felt like my skin had been stripped off, and I was a quivering glob of nerves and shame and scars and a bleating heart that had never grown beyond the years of a pitifully insecure and needy, attention-starved teen. With all of this exposed, it was apparent how undercooked the whole of me was.

"Still hungry?"

I shook my head.

He put the fish and chips in his refrigerator and said quietly, "We can throw these under the broiler when the mood strikes. I like them better like that, anyway."

He stood behind me and rubbed my shoulders. I turned and curled toward him, so he kneeled and let me.

We stayed like that, my arms wrapped around him, my face burrowed into his neck, until the late October sun slanted toward its mid-afternoon reminder that light would be fleeting for a while.

He lifted me up from under my armpits. He walked us to his room, pulled back the covers, and guided me into bed. I lay on my left side, facing a window with crimson curtains with Dandelions embroidered onto them. This wall was filled with tacked-up sketches that I guessed were his works in progress. I couldn't make anything out clearly through the tears that had snuck up on me. John lay next to me with an arm and leg draped over me. He felt like a bullet proof vest or an exoskeleton. I let my eyes close.

#

When I opened them again, it was dark except for some scattered streetlights outside. *It's Joy Division night.*

I shot up to a sitting position so fast I got dizzy. "We didn't miss it, did we?"

He glanced at his watch, shook his head and croaked, "Still want to go?"

"More than ever."

We threw the covers back and ran outside and down the hill to catch the bus to Derby, yawning most of the way. On the bus, he put an arm around my shoulder.

We reached Derby in about twenty minutes, then had about a ten-minute walk to the venue. I looped my arm through John's. The chilly evening air, strange new place, and promise of nothing ever being the same again charged me with jangly electricity, making me alert and giddy.

The Assembly Rooms building was a hulking concrete and brick structure with square sections that overhung other sections, some with vertical metal accents. Inside, the vast hallways were all carpeted with a blue and brown stripy pattern, and if I stared down at it too long, I had to catch my balance using John's arm. We found the counter to buy our tickets, and climbed the wide, squat stairs to the second floor, where the main hall was.

In between the doorways that went into the different performance spaces was a sprawling bar with draft beers and a display of multicolored glass liquor bottles.

"Want a drink?" John asked.

I nodded and handed him a five-pound note. "First couple of rounds are on me. Whatever you're having, please."

The ceilings were high, with floor-to-ceiling windows overlooking a busy street on one side, and a less busy parking lot on another. There weren't nearly as many people here as I thought there would be, but the bar was doing a healthy amount of business.

John came back with two plastic cups filled with deep amber liquid, and handed me one. We clunked our cups together and toasted to the band, then found the main hall.

A small grandmotherly-looking woman with short, curly grey hair squinted at our tickets, confirmed we were at the right entrance, tore each ticket, and handed them back to us. John asked if it was all right to bring beer into the hall.

"What's that, dear?" she said, and pulled out some earplugs.

"Should we drink our lagers out here, or is it ok to bring them inside?"

She laughed and patted his shoulder. "It's fine, love. Just don't go throwing them at anyone, please."

He looked her in the eye and squeezed her hand. "We won't, promise."

She nodded, put her earplugs back in, and waved us along.

The hall was large, and the seats were all folded up and strapped together against the walls. The stage at the far end had some speakers and microphones set up. There were maybe 30 people in the room, scattered around it, all talking to each other, acting like this wasn't a huge deal.

A few minutes later, the lights got low, and people started clapping and moving around.

"Where do you want to be?" he asked. "For the show, I mean."

"As close as we can be."

"Shows can get rough in the blink of an eye around here."

"I don't care. I'm going up front. You can stay here if you want."

As I walked across the expanse of shiny wood planks toward the stage, I started thinking about everything back home.

Trash. Loser. Whore. Tramp.

There was nothing for me to be afraid of anymore; everyone knew everything, no one had held any punches in letting me know what they thought, and still, here I was. I was fine. I was way goddamn better than fine.

I went and stood dead center in front of the stage, near a small group of guys about my age smoking and talking. I was in the front row. I almost hoped someone *would* start something. I would fight off gangs of people to keep this spot if I had to: *fucking try me.*

The familiar feeling of waiting for a show to begin washed over me: the nerves, the anticipation, the instruments and amps bolstering the excitement already bouncing around the room. The hair on the back of my neck stood up and my palms got hot.

I felt a hand squeeze my shoulder, and I turned, ready with a right hook at my side. I looked up to see John gazing down at me. I relaxed my fist.

"You all right?" he asked.

"Yeah," I said. "Sorry. Just a little edgy from the call earlier."

He put an arm around me and kissed the top of my head.

"If a fight does break out, I want to be with someone who knows how to throw a punch," he said.

I ruffled his hair and said, "I'll protect you, my delicate flower."

The spotlights aimed at the stage turned on. The four men in the band came out, picked up their instruments, cast furtive glances at each other, and talked in low tones. They were just like the pictures, but full color. Their clothes looked like they'd just come from a day at the office, albeit no office I'd ever been in; their regular pants and collared shirts were shades of grey and burgundy, they had short hair and were clean-shaven – except for the bass player, with his scraggly beard and moustache, and shaggier hair than the others, glowering at anyone who made eye contact. They all looked deceptively normal, yet aspirationally cool.

The PA switched on, the archetypal feedback that preceded every live show I'd ever been to screeched, then petered out. I felt John's warmth emanate from close by, and the greatest band in the world was right there. I took a big gulp of my room temperature beer, and energy coursed through me like electric eels sparking in dark seas.

"Good evening. We're Joy Division."

The ground dropped out from under me. The bass and drums rolled out, enveloping the room in a massive, relentless tidal wave, tossing us all around like tiny, ill-equipped ships. The guitar prickled my skin with aural jagged sleet.

The first time I'd heard them, a mere month and a half ago, I'd been hurtling toward a future that I didn't want, and I didn't believe what I did want mattered. I was almost entirely resigned to it then. I'd picked their record to review that day because the blurbs I'd read about their sound matched my mood: a glum band for a glum girl. That record was the only thing that made me feel better.

And now, here they were, mere feet in front of me. If I were less shy, or less respectful of personal space, I could have reached out and touched Ian. The voice of a dark god flowed through his throat as his tall, wiry frame alternated between grasping the mic in its stand like it was another limb, and kneeing and swatting at the air, dancing like mad, a firefly caught in a jar, his blazing eyes focused on something hovering over our heads in the air.

My bones throbbed, and my chest ached from the rawness on that stage; it made my own rawness seem that much more real, more valid, more reasonable a response to everything that had happened. All the fear, the fury, the longing, that I'd been clutching for years in my near-death grip cascaded in thick waves from the stage, the songs' healing waters barreling straight through me.

Their set lasted forever and was over in an instant like a fever dream in the throes of an illness. The last notes zipped up through the ceiling and back into the sky.

The small crowd applauded and yelled. I heard a few incredulous fucking hells, but other than that, no one talked, or at least I didn't hear them. The four men in the band left the stage. The lights came back up.

I felt unsteady on my feet, and like my brain had been stripped of language. I looked at John, who appeared similarly shaken. A larger crowd had gathered in back, there for the Buzzcocks. The small group that had been standing with us shuffled, silent, toward the exit. I looped my arm through John's, and we followed.

We wound down the soft hallways and the squat stairs to the ground level, then out into the bristling night air. The other group consisted of four guys and two girls, and as we walked across the black, cracked asphalt, one of the girls looped her arm through my unoccupied one, a boy looped his through her other one, and soon we formed a chain of eight, walking silently. I wasn't sure why I belonged here, just knew that I did; I had never been so certain of anything, and I could have wept with gratitude. Someone said, "Shall we go have a pint, then?"

"Yeah," said another. "Love the Buzzcocks, but I don't think I can bear to be shouted at by Pete Shelley after that."

The daze lifted a little, and someone laughed. Like a hastily patched-together family, we walked a couple of blocks to a pub that was similar to the others I'd been to over the weekend: lots of heavy wood, gleaming brass accents, vested barkeeps, and the faintest scent of oak hanging in the air, as if all that wood were still a living tree.

We compared what we saw and heard in the cruelly short set, and as we all talked and listened, a thought began to settle in the back of my brain: even if I never saw these strangers again, they – and of course, John – were the people I used to daydream about back in my room in Stonewald, never sure if they actually existed.

We had a couple of beers and by then it was only starting to get kind of late for a Monday, so John and I said our goodbyes, and got on the next bus back to his place. When we settled into a seat, he put his arm around me, and I leaned into him.

"Sorry we missed the Buzzcocks," he said.

"Me too, but I don't think I could've handled any more tonight."

"We'll catch them sometime."

I looked up at him. "So... That was..." I still could not find my words.

He kissed me, then leaned his head on mine. "Yeah. Yeah, it was."

When we got back to his apartment, he asked, "Hungry now?"

I nodded.

He removed the thick pieces of fried fish and fries from their wax paper in the fridge, sprinkled some extra salt over them, and stuck them on a baking sheet in the oven. He took a bottle of malt vinegar from the fridge and set it on the table.

When everything was done warming, we ate like ravenous teenagers. The fish and fries were salty and crunchy and perfect, especially with a shake of the malt vinegar, which gave them a hint of slightly sweet acidity.

"I don't know what you and Bruce were bitching about. This is the most delicious fish and potatoes anything I've ever had."

I grabbed a napkin and wiped the grease and salt off his chin. He kissed me.

I said, "Thank you for yanking me off the phone today."

"Thanks for punching out a bloke before he kicked my teeth in yesterday."

He stood, went to the refrigerator, and got two cans of cider. He opened them and set one in front of me. He hugged me, and then we drank and ate the rest of our food.

That night, lying next to him, I relived every moment of the gig in my mind; they were different from every other band I knew and loved, but I still couldn't quite verbalize how. They could have gone right there from work, to look at them. They didn't have costumes or personas or schticks. Of course I had known that this band was comprised of real people, but being in the same space with them had shaken up all the events of the past month and a half, then set me down abruptly, letting all the confetti-like pieces settle all around instead of on me, so I could finally see clear, without those bits in the way.

"You're going over every last detail, aren't you?" he said.

"How'd you know?"

"Your eyes are wide open and you're staring up at the ceiling. Plus, I've been doing the same thing."

I burrowed my chin into his neck, where it met his shoulder. The burst-open smell of rain swooped in through a cracked window.

Chapter 20

John went back to classes on Tuesday, and his office job on Wednesday. Each day when he left, I walked around, exploring Lonsdale and, inadvertently, some of its neighboring towns, including the very outskirts of Derby. The record stores I found were a little disappointing, as they weren't much cooler than the ones in New Hampshire had been, save for the occasional Bowie 45 I had never seen.

But the bookstores were a wonderland of titles and authors with bindings that I'd never seen before; standing before a wall of books, many of which had Faber & Faber imprints, it was all just so fucking British, and I loved it. At the one in Lonsdale's center, I almost bought two books by my favorite poets – Patti Smith and Philip Larkin – but decided to wait until I could get more money from savings at home, or pick up a part-time job. As I browsed, I ran my fingers through the soft, thick orange and white fur of the store cat, Teddy, the very same one John had mentioned in a letter. I felt like I was petting a celebrity. I resolved to get a cat of my own once I settled down somewhere. I really missed having one around.

Each day I wandered a little farther out, past Lonsdale's little village with shops and bakeries, into the residential areas that had more working people and fewer students. These areas were fairly quiet during the day, aside from the occasional kid riding a tricycle up and down the two-foot-wide sidewalk in front of their house with a gate and tidy, small yard. Sometimes I'd see a pretty young mother in a bright red coat walking toward town with a squinting, dark-haired toddler balanced on a hip and a slightly older child holding her hand, dragging his feet behind her. We started saying hello to each other after a few times, but that was it. She didn't look like she had much time for new friendships.

Over time, as I walked out farther and farther beyond the rowhouses to the vacant lots and plain apartment complexes with identical little playgrounds, as quiet and still and dull in their way as Stonewald was, I hoped to stumble on some piece of the puzzle that would give me special insight; something, I don't know, uniquely English that illuminated how fascinating, commanding creatures like Ian Curtis or David Bowie or Siouxsie Sioux could emerge from pale grey housing, empty merry-go-rounds, and busted chain link fences. I wanted a clue as to how their isolation made them into artists, and mine had just made me want to die because I couldn't see a way out.

I didn't find any clues, but I started to understand why certain songs resonated with me; it was because I had more in common with the songwriters than I'd realized. Home countries aside, the difference between them and me wasn't so much the types of homes and desolate environments we'd come from, but how we'd responded to them. I decided not to go further with that thought lest I decide to walk in front of a train.

When I'd get back to the flat, John would typically already be there, cooking up some form of chicken and rice or pasta. He was fine with my distaste for domestic chores, and his roommate, Albert, who I'd met the second day I was there and really liked, was a baker with hours the opposite of most everyone else. He always brought back day-old leftovers for breakfast. He said he didn't mind me being there, adding, "It's nice having a bird around the house."

John and I settled into our own routine: go our separate ways around 8:30, and reconvene at the apartment around 5:30. There were always records playing, or a radio show playing songs I'd never heard before. Then, dinner, a pint or two down at the neighborhood pub with some of John's friends from school, usually followed by falling naked into his bed and listening to the Peel Sessions on the nights it was on.

Those days were a mixture of exhilarating freedom and a gnawing, nagging thing sitting at the base of my skull, reminding me that there was a lot of shit that needed settling, and it wouldn't let me fully relax into what was trying to become my life, or perhaps just an extended vacation. But still, I liked our routine. I liked *him*.

I'd managed to get in touch with my dad – who said that he didn't want any details of the thing about me and Adrian that Mom was so riled up about – and he agreed to wire some money from my bank through Western Union each week. I'd saved enough working in the summers that I'd be ok for a little while, but I knew I'd need to either find a job soon or go back home.

After three London weekends in Claire and Sammy's apartment, and Lonsdale in between, we spent our first weekend in Lonsdale for an art installation by one of John's friends. Bruce was up from London for family things that Saturday afternoon, and we met up with him and a few of John's university friends at a pub down the road before the exhibition. We got ales and sat down at their table near the darts and pool tables, settling in for an afternoon that would get progressively rowdier. Bruce asked how I liked England so far.

"I like it so much, I'm going to try to stay for a while," I said. "Maybe a couple more weeks. I'm not sure. I like Lonsdale a lot, but I'd like to spend more time in London before I go."

"Just a couple more weeks?" he asked. "Why not longer?"

"Contrary to what the movies would have you believe, not many of us Americans are independently wealthy. I'll hang on as long as I can, though."

"You have work lined up?"

"No. I left home literally in the middle of the night to come here. I wasn't thinking about staying long, or work visas, or anything practical like that. I'm just taking it week by week at this point."

Bruce looked at John, and something passed between them that I couldn't quite read. "My record shop's looking for some help," he said. "We're coming up on Christmas. My boss has been known to pay under the table, especially 'round this time."

"Really?"

"The pay is shit," he said. "But we do get an employee discount. And I can't promise anything, of course. But I'm going in tomorrow morning, and I'll ask her. I'll call you and let you know what she says?"

"Are you sure you don't mind?"

He smiled his warm, crooked smile and said, "Anything to help a friend." He looked from me to John, then patted my hand and excused himself to the bathroom.

I turned to John next to me in the booth. "If I can get a job in a *record store* in fucking *London*, I can die happy. Do you think Claire and Sammy might let me rent the room?"

"I have a feeling," he said.

We decided to take a walk along a nearby river to talk more, and said our goodbyes at the pub. When we got to Bruce, he locked me in a bear hug, said he'd see me soon, and to call him if I needed anything. He whispered, "I've known John since we were kids. It's so nice to see him happy again."

When we got outside, blinking to adjust to the light, I looked around as John buttoned up his coat. There were poles with the symbols for the Tube, buses, and trains dotting the street, people on bikes, or walking, some with dogs, some with kids, some couples just holding hands and walking slowly, getting in everyone else's way. Down the hill and across the road at a busy intersection, a four-story brick building's edges culminated in a partial circle with windows all around it, looking more like a Victorian home than the bank it was. Street vendors sold fish and chips, Indian food, tea, coffee, and pastries and cakes, their smells all mingling in the air. At home, being able to walk to the library as a kid had seemed like big deal, but here, the whole world was just a few steps away. And this was just Lonsdale. London had so many treasures I had yet to even glimpse.

John offered me his arm, and we walked a block to a park along a small river. We walked in easy silence, watching the geese, ducks, and swans compete for food that people tossed on the ground for them.

"I haven't wanted to nag, so I've been trying not to ask. But now that this has come about, I'll risk it: will you stay if you're able?"

It was the question I'd been trying to push aside. I tried to come up with something eloquent, but ended up simply being honest. "I'd like to," I said. "But I don't have the job yet, I haven't even looked into the visa thing, and I haven't talked to my family about it – that's a whole lot of loose ends. At this point, I don't think there are any that *aren't* loose. I'll have to go home at some point. I'm just not sure when, or for how long."

He nodded and put his hands into his jacket pockets. "Of course. I'm sorry if I overstepped."

I stopped walking and put my hand on his shoulder so he would stop too. He turned to me but wouldn't look me in the eye, instead looking up at the sky. He swallowed hard, like something had stuck in his throat.

"You didn't overstep," I said. "I just wish I knew. I mean, things are looking pretty good. I didn't expect Bruce to try to get me an interview or anything, so that's... Hey, would you look at me?"

He flicked his eyes down at me, and they looked like the sky had gathered into them, making them so airy blue and bright I had to squint. He had creases in his forehead, and he kept chewing his lip.

He cleared his throat. "I think once you have a place to sponsor you, it's easier to get a work visa. Or so I've heard. Not that I've been asking around or gathering information or anything."

I lifted my fingers to one of his pretty, angular cheekbones and held them there, curving them along the bone, still in awe that I got to touch him whenever I wanted. He closed his eyes.

I wanted the job. I wanted to stay.

Don't say it out loud, or you'll jinx it. Do not get your hopes up too much.

#

Sunday morning, Bruce called, said his boss knew about my situation, and had agreed to interview me at 10:30 Monday morning.

I hung up and told John he could come out of hiding. He stepped into view from the living room.

"Bruce said his boss will talk to me tomorrow morning."

"Shall I call Sammy and Claire?"

"It's so last-minute," I said. "Is that too much, do you think?"

He dialed their number, and Sammy answered. He asked if we could bother them for their spare room that night, a Sunday, which we didn't usually do.

"Great, Sammy. Thank you," he said. "I was also wondering, are you guys still looking for someone to rent the spare room till I can get there in January?"

Now it was my turn to pretend that I wasn't listening intently.

"Yeah, actually my – friend? – who's coming with me later, Viv. She's been with me for I guess three weeks or so now, and she's quite easy to get along with. I think you'd all get on very well." He smiled at me.

He made some agreeable, pleasant sounds, said some rights and okays, and then hung up. "They think it's a great idea. We can go this afternoon, get you settled, and I'll come back here tomorrow."

I cupped his face in my hands, and said, "You're amazing."

John told me that I'd practically have the place to myself during the week; Sammy was a chef and Claire was a seamstress for a big theater and they both worked nights. And as he'd mentioned, they were usually gone on the weekends. John would be done with classes Thursday afternoon, and would come down after that, probably early evening, and stay till Monday morning.

I went into John's room to gather up my things. As I did, I took in every detail: his friends' drawings and paintings, his sketches tacked up on the wall, and his works-in-progress on the desk. I loved his sketches; they were snatches of his thoughts in ink.

One of the pieces on the desk caught my eye. I hadn't seen it before; it was still in its early stages, but there I was from the back, my hair swinging as I swayed, arms at my sides. I never understood how artists could capture movement like that in a static image. Beyond me was a raised stage with the four developing shapes of what I assumed were Joy Division.

I stood gazing at it, and at some point, John came in, wrapped me in his arms, and kissed the back of my neck. Citrus and plants wafted up from him, and I breathed him in like the second chance at a memory.

"Meant to tell you about that," he said.

I turned toward him. "You did this after the Derby show?"

"Yeah," he said. "Do you like it?"

"Do I like it," I said. My mouth trembled and I covered it with a hand. And then I was crying. Going away felt like hacking off a chunk of skin.

John's face morphed from that of a very happy guy who'd been having a lot of sex lately, to that of a concerned and somewhat frightened person.

"What is this?" he asked. "What's happening right now?"

"What am I going to do in London by myself? I'll get lost and end up in some part of town with ruffians and pickpockets or chimney sweeps or something."

He laughed. "Times have changed since Dickens novels, darling."

He'd never called me that before. I liked it.

"I mean, other than neo-Nazi skinheads, are you telling me there's bigger threats than plucky, dirty-faced kids in tweed caps saying 'Oi, love,' to charm and distract me while they sneak a hand into my bag and rob me blind? And what if it turns out that I can't fight if you're not there with me? I'm completely unprepared for London solo." I sniffed and wiped my nose on the back of my hand.

"I don't *want* you to go. But... It's what you need to do right now, yeah?"

"Yeah. But I don't know anything about living in a city, let alone *that* city. I used to get lost in *Boston.* London's going to eat me alive."

"No it won't," he said, brushing away my tears. "Sam and Claire will help you. They know the neighborhood well and can tell you how to get anywhere in the city."

A reminder that I wouldn't be alone was a comfort. And if John trusted and liked them, I was sure I would, too. I decided that if it all went horribly wrong, I could hop a train back here, or a plane back home and then face the fact that I simply was not the person I always hoped I would be if I were in this situation.

#

Later that day, after I did my laundry and packed it back into my hobo bags, as John had taken to calling them, he returned, packed, and we walked to the train bound for London. I hadn't been sleeping through the night, and was exhausted, so I slept on the way, using John's shoulder as a pillow. Light, sound, and life all around helped me relax.

Sam and Claire were at their apartment when we got there around six, each about to head out to their nocturnal jobs. Claire had long, blue-black hair the color of a Raven's feather turned toward the light, short 50s style bangs, and a round face that looked like she laughed a lot. Sam had close-cropped hair, bright hazel eyes, deep brown skin, and freckles. He wore black pants, a white dress shirt, and a skinny black tie, and looked like he just stepped off a Specials record jacket.

"Love your hair," Claire said. "Very Louise Brooks."

We agreed that paying rent by the week was best, as I still didn't know how long I'd be in the country. They showed me where all the cooking stuff was, and towels, and the washer and dryer in the totally haunted dirt basement below. And I'd thought the Windsor chair at the station was something. It *was*, but…

"We're headed to work and won't be home till the wee hours," Sam said. "But this is your home, and it'll be John's home come January, so go ahead and make yourself comfortable." I thanked them both, and they hugged me before leaving.

"The record store's open till eight tonight," John said. "Want to go scout it?"

We headed out a few minutes later. I brought a notebook and took detailed notes: go right out of the front door, down the hill about ten minutes to the bus stop, then look for the one going to Elm Street. Ride that for about 15 minutes to the Teppingham stop. Ride that one for about 12 minutes to Potsdam Row. Get off, go to the movie theater, turn left, then straight ahead to the plaza with the record store. I'd plan on an hour to get there in the morning to be safe.

The front looked like a combo storefront/apartment unit, set aside from the neighboring buildings. But the space inside was vast; matte black wood bins stretched to the far wall, with the right-hand side elevated, with more bins and a quivering metal spiral staircase leading to the second and third floors, all filled with bins. Used records were on the third floor, which you'd have to hop off the stairs and over a little gap to get to. The second floor had extensive Jazz and Classical, and the first floor was jam packed with my import record fever dreams—records I didn't know existed by bands I thought I'd already heard everything by. And of course, here they weren't imports.

There was a register on each floor, staffed by people wearing clothes ranging from corduroys and sweater vests, to Bruce's own standard jeans and tall boots. Bruce had gone on break just before we got there, the girl with short fuchsia hair and a nose ring told us.

"I don't want to get caught sneaking around," I told John. "I think I get the gist."

We walked about a block to a little pub called The Cat & Kin. The setting was familiar: woody, gleaming brass, cozy booths lining the walls. But there were two striking differences: it smelled of lavender and lemon, and all the staff were women, even the bar keeps. Each of them had different looks, and none of them appeared self-conscious or apologetic about anything, whether they were tall or short, thin or fat, pale or dark.

Melody, our waitperson, was from Wales, and just a little taller than me. She wore faded jeans and a grey t-shirt, had long, dreadlocked, wheat colored hair, and indigo eyes I could have tried to figure out all day. When she left with our drink orders, she stopped by a nearby table of businessmen and handed them their check. One of them said something, laughed, and pinched her ass. She grabbed his hand, twisted it and his arm behind him, and pinned it and him onto his leftover bread crusts. "That's not how we do things at The Cat & Kin," she said. Then, addressing the rest of the table, "Boys, control your *friend*." They stammered their apologies and berated him as soon as she left. The man whimpered.

I couldn't fucking wait for my new life here.

Chapter 21

Monday morning, I tried to keep my mind busy with what to wear for an interview at the record store; surely the dress code would be different here than at home, but despite what I'd seen, I wasn't confident enough in Bruce's advice of "Just jeans or whatever."

I hadn't brought the clothes that I'd forced myself to wear when I interviewed for the bookstore job at home: tan pants that made my thighs and hips look like they weren't interested in rock & roll, thank you very much, and a black, collared shirt that I had hoped would project the Studious and Serious Me, but instead showcased every little piece of lint and yarn I picked up in a 30 foot radius, and gapped at my boobs, no matter how many times I ironed it.

It was getting chillier. I went with a just-above-the-knee-length black pleated skirt, black tights, my weathered but trusty big black shoes, and a charcoal grey V-neck sweater with a white collared shirt (which also gapped at the boobs, hence its banishment to an underlayer; sometimes I learned from experience).

I went downstairs to meet up with John and walk with him to the station, get him on the train north, and then catch the bus. I checked in my coat pocket to make sure I had my notes I'd taken yesterday. He was in the kitchen, washing the last of the breakfast dishes, and when he turned and saw me, he smiled so sweetly, I was sure I'd cry.

I stammered, "I have no idea what to wear."

"I like it. Got a spooky schoolgirl from the 20s look going on."

"I can't do this."

He reached out and came over to me. "You can."

I leaned against him. "I don't want you to go."

"Then I'll quit university and stay here with you."

I pulled back to admire the fullness of his cheeks when he made one of his subtle jokes. "One of us should probably finish their degree."

He sighed. "Fine. I'd rather not go. But it's just till Thursday."

When we got to the station, the reality of not having him there at night for the first time since I'd been in England, most especially in this incomprehensibly big city, hit me, and my throat tightened.

His train was just about ready to go. We stood on the platform as discarded tickets and candy wrappers, blown around by the incoming and departing trains, swirled all around. We kissed, and I realized I was clutching the back of his jacket collar.

"I'll be back before you know it," he said.

He got on the train and sat in a window seat. Before he saw me watching him, he wiped at his eyes with the back of his hand. I forced myself to stay put, and not run on after him. He looked up, smiled, and waved at me from his seat. I waved back, blew him a kiss, and knew I had to walk away immediately if I was going to make myself seem stronger than I felt.

I took a deep breath and walked toward the long line of buses across the expansive lot. There were so many buses and people, and newspapers blowing around like Dandelion seed heads, I got disoriented. But I found it eventually. The bus was already waiting, boarding a long line of passengers.

I stepped on to this bizarre interpretation of safe public transportation, the double-decker bus. Everyone ahead of me plunked coins into a plastic tube. I looked in my bag for my proper British money and came up with a twenty-pound note. I presented it carefully to the plump, merry-faced driver, and smiled.

"You must be joking," he snorted, and waved the bill away.

The line behind me grew, which I only knew because I could feel it in the hairs on the back of my neck. My face got hot as I fished in my bag, looking for any smaller bills or coins, but I didn't have anything. I stammered, "I'm sorry, I don't have - "

"Step aside miss," he grumbled. "Go buy some sweets and catch the next one."

I kept digging in my bag, hoping it would either produce some magic coins or swallow me into it arm-first.

"I've got it," a woman's voice said, plunking coins into the tube. "Don't be such a grumpy old bastard, Phil."

Her head was shaved, and her expertly applied black eyeliner set off her light grey eyes. Her right eyebrow had a single, silver hoop, and she had the leather jacket and ripped up jeans that many in London had, each person with their own twist: different band name, different metal accents, different quotes about anarchy. Hers had a stark drawing of the singer Siouxsie Sioux, and under that, the words "Break the patriarchy."

"*Thank you*, Mitzy," Phil the driver said.

"Yeah, yeah," she said, and made her way back to her seat.

"Go on, Miss Twenty Quid, find a seat," Phil said to me.

The bus was packed. I was so nervous that it didn't even occur to me to look upstairs, not that I could've figured out how to get up there – all the buses I'd ridden so far had been single-level. I just stood there like a scared rabbit, looking for a space while passengers piled up behind me, swearing.

I heard a whistle, and noticed an arm in the air, index finger pointing down. It was Mitzy, who had a space next to her. I shuffled down the aisle and dropped into the seat beside her, keeping my head down. "Thank you," I said. "You really didn't have to do that."

"No problem," she said. "Don't let him rattle you. He's from the old days, likes to enforce the rules with an iron fist and all that. You American?"

"Yeah. It was probably obvious before I opened my mouth."

She smiled. "Nothing to be ashamed of. People come here from all over."

"I love your jacket."

"Thanks," she said. "My mum made it for me."

I love this city like crazy.

Her stop came up a few minutes later, and she scrambled out of the seat. She said, "Nice meeting you. Welcome to London."

I moved to Mitzy's seat next to the window. As the bus got moving again, I looked out at the streets filled with people – most were in suits, hats, and belted trench coats, on their way to some job in some important office somewhere. Everywhere in this city seemed important.

The younger people ranged from jeans and ragged sweaters to groups of laughing, leering, colorful punks gathered around coffee and tea stands. I loved seeing them in the real world, but their loudness kind of scared me; walking by a group of them on the street always made me nervous because I thought sure they'd make fun of me and my squareness. No one had yet, but it seemed like it was just a matter of time.

When the bus slowed enough to be able to look closer, behind the people nearest to the street, and back to the almost hidden people clinging to building walls so as not to catch the faintest trace of sun that wasn't perceptible to the rest of us through the overcast sky, were the most delicate, ornate Goths I'd ever seen with the naked eye: black or platinum hair teased high as a church steeple, fishnet peeking out from under expertly placed holes in black jeans and fluttery shirts, or conversely, the more buttoned up factions with wrinkle-less, lint-free velvet jackets and white, high-collared shirts. Almost all wore a variation on black, heeled boots as jagged as a gravedigger's shovel, with silver buckles or buttons and straps. Even after an entire night/early morning out clubbing, their makeup – men and women alike, embracing androgyny as comfortably as glam rock had – was perfect; there were precise black slashes at points along the eye contours, crimson streaks along those damn cheekbones I always wished I had instead of my apple cheeks, and lips the color of blood, or death, or Heaven. Unlike the punks out there, they appeared to be silent, though some in pairs whispered into each other's ears. I couldn't believe my luck seeing them during the day – if I had had to catch the later bus, not only would I have missed my interview, but these creatures of the night would surely have been back inside, somewhere safe and sinister. They made Kelly in Marblewell look as daring as First Lady Rosalynn Carter.

I almost missed my stop, engrossed in my spot-the-Goth game, but I made it off just in time. Phil the driver grumbled something at me as I exited, but I couldn't understand him, and I still felt like an asshole, so I didn't look back.

I didn't want a repeat on the next bus, so I found a coffee stand and bought one, and asked for as much small change as they could spare. I scanned the buses while clutching the small Styrofoam cup, and sipped. I am not picky about coffee. I came of age on Maxwell House in the blue can, or whatever else happened to be around. But this coffee was oily, chunky with grounds, yet also weak, a liquid "fuck you" to everyone who had ever enjoyed coffee.

Phil had shaken me much more than I wanted to admit, and Mitzy's kindness had briefly taken my mind off it, but as I approached the next bus, my vision blurred, palms got sweaty, and my eyes kept blinking. I couldn't even see what I was doing. I felt like a toddler dropped off in the middle of a department store, and I desperately wished John or Mitzy were there to bail me out of this. I found two coins, dropped them into the tube, and waited for the berating. Instead, the driver handed me back three smaller coins, said thank you, and I shuffled along. This time, I found a seat near the front. As I sped toward this uncertain thing, I missed John's arm next to mine on the armrest.

#

Victoria, Bruce's boss, was funny, sarcastic, intimidating, and five feet two inches tall. She liked that I knew about both post-punk and classic country and agreed to hire me for about 20 hours per week under the table. I would start the next morning.

I went over to the Cat & Kin for lunch. I sat at the bar, alone, drank my beer, and picked at my Ploughman's Plate with apple, two different kinds of strong cheese, sausage, hearty bread, and some sort of dark nutty spread. The bartenders were attentive but not overbearing, and not a single other patron bothered me. I read a local paper and felt, for the first time, like an actual adult with my own space, time, and decisions to make or not make.

When I got back to the apartment, Claire and Sammy were sleeping. I put some water on the stove to boil, tiptoed upstairs to my room to get my copy of the *Hitchhiker's Guide to the*

Galaxy I'd got at a bookstore in Marblewell a month or so earlier, but hadn't had the attention span or will to read for more than a couple pages at a time. I picked up the thick book from the nightstand and looked around the little yellow room; the rainy afternoon light politely seeped in, my suitcase and ragged old duffel bag both still zipped and lined up along the wall. But this time, John's olive drab backpack wasn't next to them on the floor, and I felt a pang in my stomach. I glanced over at the bed – he had made it before he'd gathered his things and left with me. I heard the kettle start to whistle, so I rushed back downstairs to the kitchen. I got the big, red and white speckled tea pot down from the top of the refrigerator and put enough PG Tips tea bags in to make a full pot, like John had showed me, in case Sammy and Claire got up and wanted some. I put the tea pot, milk, sugar bowl, and three cups on a tray, and very carefully carried it all upstairs to the living room and set it down on the coffee table.

The living room was small, but comfortable, with large, deep green house plants crowding around the big picture window and smaller windows flanking it. The overstuffed burgundy easy chair in front of the window and nestled between two Ficus trees beckoned to me. But first, music. Their bedroom was far enough away and down a little hall that it shouldn't disturb them, as long as I kept the volume reasonable.

I went to the stereo across the room. Its two big speakers with wood cabinets almost as tall as me stood on either side of the turntable and receiver, and I flipped through their records in wooden crates. I saw the Tom Waits record, *Small Change*. Perfect. It made me feel a strong sense of – dare I say it – pride to see my home country represented here by the gravel-voiced, rumple-suited, muse-ridden, grouchy poet/piano bar singer.

The rain outside came down harder, and a small breeze shimmied in from off the street, as if in approval; it was a little chilly to have an open window, but the sound of rain and cars splashing by was a sweet song I couldn't resist. I put the needle down on the record, walked to the easy chair, and poured my tea, milk, and sugar into the mug.

This record always made me think of Keaton, and one early spring Saturday afternoon a bunch of us radio station nerds were hanging around his apartment, drinking whiskey and coffee, ignoring homework and boredom and boyfriends and girlfriends. Keaton had grumbled along intermittently with the songs about strippers, drinking, and lost loves in an uncanny Cookie Monster impression.

I leaned back, closed my eyes, and exhaled deeply, sinking into the chair. I picked up my book and read for a while, until Claire came wandering out, yawning and looking like a movie star in an old, brightly colored silk robe.

"Morning," she said.

"Would you like some tea?"

Her eyes widened. "Yes, thank you. I always have to make the tea."

A few minutes later, Sammy shuffled out of their room in plaid pajama bottoms and a white t-shirt.

"Darling," Claire said. "Come have some tea. Viv made it."

He grinned. "And John said you were helpless in the kitchen."

"I am," I said. "But I did pay attention when he made tea. I figured I'd be kicked out of the country if I didn't at least know how to do that."

He sipped. "It's good. Not too strong, or worse, too weak. This might be your daily household task if you're not careful."

I told them about the interview and how I'd like to stay if I could, but I wasn't sure how to make it happen.

"Seems like there must be lots of paperwork and documents or something involved," I said. "I wouldn't even know where to start."

"We could go with you to Immigration Services if you like," Sammy said. "A lot of cooks at my work came here from other countries, and I've helped many of them get settled."

"Of course," Claire added, smiling, and patting Sammy's chest, "we're not pressuring you. Just know it's something to consider. Let's rephrase the question: do you *want* to stay?"

Sammy said, "I haven't seen John this happy in a long time. Just for what that's worth."

Claire said, "Poor guy was in rough shape when…" she trailed off.

"When Lorelei left him for a coven in Scotland?" I said.

"He did tell you about that," she said. "Good."

I nodded. "He said he was planning on asking her to marry him before she left. Sammy came back to the room and found him." My eyes teared up.

"Yeah," Sammy said, and sipped his tea. "He's my best mate. Don't know what I would've done if they hadn't been able to save him."

"One day, he's all glowing and smiling, saying he knows what he wants to do with the rest of his life," Claire said. "Then that slag doesn't come back, and doesn't come back, and fuckin' moves to Scotland without telling anyone. She finally calls John and tells him, and it was like the light in him just went out."

"Even knowing all that about his mum," Sammy said, "She just fucking vanishes without thinking about how that would affect him."

"What about his mom?" I asked.

They glanced at each other. Claire stood and said she was headed to the shower.

"Sorry," Sammy said, and patted my hand. "Typical John. Buries the lead. His mum left when he was four. Just after Noel was born. Never really found out why."

He'd mentioned a stepmom, but I never found the right time to ask him about it.

Sammy continued, "He told me he had only one memory of her. He said he was sitting on a blanket on a porch, playing with blocks. He heard some wavering sound and looked in the direction of it. His mum was sobbing while she held his baby brother and fed him a bottle. He doesn't recall seeing her again. John's dad told him she left a couple weeks later."

My mother was judgmental, unforgiving, and rigid, but at least she'd been around. And as much as I adored my dad, I couldn't imagine him raising any of us on his own. "What did his dad do?"

Sammy sipped his tea, then set the cup down on the side table. "Just got on with things, I suppose. John said he remembers lots of Aunts and older cousins coming 'round, everyone being extra nice to him, that sort of thing. His dad's a good guy – always did his best for his boys."

The phone rang, and Sammy got up to answer it.

I went back to reading, or tried to. *Poor John.* His mother's absence must have felt like a wall in his house had a huge hole in it. He'd done nothing wrong and got abandoned anyway. Twice that I knew of. It put everything with Lorelei in an even more painful light. If Sammy hadn't gone back to the room that day. If John had died, and…

If John had died. A gut punch. I needed him to know... I glanced at the clock. 5:30. He'd be home by now. When

Sammy got off his call and started getting ready to go to work, I sprang up and ran to the phone.

"Hello?"

"Hey. It's Viv. Did you just walk in the door?"

"Yeah. How was the interview?"

"Good, good. Hey, I've been thinking… I know it's different, like with me here and you there, but - "

"But you're only a train ride away, and not across the bloody ocean."

"True. And it's only for like another month or – whenever it is you're done up there. And you'll probably want to see your family at some point. But then…"

"Yeah. But then."

"I just – I needed to hear your voice." *I needed to know you were safe.* "I talked with Sammy and Claire about the whole... you almost dying thing. I hope that was ok."

"Sure."

"And Sammy told me – " *This is none of my business. Maybe I should just keep this to myself.*

"Sammy told you what?"

No. Don't keep anything from him. "He told me about your mom. How she left when you guys were little."

It was silent on his end. It was silent a bit too long.

"I'm sorry," I said. "I know it's none of my business."

"It's all right."

So stupid. What was I hoping to accomplish by bringing this up? "Are you – I just need to know if you're ok."

"Yeah," he said. "It's not like it just happened. I barely remember it."

"But doesn't something like that seriously affect you?"

Again, quiet.

I stumbled ahead. "I just want to make sure that you know you can tell me these things. Even if you don't know what to say about them."

"I didn't want you to think of me as just another broken guy with mother issues. It's a bit trite."

"Hey, I've got mother issues myself," I said. "Just in another direction."

"That you do," he said.

"You are so not broken. And I need you to know that you can trust me."

"I do," he said. "I just – it was so long ago, you know? And it's not like I didn't have my dad. I had everything I needed. And after the Lorelei situation, I worked out a lot of that *and* this in counseling. Perhaps not everything, but enough, I think."

"But did you ever find out why she left? I think I'd want to know."

I heard the creak of a kitchen chair as he shifted. "All Dad ever told me was 'Some girls aren't cut out to be mums.' He wasn't angry, and never said anything bad about her. I suppose that was all the explanation I needed."

Instead of letting his experiences of being left with no explanation turn him angry and cynical, he learned acceptance without judgment: me and my mess, for example.

"Your dad sounds like a sweetheart."

"Yeah," he said. "I was happy for him when he eventually married my step mum. They'd been friends for ages, and she always knew how to make him laugh. She still keeps him light."

Claire and Sammy walked by and whispered that they were going to work and that they'd see me later. I waved.

"So is that why you called?" he asked. "To hear my woeful tale of maternal abandonment, and make sure I wasn't sitting 'round crying into my lager?"

"Something like that." I leaned back in the chair and pulled a brown leaf off the Ficus. "I just can't – the thought of you being sad to the point where you might not be here today – it's been on my mind. I worry sometimes."

"Worrying's not very punk rock. No future and all that."

"I just need you to know that if something happens and I end up not being able to stay here – for whatever reason – that it's not because I don't want to."

"So... You *do* want to?"

"Of course. But that's not the point - "

"I don't care if it's the point, I'm just glad to hear it without any qualifiers."

"I did say 'but.'"

"But it wasn't in reference to whether or not you wanted to stay."

I laughed. "You are *very* nit-picky tonight."

"Very well. I'll try not to interrupt again."

"The point is that I just want to know that no matter what happens, that you'll keep going. If I've learned anything over the past few years, it's that relationships – that's such a lame word, but whatever this thing is that's been happening with you and me – they're usually all conditional and precarious and can change in an instant, like with one person not even realizing it. Like what happened with you and Lorelei, and what happened with me and Ade, and other people before all of that."

"I made you a promise when you were still in the States. Remember?"

"Yes."

"I take promises seriously. They're more important than however dreadful I might be feeling on a given day. And I have to add that lately, I haven't been feeling even a little dreadful."

"But I saw you wipe your eyes earlier when you got on the train."

"I was hoping you hadn't seen that. I was trying to be the strong one."

"I wanted to run after you," I said. "You looked so sad."

"Well, I *was* sad. You've now been in England for nearly as long as I spent wishing I could see you again. I just – got choked up thinking how you wouldn't be at the flat later. I'm not reliving a trauma or anything. This is different because I know you'll be missing me, too."

"I will. I am." I exhaled and stretched my legs out. "So I don't have to worry?"

"No," he said. "I promise to keep trudging along, however joylessly."

"OK. Good. Me too."

I didn't sleep at all well that night. I kept reaching for him, and when my arm landed on an empty pillow and the hand that tried to grasp his shoulder held only blanket, I'd remember.

Chapter 22

The record store training consisted of Bruce showing me how the cash register worked, then leaving me while he ran errands. A couple of customers yelled at me when I asked them to repeat themselves, saying things like "You'd best learn how the Queen's English works while you're in the Motherland, *pet*." And "I hear your next President's going to be a former Hollywood actor, for fuck's sake. 'Bedtime for Bonzo,' yeah? You lot don't deserve your independence." I apologized for everything. I didn't even understand what for half the time, but it was my kneejerk reaction to being yelled at.

Wednesday and Thursday were much the same, only a little worse; I was pretty sure word had gotten out that I worked there, and lots of middle-aged men came by to hurl insults at me, the unwilling Miss America. When people told me to go back where I came from, I did my best to ignore them and look unaffected. My co-workers stood up for me and told me to pay them no mind, but it did remind me that as much as I loved London, it was utterly indifferent to me. Phil the bus driver kept calling me "Miss Twenty Quid." But Thursday, I knew that at the end of it all I'd get to see John; it was only three days and nights since he'd first left to go back to Lonsdale, but it was the longest we'd been apart since I'd gotten here a month earlier, and something in me ached being without him, especially at night and waking up in the morning.

I had to work until seven, so when I got back to the apartment, he was already there. I was so excited to see him that my hands shook as I put my key in the lock. I heard rapid footsteps inside. When I opened the door, he wrapped me in his arms, kissed me, then picked me up, and swung me around. Goosebumps erupted everywhere, and I held onto him as tightly as I could.

"You're even lovelier than I remember," he said.

"So are you." I kissed him again. The most savory smells from the kitchen filled the hall. "You're cooking?"

"A little," he said with a grin. "Happy Thanksgiving."

"Huh?"

He crossed his arms over his chest, examining me like I'd made a joke he didn't get. "What, you're so fucking British now you forgot about your own national holiday?"

"I guess so, *pet*."

"Good thing we remembered," John said. "Everything's about ready: turkey, mashed potatoes, peas. Cranberry 'sauce' straight from the tin. Gravy, stuffing, fucking all of it. Pies, too. Sammy and Claire helped me with all this. They had to go to work before you got back, but they said they'll ravage the leftovers later. Hope you didn't eat crisps on the way back and ruin your appetite."

"No. I didn't have enough money for crisps today."

He took my hand and led me to the kitchen. The table was set, with a tablecloth and candles and so much food there was hardly any bare space. It smelled just like home – turkey, Rosemary, the starch of the potatoes... Home. A longing gripped my chest. My eyes filled with tears, and a sob burst from my throat. He turned and looked at me with some alarm.

I sniffled. "This is amazing. I don't know what to say. I can't believe I forgot."

He put his arm around my shoulders. "Want to call home? I have some carving and such to do."

"I'm not sure. I haven't talked to my mom since… you know, *that* call. I'm afraid she's learned some synonyms for 'whore' to try out on me."

He wrapped his arms around me. “You don’t have to. We don’t even have to call it ‘Thanksgiving.’ We can just call it Thursday. Course, then I’d have to do this every week, and it’s a bit time consuming, but if it makes you happy, I’ll do it.”

I buried my face in his neck, wanting nothing more than to grab a couple of turkey legs and a bowl of mashed potatoes and crawl into bed next to him and forget the entire rest of the world existed.

“I guess I should call.”

He kissed the top of my head and held his lips there. “Don’t let your mum be cruel to you, or I’ll have to intervene again.”

I groaned and went upstairs to the phone in the living room, brought it over to the easy chair, and sank back. The streetlights outside twinkled, and a gentle rain coated the world in a gauzy haze.

They probably just finished eating, and were piling dishes in the sink; Mom always liked to do Thanksgiving in the early afternoon. I dialed and held my breath. She answered.

“Mom? It’s Viv.”

“Oh my god – Bill - it’s Vivian. Pick up – pick up the other phone. Where are you?” She sounded so happy to hear from me that I wondered if she’d taken up heavy drinking.

“Still in England, Mom. I just – I wanted to call and say Happy Thanksgiving.”

I heard Dad pick up the other phone in the basement. “Hey Viv?”

“Dad!”

“Everything all right?” he said.

“Yeah, everything’s fine. I was thinking of you guys today.”

“The Brits don’t celebrate Thanksgiving,” Mom sniffed.

I decided not to tell them I'd forgotten, because the wave of homesickness I was having right then more than made up for it. "Not usually, no. But I got back to my apartment after work, and my… friend and roommates had cooked up a big turkey dinner so I wouldn't feel as far from home."

"But you *are* far from home," said Mom.

"Elizabeth, don't start."

I sniffled. "I really miss you guys."

"Us too, sweetheart," said Dad. "What was that about work and roommates?"

I told them about the record store and London and Claire and Sammy. As little as possible about John and our arrangement.

"John, huh?" she said. "He's the other man, isn't he? *And* he was rude to me on the phone."

"That's enough, Elizabeth," my dad said.

She sighed. "When are you coming back?"

"I'm," I paused. "I'm not sure I am. I really like it here."

"Oh, for Heaven's sake," she said.

Dad spoke up. "We're glad you like it there, honey, but you're going to have to figure out what you're doing about school, and you'll need to do a bunch of paperwork and – you know, moving to another country could take some time."

"You're coming back for Christmas, at least," she said.

"I don't think I can. Christmas is the record store's busiest time. They'll need me there."

There was a pause. I couldn't imagine not being home at Christmas, but then, I'd also never thought I'd actually be *here*.

"I'll come home after, though. Maybe the first couple weeks of January?"

"I've got to go," Mom said. "Things to do." She hung up the phone.

"I'm still here," my dad said.

"Sorry, Dad."

"You know how she gets about holidays. I understand about work. Be in touch when you have some dates, ok?"

"I will."

I pictured the kitchen, cramped with the fold-out leaves of the table, the extra, mismatched chairs, the dishes and platters and serving utensils all piled to the right of the sink. We said our goodbyes, and I went downstairs.

"How did it go?"

"Better than it could have."

"Hope you're hungry."

"Wicked."

He pulled out a chair and indicated that I should sit. He sat across from me. We filled our plates with thick slices of turkey, mashed potatoes, gravy – fucking all of it, just like he'd said.

When it came time for him to leave Monday morning, it wasn't any easier than it had been the week before, but this time there wasn't the fear of being alone in a new place; only the wish that he could stay.

Chapter 23

On December 21, the Friday before Christmas, I was scheduled to go into work. I didn't usually work Fridays, but Victory Records was crazy from open until close with shoppers loading up on presents, and they needed the help.

Per usual, John had come on Thursday, but this time he wouldn't be going back to Lonsdale the following Monday because he'd finished university. I hated to leave him, but I needed the money, so I took every hour that was offered. Around noon on Friday, I kissed him goodbye and headed toward the bus. He was going to spend the afternoon drawing, then come meet me when my shift ended around eight, and we were going to grab some dinner and drinks at The Cat & Kin.

When I got to work, Victoria asked if she could talk to me. She spoke slowly and quietly, two words that I would never have attributed to her before.

"Am I in trouble?"

"Come back to the office?"

She led me back to the small, windowless room where I'd had my interview – I hadn't been back there since. The blue and black speckled carpet felt spongy underfoot, and a cold damp seeped in from the brick walls.

Victoria sat at the little green metal desk that looked like it must be older than she was, and gestured for me to sit. There were no other chairs, so I pulled up two stacked milk crates and perched on them across from her. A single, unadorned light bulb dangled overhead. I folded my hands in my lap and twiddled my thumbs, bouncing my foot as I waited for her to speak. I tried to remember if I had done anything bad, like accidentally shoplifted somehow.

She put her elbows on the desk and leaned forward. "I am so sorry to have to do this, especially right before Christmas, but I have to let you go."

My bottom lip trembled. "How come?"

"It's nothing about you, honest," she said. "Some twats from Immigration started sniffing 'round, asking people questions. Since fucking Thatcher took office, they've been cracking down like I've never seen. I wasn't too worried till a couple people here mentioned an officer asking them invasive questions about their co-workers."

Shit. This was the worst news possible.

"I understand," I said, attempting to keep my bubbling-up blubbering to a minimum.

She handed me a tissue. "Once you get your papers sorted, come back and see me, yeah? If I can take you on, I will."

I nodded and blew my nose.

She handed me an envelope. "That's all your wages from this week, plus a little extra as a thank you for working so hard. I really am sorry."

I thanked her for her kindness, put the envelope in my bag, and left, trying to get out of there with a tiny bit of dignity.

I was in shock. I wandered toward the bus, and climbed in. I leaned my face against the cold glass, watching the buildings and people roll by. *What am I going to do?* Getting a visa would probably take a while, and I kicked myself for not starting the process before now. I'd come to love that job; I got to be around records all day, and listen to new ones before almost anyone else. And that employee discount...

I decided to go back to the apartment and calm down. Sammy and Claire had left for the weekend, but when they got back on Sunday, I would ask Sammy to take him up on his offer to help me with paperwork and the next step. I would figure this out. I *had* to.

When I got back, the door was unlocked, which was weird; we were always very careful to lock everything, especially on the ground floor. I stepped inside, and heard voices from the living room upstairs; John's voice and a woman's. It wasn't Claire. I listened, but couldn't quite hear any distinct words. I crept carefully up the stairs, avoiding the creaky spots, and listened from the top step.

She said, "I had no idea you went through all that. None of your friends would talk to me. My God, John. You poor dear."

"It's all in the past," he said. "You don't have to be sorry."

"I suppose it's good that that's all in the past," she said. "But I've thought about you a lot since then. And especially since... you know, last time we saw each other."

Last time? I got cold. I craned my neck and peeked around the corner. A woman with long, wavy red hair sat on our couch, smiling and leaning over toward John, her porcelain hand on his forearm. I smelled the rich, otherworldly scent of sandalwood. Fucking Lorelei was in *my* apartment.

I'm not supposed to be here right now. I'm not supposed to be seeing this. They're reconciling. Of course they're reconciling. You don't belong here, Viv, and you know it.

I stared at them, her touching him, him gazing at her, and froze. They made a staggeringly beautiful couple. John looked up and saw me.

I felt lightheaded, lost my balance and nearly fell down the stairs, but caught myself on the bannister. I turned and flew down the stairs, out the front door, and down the brick steps. I heard him call my name. I ran faster than I ever knew I could.

When I was a few blocks and side streets away, I paused to catch my breath and leaned against a wall. A sharp twinge let me know that I'd pulled something in my back when I'd almost fallen down the stairs.

Shit. Shit. Shit. They were seeing each other again – why the fuck else would *she* be there when I was supposed to be at work? This had to be what they called "karma." Of course he was getting back together with her. She got whatever it was in her system out, and now was ready to come back to him, because why on earth wouldn't she? I knew something like this would happen, I just hoped it wouldn't.

I thought of everything I had dropped at home: school, friends, my family, the radio station, my future. Of all the stupid shit I had ever done, thinking I could just up and move here was the stupidest. I couldn't make it here.

I headed to a pub I'd never been to before, ordered a Jameson and a beer, and found a table in the corner. I drank the whiskey in one gulp; the fire shot down my gullet, warming me as it went. I took a deep breath and put my head in my hands. I had to make a plan. When I looked up, I noticed that I was sitting next to a Christmas tree, its fragrant Pine branches heavy with old-looking, multicolored glass ornaments, gold-edged thick velvet ribbon, and delicate, twinkling lights.

My dad and I used to walk in the woods together to pick out a tree at home; it was always too tall, and by the time enough was sawed off to fit, it wasn't like a triangle at all, more like a column of branches. Dad would spend the next hour trimming the branches to form something closer to an upside-down V. During that time, whatever woodland creatures that had made the tree their home would make themselves known; one year it was a red squirrel, another it was a family of mice, another it was two chipmunks. Mom and I would run away screaming. Dad would open the door to the outside, keep at his branch trimming, and assure us that they'd find their way out. Mom and I would end up hiding in their room with the door closed until he hollered, "They made it out. You girls can come out now."

As I regained awareness of my surroundings, Bing Crosby sang about silver bells. Dad loved that song, and always sang along with it when it came on the radio. I cried into what was left of my beer before draining the glass.

"Pardon, miss?" The waitress had come and stood next to me. She placed another lager and whiskey down on my table. "I saw you crying – this time of year is rough on lots of people. I've been there. This one's on the house." She had an Irish accent.

I wiped my eyes. "That's so nice of you. Thank you."

She patted my shoulder. "Gets easier, promise."

I shot the whiskey and started in on the beer. I went to the phone booth at the back of the pub and dialed Dean's number followed by my calling card number, which I now knew as well as my parents' phone number. I wanted Izzy to tell me it was ok to come home. When Dean answered with his corny "Yello?" I slumped against the wall.

"Hey Dean. It's Viv."

"Viv?" he said. "No kidding! Izzy – hey, come here. Viv, how the hell are you?"

"Pretty good," I said.

"No, no you're not," he said, "your voice just went up like two octaves. What's going – ok, Izzy, fine, take the phone."

"You're talking squeaky," she said. "What's happening?"

I exhaled. "Have you guys been getting my letters?"

"Yeah. You've been having a great time, right?"

"Uh huh," I said.

I stood up as straight as I could with my aching back, and turned toward the corner so no one could see me crying. I told her about losing my job and going back to the apartment and seeing Lorelei there, and how I was in over my head and I was an idiot to think it would turn out any different.

"Whoa," she said. "OK, I need you to think: when you two were basically living together, did he hide any mail from you? Take calls privately? Go out when it wasn't for school or work?"

"Not that I can recall, detective."

"Is it possible that she initiated this visit? Or that it happened randomly? Or maybe she was casing your apartment and moved in when you left?"

"I don't know. Seems a bit creepy if she was watching us."

"OK. Was he touching her?"

"She was touching him, and he was, like… *looking* at her. Gazing, in fact."

"Have you asked him directly what the hell was going on?"

"Of course not. I panicked and ran out."

"Huh."

"Iz, come on. He's way too great for me. Of course he'd bide his time with a smitten American till his real girlfriend came back."

"Why do you say that?"

"Because I'm plain and childish and selfish and stupid."

"That's your family talking. Ade too, gross. That's not the woman that I know."

"I'm a kid, not a *woman.* And I can't make it in a city."

"That's definitely your mother talking. She's wrong."

"But – what if John does want to be with Lorelei? What am I going to do?"

She sighed. "Who cares, ultimately?"

"What?"

"You've been in love with that city for longer than you've been in love with any guy. Right?"

It had been four and half years since I listened to Ziggy Stardust on my brother's couch and rediscovered the will to live. I was *there,* where that record was conceived and written. I had to remind myself, I was *there*. "Right," I whispered.

"So even if John turns out to be an asshole, you're where you want to be. Things fell into place, and then they fell out of place, but something else will happen, and they'll fall back in. Just like Keaton told you that time; the boy is almost irrelevant."

"Yeah…"

"You're *there* now. That's where you should be. Don't chicken out."

I sighed. "So what, I can't go home?"

"You can, but I don't think it'll be comfortable anymore."

"I was hoping you'd tell me to come back because you miss me too much."

"I *do* miss you," she said. "But this has been building for a long time – before I even knew you. Don't give it up because you're scared."

We said our love-yous and goodbyes.

If John wanted to be with Lorelei, then he should be.

I wanted him to be happy; if that was with me, great; if with Lorelei, I'd have to accept that. More than anything, I just didn't want him to be sad again.

I went back to my table and settled into the booth. More people had come in, but it wasn't dense yet. I wasn't quite ready to go back to the apartment and face my fate, so I took a big swallow of my beer, hauled my *Hitchhiker's Guide to the Galaxy* out of my bag, and read. I only got through half a chapter before I had to admit I just couldn't focus.

Might as well get this over with.

I closed the book, put it in my bag, and drained the rest of my beer. I stepped out onto the narrow sidewalk and buttoned up the top button of my coat. The air felt wet and raw now, and I wished I had a thicker jacket. I tried to remember which direction I'd come from. None of the signs or buildings looked familiar, and I wondered exactly how far I'd run in that blind panic. I decided to go right, to where the street met up with another at the next corner.

When I reached the next street, I saw a small bookshop across the road. There was a sign in their window: HELP WANTED. EXPERIENCE PREFERRED, BUT NOT REQUIRED.

I have experience working in a bookstore! Maybe they'll sponsor me and help me get my visa.

I decided to go in and look around, maybe get an application. I looked left, then right, then left again, and stepped off the curb.

I heard a squeal of tires on pavement, and my right hip got pushed out from under me. I felt rolling and slamming and metal and cracking glass, then asphalt, as my breath got shoved out of me, evaporating in the foggy air above.

I heard shouting, but my vision blurred, and I couldn't see where it was coming from. The left side of my face felt wet from hitting the pavement, and my elbows and wrists burned.

"She wasn't even looking," someone yelled, "just popped out into the street from between parked cars. I didn't *mean* to."

I rubbed my eyes and was able to just make out three people standing around a car, its driver-side door open.

Oh, fuck. I forgot to look right again.

"Would someone call a fucking ambulance?" a woman in a long, wool emerald coat yelled, and then approached me. Her face was blurry and my skull pulsed. I saw that she was touching my arm, but I couldn't feel it. She said, "You were hit by a car, dear. Can you breathe?"

I tried to pick my head up, but she and another person who had come over said "No, no, don't move, please, just stay put."

When the ambulance arrived, the fog hovering over us turned pink, then red.

Chapter 24

My left inner elbow felt like it had a splint rammed into it, but when I looked, it was just a tube connected to an IV. Both my wrists were heavily bandaged. I tried to use them to sit up, but the slightest pressure sent spears of pain flying up my arms. I managed to scoot myself to an upright position and looked around a cavernous grey room with dim lights and identical beds with arched metal slatted headboards and footboards. Each had red and silver sparkly garland looped through them, with metallic green balls dangling. Across the room stood a large Christmas tree similar to the one in the pub. A lump congealed in my throat. I'd never been in a hospital overnight before.

The beds nearest me were empty, but the rest were dotted with people groaning and crying. My stomach tightened, and my neck tensed. It looked to be nighttime through the windows lining the far wall. I couldn't stop shivering.

There was a button next to my bed. I pushed it. A nurse came striding out from a room cloaked in white curtains.

"Hello, Miss Pierce," she whispered. "How are we feeling?"

"What happened?" I croaked.

"You were hit by a car, but luckily, the bloke wasn't going fast. You have a mild concussion, though I'm sure it doesn't *feel* mild."

She also told me that both wrists were badly sprained, I lost patches of skin here and there, and got some cuts and bruises. Oh, and that my left shoulder would probably feel tight, as I crash-landed on it at some point. Also, that my right hip, where the initial impact was, would cause me to limp for a while.

"You're lucky to be young and bouncy," she added. "No major damage was done, but as the painkillers wear off, you'll be quite uncomfortable. We'll get you a prescription to help with that."

My right cheek throbbed. I brought my hand up to feel a chunky bandage and tape.

"Got a cut there, too – required four stitches. It will leave a scar, but nothing a little cover-up won't be able to camouflage. Eventually, anyway."

"How long have I been here?"

"They brought you in the ambulance around 3:30 this afternoon, and it's nearly two in the morning now. Just need to rest a bit and get looked at by a doctor in the morning before we let you go. Is there someone I can call for you?"

I gave her John's name and the number to the apartment, and she went to make the call. All I wanted was to see him, even though I was still mad and confused; I was also scared and needed my friend.

I stared at the garland on my footboard until it got blurry. I must have dozed off, because when I opened my eyes, John was sitting in a chair next to my bed, holding my hand. He looked exhausted: his eyes were red-rimmed and puffy, and he wore the jeans and loose grey sweater with unraveling neck seams from the day before. I loved that sweater on him. He had draped his black wooly coat with the pewter buttons over me like a blanket.

"Hey," he whispered. Tears spilled down his cheeks.

I was so relieved at the sight of him that I sprang up and hugged him, ignoring my roaring pain receptors. I let out long breaths I'd been sucking in since I'd initially left the apartment to go to work.

"I couldn't find you," he said. "I was terrified. I was out all night looking. Claire called out of work so she could stay home in case you came back or called. I'd come back to make some coffee when the Nurse called. When she said you'd been *hit*, I just... I'm so relieved you'll be ok."

He squeezed a little tighter, and my entire back radiated a stiff heat, and I winced. He loosened his embrace. I pulled away and carefully moved back so that I was sitting up against the headboard.

"Everything hurts right now," I said.

"Sorry," he said. "Why did you run off earlier?"

"This... whatever this is with you and me, it's run its course, right? Lorelei came back for you."

"What?" He shook his head. "Wait, you honestly think..."

"Why was she there, touching you?" I remembered her porcelain fingers on this, my favorite sweater of his. "And you were *gazing* at her, you dick. And she said something about a 'last time.' What the hell was that?"

I didn't care that I was a gigantic hypocrite, being mad that he was reconciling with his ex. My eyes felt heavy. He held my hand with one of his, and smoothed my hair with the other. I closed my eyes and braced myself.

"The 'last time' she referred to was one night at the pub a couple weeks back; I was meeting you there after you got out of work. She approached me and said she wanted to talk. I'd seen her out and about a few times since the whole… thing I told you about, but she'd always looked away and avoided me. So I didn't understand why she wanted to talk all of a sudden, and frankly, I wasn't interested in finding out. I'd made my peace with things some time ago. So I told her no, that I was meeting my girlfriend there, and there was nothing we had to talk about."

Girlfriend.

He added, "And I wasn't *gazing*. I was glazed over. For a Witch, she can be incredibly dull. Talks about herself constantly. I'd not noticed that before."

"So why was she in our apartment? And when I was supposed to be at work? Can you understand why I freaked out?"

He brought his face down to my hand, which he was now holding tightly with both of his. "Yeah, I understand. She asked around mutual friends until she figured out where I was staying. She phoned a little while after you left, said she just happened to be in the neighborhood, which was more than a bit creepy to me, but I thought, 'Fine, let's just settle this now.' So she came over."

"That was dumb," I said. The painkillers were making it impossible to hold much of anything back.

"It *was* dumb, but she caught me off guard before I could suggest meeting somewhere more public. I'm sorry. I did phone the record shop to tell you what was happening as soon as I knew she was coming over, but they said you'd just left. Didn't tell me why, though, and told me to fuck off and mind my own business when I asked where you'd gone. I figured Victoria must've sent you out on an errand."

I closed my eyes. "But why was she touching you? Why were you *letting* her if you really didn't want her there?"

"In the interest of getting things over quickly, I told her everything very matter-of-factly. She'd only heard pieces here and there; only my closest friends knew all of what happened, and they wouldn't tell her anything. She hadn't known about the pills or the ring or how devastated I'd been. She felt awful about it all, and she's a very touchy person."

"She *should* feel awful. Did she at least tell you why she left?"

He let out a long exhale and shifted in his chair so that he could look at me easier, without twisting his neck. He squeezed my hand. "She was, come to find out, nowhere near as serious about us as I was. She said as she got deeper into a life in Scotland, that it didn't even occur to her to contact me. She just… forgot about me."

I shook my head. "What kind of space cadet just forgets a person? About *you,* especially? It doesn't make any sense. I'd only met you once, and I could barely stop thinking about you for like a month and a half." *No no no. Shut up.*

He smiled. "Really?"

I rolled my eyes and looked down at his hands holding mine. "Yeah. Can we please go back to you talking now?"

He dragged his chair closer with a loud scrape. One of the other patients yelled to keep it down. We both mumbled "Sorry."

John brought his face closer to mine and whispered, "She came to talk about ghosts from the past. I told her I wasn't haunted anymore. I told her about you – that you've inspired me to do things I've always wanted to, but never quite dared. That you're hilarious and fearless and even more obsessive about music than I am – definitely more eloquent about it, as well. Then I told her goodbye, showed her to the door, and went out looking for you."

I was *so* not "fearless."

"But when I saw you two sitting there together talking, you looked like a real couple. She's even prettier than I imagined, and now that everything is out in the open with you two, this could be a second chance for you with her. I'm just this bumbling oaf who had a crisis and came staggering into your life, and I'm just really afraid that because you're so incredible and supportive, you feel some sort of obligation to me, and it's holding you back."

He shook his head, but I continued, “My point is, I have no idea what I’m doing. As harebrained as it was when I got on that plane, it was the most excited I’d been about being alive in a long time; I *liked* not knowing what I was doing. And even though *this* thing happened, I’ve fallen in love,” I swallowed, “with this place, and I’m not leaving unless something I can’t control makes me. I’ve never been more sure than I am now that I don’t want a normal life. And if you do, I am not going to hold you back from someone who can give you that. You deserve only good things, John. Jesus H. Christ, I’m tired.”

I sank down on the bed, feeling sleep curl around me.

“You’re not holding me back,” he whispered. “You’re propelling me forward. As long as I’m with you, I don’t need to know where.”

I couldn’t keep my eyes open anymore. I smiled at him just before my lids fluttered shut. *It’s not just this city. I love you like crazy.*

#

It was daylight when I came to, and sunny; I glimpsed an aching-blue sky beyond the trees, through the windows at the far end of the long room. The IV was out of my arm, a bandage in its place. John was still in the chair, holding my hand with both of his. He was hunched over, asleep, his head resting next to mine on the scratchy pillow. Just to look at him made my neck hurt more. I brought my other hand over and placed it on his dark hair. He stirred and flicked open his eyes. He kissed me.

“Morning,” he said. “I love you too. Like crazy.” He drew out the “a” sound as he did whenever he impersonated my American accent.

My eyes got wide. “I said that out loud?”

"You're on some pretty heavy painkillers."

"Your breath is terrible."

"Yours is worse," he said. "Regardless, it's too late now. You can't take it back."

My wrists burned and the stitched-up cut on my face throbbed. "Neither can you. You're not even on anything."

Chapter 25

March 24, 1980

Dear Paul,

I'm all settled in back in London, and things are evening out. The work visa situation finally got squared away. Victory Records doesn't have any openings right now, but I'll keep checking. In the meantime, I'm waiting tables and learning a little bartending at this place called The Cat & Kin; only women work there, and no one takes any crap from customers. It's all new to me, this standing up for myself thing, not to mention the logistics of waiting tables. It's hard sometimes, but I love the people I work with, and I'm learning a ton about – well, everything, really.

Rent is pretty cheap with the four of us living here, so I can save a little money. Don't tell Mom and Dad, but John lives here too. I'm sure they know, but we don't talk about it. You know the drill.

I love London; there is *so* much history everywhere, even just walking down the street. There are plaques everywhere with names and dates and horrific tragedies I remember hearing about in European history classes. It's all very humbling and inspiring at the same time.

I never jaywalk anymore, and always remind myself to do the exact opposite of how they taught us to cross the street at home as kids. There are some pink, shiny patches where regular skin used to be before the accident, but the Doctors told me it'll look closer to normal someday.

I'm still dying to see David Bowie, but I think he must be making a record or something, because I haven't heard of any concerts. I keep my eyes peeled whenever I'm out, though, just in case he's running to the store for some snacks or something. I'm sure I'd pass out if I saw him.

Speaking of going to shows, some girls from work took me to see this band called The Slits; it's three girls up front, and a guy on drums. They were loud, sweaty, and aggressive, way more so than any other band I've ever seen. They sound like Punk mixed up with Reggae in a lawnmower falling down several flights of stairs. You probably wouldn't like them, but I love them.

Also, there's a little independent, or "pirate" radio station near my work that I've started hanging around the past few weeks; a girl I know from the record store has a shift there, so I've been hanging out with her while she's on the air. I'm working up the nerve to ask about getting my own shift. I miss WCNH.

I'm glad you like the Peel Session tapes I've been sending you. There's another one enclosed here. I know that not all of them are your bag, but it's like you said: it's good to keep an open mind.

Things with Mom continue to be awkward and uncomfortable. I hope to be able to be on the phone or in a room with her someday without arguing or biting my tongue so hard it bleeds, but until then... Sherry still won't talk to me, and I'm going to give up trying. I miss Dad a lot, but I'm always afraid to call in case Mom answers.

John's drawings have been in a few exhibits, and quite a few have sold. He has a few more small exhibits lined up and seems to be gaining some momentum. He's so good that you don't even have to know anything about art to get something out of his pieces. I need to show you this drawing of me he did last fall. I'll take a picture of it and mail it with my next letter.

Speaking of John, things there are really good. There are times when I don't even have to say anything, and he knows what I'm thinking (poor guy). I don't know how I got to be so lucky, but I'll take it.

I love and miss you boatloads. But I'll be back in August for my friends Dean and Izzy's wedding, so I'll see you in a few months. I'm really excited for you to meet John. I know you'll love him as much as I do.

All My Love, Viv

#

On a postcard featuring a red double-decker bus:

April 7, 1980

Dear WCNH,

First, these things feel like death traps, and I avoid them whenever possible. Which, unfortunately, isn't often. They're fucking everywhere.

Second, I've been thinking about the radio station a lot lately, and missing you all terribly. That little dusty station saved me. It let me become who I was but didn't realize yet. And it's all thanks to Lenny for walking up behind me and scaring the shit out of me that first night I wandered up there. To all of you for never laughing me out of there, I owe you so much, but for now, a THANK YOU from the bottom of my heart will have to suffice. Take good care of that place.

Love, Viv

Elegia

I talked to Izzy earlier in the day, and she confirmed that she and Dean would be at Joy Division's US debut in New York City on Wednesday. It wasn't like we'd ever met the band or anything, but having seen them so many times, each show a unique religious experience, I felt protective of them, and was glad that Dean and Izzy would be there since we couldn't be.

John had graduated university and had a few more exhibits lined up. I'd be turning 22 in a few days, and we decided to take the week off and do some traveling.

Just before ten that night, I went downstairs to see what John was up to. He had the radio on, and was washing the last of the dishes. I walked up behind him and wrapped my arms around his waist.

"I love you," he said. "Hasn't gotten old yet."

"I love you, too." My guts still felt like they were made of delicious, melting cheese when we said it. "When we get back from up North, I'm going to the animal shelter to get a cat. You're still cool with that, right?"

"We'd better get two so they can keep each other company."

"Even better. I should probably make sure Claire and Sammy are still on board with that. Did they go to work?"

"They've got the night off. They were going to meet Bruce at the Bull for a pint or two. Want to go?"

"Sure," I said. John went to the hall to grab our jackets, and the now-familiar voice of John Peel came on the radio. My John came back in and helped me with my jacket, as my left shoulder still wasn't back to normal. I said, "Can we wait just a minute? I want to hear who's going to be on."

We paused, listening to the little radio on the kitchen counter.

John Peel began to speak in a somber tone. He'd been told that Ian Curtis had died. My stomach dropped. He said he didn't have any details beyond that. That he offered sympathy to Ian's friends, family, and band mates. I was frozen in place, willing time to move backwards and hoping I'd misheard him. He played "New Dawn Fades," a heavy dirge of a song that had always made me somewhat uneasy. I couldn't breathe.

A warm, rainy spring breeze wafted through our small kitchen, but I was freezing. Every word and phrase that we'd just heard snaked through my mind. I tried to make sense of them, but they ended up like puzzle pieces that didn't fit together. I silently pleaded with the radio to tell me what had happened.

Except for the now-elegiac song playing on the little countertop radio, all was quiet. The air around us shivered.

John and I stood staring at each other, our eyes wide and shimmering. He put a hand over his open mouth, then squeezed his eyes closed. I could tell that he had suspicions that mirrored my own about what had happened; there had been talk at their shows of depression, epilepsy, and a complicated personal life.

Ian Curtis had spoken to both John and me during desperate, dark nights. David Bowie saved my life at 17, but four years later, Ian made sense of it when I'd lost my way. Some of his lyrics had been warnings, and I had listened. I wished I could have thanked him.

He danced like a firefly trapped in a jar, eyes blazing, seeing flashes both terrifying and divine that not everyone could, not even all the people who adored him. And just like that, he wasn't in the world anymore. That voice that had given both John and me hope, made us feel seen, made us feel like our struggles, our loneliness, our fears, were valid… That voice was now gone. He was only 23. It didn't seem possible. It didn't seem real.

I thought of how close John had come to that point. How close I had come to that point. We wrapped our arms around each other. I'm not sure how long we stood there, not speaking, not needing to, just holding on.

A while later, I said, "John?"

He sniffed. "Yeah?"

"Want to get married?"

He pulled back to look at me. Our cold noses touched. A trace of a grin cracked through his solemnity. He wiped his eyes with the backs of his hands. "What?"

I took his face in my hands, and looked into his eyes. "You're the most important person to me. I don't ever want to be without you. I need you to know that I will never voluntarily leave you."

"I know," he said. "I don't ever want to be without you, either. And I love you far too much to make you a missus."

I closed my eyes and put my arms back around him. The peace that settled into my bones at that moment was as thorough as the grief that sat heavy on us both.

Acknowledgments

Bottom-of-my-heart thank yous to:

My dad Bill, the voracious reader, who I wish was here to see this moment.

My mom Dorothy, who thankfully, was never anything like Viv's mom.

My husband Dave, who never stopped believing in me, even when I did.

Steve Ingram, Dave Perrin, Juliette Rogers, Rick Doody, Terri Alexander, Dave Brigham, Kim LeVasseur Hartgrove, Emily Benson, and the faculty and students in the Mountainview MFA program for helping this novel get where it is today.

Matthew Sharpe for his insightful, discerning, invaluable developmental editing.

Joy Division Central (http://joydiv.org) for the like-minded community of fans, and for the thorough historical information, especially about concert dates and individual narratives about each gig when available.

And, of course, Ian Curtis, Peter Hook, Stephen Morris, and Bernard Sumner for unleashing Joy Division on the world in the late 70s, and to Gillian Morris (née Gilbert) for going forward with New Order when it was time.

CPSIA information can be obtained
at www.ICGtesting.com
Printed in the USA
LVHW010742100221
678897LV00002B/198